Sparkle & Shine

Try Again Series, Volume 2

Marla Holt

Published by Marla Holt, 2019.

eBook ISBN: 978-1-7322754-6-1
Paperback ISBN: 978-1-7322754-7-8
Cover Design by: T-Rex Cover Design
Tiny Dino Publishing
Topeka, KS
To Find out more and for exclusive sneak peeks at Marla's newest work,
sign up for her newsletter[1]

---

1. https://dl.bookfunnel.com/kxq14cdo4n

To Audrey

The only woman I know who could best Alex in the
art of badassery. Thanks for being my sister.

SPARKLE

&

SHINE

MARLA HOLT

Chapter One

Jab, cross, jab. Slide right. Uppercut. Back. Left hook.

Alex ran through the sequence three more times as she pummeled the bag. Her trainer watched with his arms crossed over his gigantic man chest. He hadn't told her once to keep her chin down or her elbows in or her feet wide. When she finished, he steadied the bag then raised one eyebrow and said, "Ring?"

Alex pumped a gloved fist into the air.

She had joined the boxing gym a year ago, and despite her enthusiasm, the sport had not come easily to her. Stepping and punching at the same time had taken Alex weeks to master. Of course, it had also taken Alex two other trainers and innumerable flashes of her middle finger to the other gym members before she'd found Dale.

Alex had only been in the ring a handful of times, even though Dale had been pushing her to join the Saturday sparring sessions. It was something she hadn't even considered. She was too busy with school and running her own jewelry business to squeeze anything else into her Saturday. She'd think of a new excuse not to come after she graduated next week—if she had any brain cells left.

For now, she was going to pretend she could kick Dale's ass.

Dale held the ropes apart for her to jump in, then took up a defensive stance. He wasn't tall, but he was broad, and had to be a heavyweight with all those bulging muscles. In any other circumstance, Alex might have taken a moment to admire those muscles but standing opposite him as he bounced on his toes, Alex's heart thrummed in her throat.

A hit from this guy would hurt like hell.

She swallowed, and Dale grinned. "That Chinese crap you had last night catching up with you?" he asked with a wink.

Ticking her off was Dale's favorite way to push her. Nagging her about her diet triggered all sorts of other issues, but that was part of his game—trying to throw Alex off of hers. Alex shook off her nerves, and took up her offensive stance, focusing her anger into power instead. Dale's grin sharpened, and he bobbed side to side, teasing her as she approached him.

"Show me what you got, Stafford."

Alex made her move, and even though Dale's blocks were more jarring than hitting the bag, she slid through the sequence just as easily as she had before. She even slid to the right just in time to avoid Dale's left hook.

"Again," Dale said.

Alex did it again and again until Dale tripped her up with a surprise uppercut just after she'd dodged his left hook on the sixth time through the sequence. Alex blocked, barely, but the force made her teeth clack together. She had to backpedal halfway across the ring, but Dale didn't let up. He loosed an onslaught of punches that had her huddled down with her gloves covering her face as she tried to keep her footing.

"Don't lock your knees," he said, not even winded by his assault.

Alex hadn't realized she'd zipped up her legs in an effort to take up less space, she jumped back onto her toes and tried to dance away from Dale, but he was backing her into a corner. Alex didn't know what to do about it. She was barely keeping her brain from panicking.

"Come on, Stafford, I'm leaving my torso wide open."

When Alex peeked between her gloves, she saw that he was indeed leaving his left side open every time he threw a punch. He'd deliberately left her an opening and she'd missed it. Alex slid to her right, again avoiding his cross, then hit his open ribs, using more force than usual because she was pissed. She was angry at him for tricking her into sparring, and angry at herself for missing the blatant opening.

Dale, being Dale, danced back, the blow not even making his breath come hard, and they slid right back into Alex's rehearsed routine until Alex was panting and covered in a fresh layer of sweat. Even Dale had a little glistening sparkle to his skin.

"You suck," Alex said between breaths.

Dale only shrugged. "You eat Chinese, I'm gonna make sure you put the calories to good use."

"I was in the studio for fifteen hours yesterday. I had to eat something!" Alex kicked at his shins, but big as he was, Dale was nimble, and jumped back, laughing at her.

"Hey, you agreed to the meal plan."

"I agreed to your recommended adjustments to my diet. I did not sign away my right to eat junk food forever."

"You might have dodged that surprise uppercut if you'd had the proper fuel."

Dale pulled off his gloves and held the ropes apart so Alex could squeeze out of the ring. She socked him in the gut as she ducked down with her gloved right hand, not hard, but hard enough for him to grunt in surprise. "Don't pin your underhanded tactics on me. I know how you are."

"Seriously though," Dale said once he'd joined Alex back on the practice mat, "there is absolutely no reason why you're not sparring."

Alex rolled her eyes and followed Dale toward their station. She pulled off her gloves as they walked. They were pink and had sparkles on the piping. They made her smile, even as Dale tried her patience. "Can we have this conversation again after I graduate?"

"And then you'll be visiting your grandmother, and then your new jewelry line comes out, and then you have your friend's wedding and after that—"

"You know way too much about my life. Are you stalking me?"

Dale traded her the gloves for a bottle of water and towel. "If you treated me more like a trainer and less like a psychiatrist, there wouldn't be so much to know."

"Hey, hitting things is therapeutic."

Dale downed his own bottle of water in one, and Alex wandered if he'd ever posed for a hot boxer calendar. She'd buy it.

"You probably should be in regular therapy too, you know. It's not so bad. I know a good therapist." Dale almost sang the last part, teasing like they were still in grade school.

Alex tossed her towel at him. "Yeah, let your husband drum up his own business, okay?"

Dale shrugged and tossed her towel right back. "You know where to find him when you change your mind."

She wiped the sweat from her face and said, "Speaking of, I stress baked when I got home last night and brought you some cookies. They're in my locker."

Dale frowned and shot her a look that said a lecture on how sugar made her weak was in her future.

She held up both hands. "Don't look at me like that. They're macaroons, so they're mostly coconut with just teeny bit of honey to hold them together." She held her thumb and forefinger so there was barely any space between them. "Totally meal plan approved, I swear."

"Then thank you," his frown tilted up into a near smile as he leaned in to peck her on the cheek. "You're a doll, Alex."

She shrugged and patted Dale's boulder of a bicep. It wasn't a big deal. As much as she complained about him, Dale had become a friend. And she'd been feeling short on those lately.

"Leave them in the office before you go. And I'll see you Thursday. Six A. M. Don't be late."

"We still on for dinner with Ben on Friday?"

A terrifying look of glee stole over Dale's face as he rubbed his chin. "Of course."

Dale was a little too excited to meet her boyfriend.

Alex shook her head and turned toward the locker rooms. One of the benefits of there being only a handful of women at the club was not having to wait for a shower or share the mirrors as she got ready for her day-which was going to be spent in her studio at school-again. She only had four more days to finish her final collection before her senior show, and after that, it was graduation.

She wasn't new to jewelry making. She'd been working with beads and stones and wire since she was sixteen but hadn't tackled full blown metalsmithing until she'd gone back to school more than a decade later. Alex was still working on perfecting her bezel settings, which made how they featured prominently in her final project all the more nerve-wracking.

Alex showered, but didn't bother with her hair or makeup and changed into black yoga pants and a gray gym t-shirt. She knew by the end of the day she'd be covered in dust and metal shavings and whatever grime had accumulated in her school studio over the last nine months. She did make the mistake of checking her messages, and there were a lot more than she expected there to be at eight o'clock on a Tuesday morning.

Gran had already called for their twice weekly chat. She'd left a voicemail saying she hoped Alex was out of bed by now and not sleeping off a hangover like a cretin. Juliet had also called even though it was an hour earlier in Colorado.

Juliet had once been Alex's best friend, and maybe she still was. They talked almost daily, and while Juliet had made the eleven-hour trek from Colorado to visit Alex a couple times, Alex had never gone to see Juliet in her new home. Alex been too busy with school and her ever expanding jewelry business, and any free time Alex had, she visited her Gran.

Besides, Juliet was happy in Colorado. She had Ethan and a job she loved, she didn't need Alex anymore. Alex had known how to take care of Juliet back when she'd been in school and working with a single-mindedness that hadn't left room for necessities like eating or sleeping. Alex had cooked most of their meals and paid most of their bills and had a best friend to drink wine with and to dance with and complain to in return. Even when the reason Alex was complaining was because Juliet had woken her up at dawn to do yoga and "greet the sun," she'd loved having Juliet around.

Alex wasn't sure what to do with this happy Juliet. Her voicemail was one run-on sentence about the baby she'd just caught, and how she'd just picked out her wedding favors, and could Alex help her by putting them together? Her friend's needs had changed so much, and Alex wasn't the one who met them anymore.

Alex wanted Juliet to be happy. Of course, she did. And Alex liked Ethan a lot. It was just, living so far apart from each other, and being in such different phases of life, talking to Juliet always made Alex feel a little obsolete. Like maybe the whole Maid of Honor thing was more of a nod to what Juliet and Alex had been to one another before rather than representative of who they were together now.

Drifting apart was solely on Alex's shoulders. Everything changed the moment Alex had slept with Rich. It had been a stupid thing to do, she'd known it at the time. There were some things you didn't do and sleeping with the guy your best friend had almost married was pretty much first thing on the list under *Thou Shall Not Murder*.

Sleeping with Rich might have been forgivable offense if she'd only done it the one time. But the affair had gone on the entire summer. At the time, Alex had told herself it didn't matter. Juliet had just started dating Ethan, so Rich was fair game—and it wasn't like Alex had been looking for anything with Rich. She'd started it to keep Rich's attention off Juliet and then it had snowballed from there. It hadn't helped that Rich was the definition of tall, dark, and handsome. His olive skin and dark, wavy hair and sharp jaw practically felled most women who looked at him too closely. When he'd turned his whiskey colored eyes on her, maybe she'd lost her senses a little bit.

If pressed, Alex could admit that she'd been lonely, and having an attractive man pay attention to her instead of her friend had been flattering. She didn't have excuses. Was the sex good? Phenomenal. Was Rich a douchebag who'd cheated on her best friend repeatedly? Absolutely. Should Alex have run in the opposite direction as fast as she could? No question.

But she hadn't.

Instead, she'd taunted him. Alex had flipped her hair and flirted and dared him to make a move, all the while asking herself *what could it hurt?*

She should have been telling herself *don't go there.* Then she should have been saying *get out while you can,* but it had taken *your best friend can't even look at you* before Alex had ended whatever sort of quasi relationship she and Rich had started. By then, it had been too late, everything had already been ruined.

Alex didn't want to think about that anymore. She'd spent most of the last three years trying to work past the fallout and prove to herself that she was a good person. Yes, she'd made some mistakes, but she deserved to be happy too. It didn't matter that she wasn't there yet.

Alex slid into her car and plugged her phone into the speakers, telling it to dial her grandmother as she made the thirty-minute commute to the University of Kansas in Lawrence.

"It's about time," her Gran said instead of, "Hello."

"Good morning to you too, Gran. How are you feeling?"

"I'm fine, just like always. Where have you been?"

Gran hadn't been fine. She'd been sick over the winter, first with the flu, then she'd had pneumonia bad enough to put her in the hospital. She insisted she was better, but there was a new wheeziness to her grandmother's voice that worried Alex.

Her Gran wasn't young. She'd had Alex's mom late in life. Alex's mom had been thirty-five when Alex was born and with Alex turning thirty later this year, her grandmother was in her nineties.

It wasn't like Alex expected her grandmother to be around forever, but she was also the only real family Alex had left. Crotchety as she might be, Alex loved her for stepping up and taking care of her when Alex's own mother hadn't.

"I'm only a couple of minutes late. And I was at the gym, you know that."

Gran liked to nail down how Alex spent her days—not that Alex told her Gran everything—but it was just how she was. She wanted to know, and Alex didn't mind. It was nice to talk to someone about everything, even if it was mundane most days. Alex told Gran about sparring with Dale at the gym, and her plans to meet Ben the next day for dinner.

"Has he agreed to come see me yet?" She asked, interrupting Alex's musings on whether they'd go out or grab some takeout and watch a movie since they were both bound to be exhausted from working on their final projects.

Alex suppressed a groan. The answer was no, Ben didn't want to drive all the way down to Pittsburgh, Kansas just to visit a ninety-three year-old lady on the short break he had between finishing this semester and teaching over the summer semester, but Alex didn't know how to explain that to her grandmother, so she settled on, "I'm working on it. Probably my June trip, or the July one if that doesn't work out."

"I need to meet your young man," he grandmother said.

"I know, Gran, but he'll be at graduation. Is Elise still able to bring you?" Elise was her grandmother's neighbor. Like Gran, Elise was widowed with grown children, but Elise was only in her seventies and while the two old women were friends as far as Alex could tell, Elise acted mostly as Gran's chauffeur.

"Oh, I'm not going to bother Elise with that."

Alex furrowed her brow and signaled to pass a semi that smelled like cow manure. "But I thought Elise wanted to come. She was excited to see Allen Fieldhouse and visit the bookstore downtown last time we talked." Because yes, Alex did call Gran's neighbor. Sometimes that was the only to make sure she knew the truth about how Gran was doing. It was how Alex found out her Grandmother was in the hospital at all last February, since Gran had called and pretended there was absolutely nothing wrong.

"Well, now she has to watch her grandchildren that weekend, and I'm not riding in a car with those demons for three hours."

"They can't be that bad, Gran."

"They're the spawn of Satan, I bet my life on it."

Alex had to bite her lip to suppress her giggle. "Fine, I can pick you up Saturday, and bring you home on Monday if you like."

"You don't have time for that nonsense. I'll be fine right here."

Gran was right. Alex didn't have time to drive back and forth to Southeast Kansas next week, but if it meant Gran could watch her graduate, she'd make time to do it.

"That doesn't matter, Gran. I'll figure it out."

"No, you won't. You'll concentrate on getting your schoolwork done and spending time with your friends."

"But I want you there."

Gran muttered something under her breath that sounded a lot like the kind of words she would have washed Alex's mouth out with soap for saying. When she was done with her whispered curses, Gran heaved a sigh into the phone. "Alexandra, I'm not coming. I don't want to climb up and down those hills and be in a crowd of people all day. I was trying to be nice about it, but there it is. I don't want to go."

Alex sucked in a breath as tears sprang into her eyes, even as her grandmother fought off a coughing fit. Gran wasn't coming to her graduation. She didn't *want* to come to Alex's graduation, just like everybody else.

That was fine. It felt like someone had stuck an ice pick through Alex's chest, but she would be fine. With everything she'd been through, she'd always been fine in the end. And really, this wasn't even that big of a deal. So her grandmother wouldn't see her walk. Neither would her mom. And she couldn't ask Juliet to come so soon before her wedding. She would have content herself with Ben being there.

The longer Gran's coughing fit went on, the pain of rejection dulled in favor worry over Gran's health. Coughing like that wasn't normal, was it?

"Gran, are you alright?" she asked when the coughing ceased.

"I'm fine, child. I choked on my coffee is all."

But Alex didn't think that was all, and mentally added calling Elise to her never ending to-do list.

Chapter Two

Most weeks, Rich looked forward to Wednesdays. Other single men probably considered having dinner with their sister and her family a chore, but it was the highlight of Rich's week.

Gina was two years older than Rich and had been married for ten years. She had two kids, Noah, who was five, and Isaac, who had just turned three. With the kids around, his visits weren't always relaxing, but Rich liked his nephew's energy. All night, Noah had been spelling their names while teasing his brother for being too much of a baby to know the alphabet. In response, Isaac had tried to recite the alphabet and got stuck on the letter 'G.' Rich has tried to distract him from tears by reciting all the G-words he could think of.

Once Gina and Colin had joined in on the game, Noah had too, and they'd ended dinner laughing around the table as they each made up the most preposterous sounding G-words they could think of and assigning meanings. Together, they'd written a whole new page of the dictionary and Rich's cheeks ached from laughing as he helped Gina clear the plates.

Despite their mother teaching them both to cook, Gina's husband did most of the cooking in their house. Colin worked for a local brewery, and Gina was a freelance journalist who stayed home with the boys during the day. The second Colin returned home from work, Gina dashed up to her office to work until dinner was ready. On Wednesdays, Gina and Rich cleaned up together after dinner for a little brother-sister alone time. It was one of the only times Rich got to speak Italian outside of class. While he loved teaching, speaking to his sister in their mother's language was like coming home.

The siblings had grown up speaking three languages at home. Their parents had been born in Europe, their mother in Tuscany, their father in Paris. Their mom had taught them English and Italian, and their father had only ever spoken to them in French. But since Gina had never forgiven their father for moving back to France when they were teenagers, she'd outlawed the language in her home.

They were talking about her latest article, a profile piece on an anonymous illegal immigrant family as Rich returned the stock pot to its home in the cabinet over the refrigerator, when he saw it.

His heart stumbled in his chest. His arm froze with the heavy stainless-steel pot over his head as he read the little piece of white cardstock.

It was a wedding invitation. To Juliet's wedding.

Rich felt like his lungs had stopped working, and he had to struggle for a breath as he closed the pot away and stepped back to pull the invitation from beneath the magnet. He wasn't aware that he'd crossed the room and sunk into one of the chairs around the small kitchen table until the wooden seat stopped his downward momentum.

Juliet was getting married.

It wasn't like he hadn't known this was coming. She'd been with Ethan for three years now. The man had left his life in Kansas City and followed her to Colorado.

But still.

His Juliet was marrying somebody else.

Rich inhaled deeply through his nose and rubbed his jaw. The stubble scratched at his fingers as he tried to wrap his mind around how far off course his life had veered.

Gina's hand landed on his shoulder as she pulled out the chair next to his. "I take it you didn't get one then."

He barked out a surprised, sarcastic laugh. "No. I didn't expect one—it's just."

Gina squeezed his shoulder and offered him a sad smile. He was glad his sister had been invited. Glad that the two were still friends even after all these years.

Rich shook his head and rubbed his eyes. He hadn't seen Juliet in years. He hadn't even talked to her outside a few messages on Facebook. Gina had given him periodic updates of course. She loved her new job, she'd learned to ski, she and Ethan had bought a house in the mountains. But no one had mentioned a wedding.

"You okay?" Gina asked him Italian.

Rich blew out a breath. "I'm fine—or I will be. It's just a surprise is all."

Gina's mouth quirked to the side, signaling that she didn't believe him. "You should be happy for her."

"I am—or I will be. It's just—"

"You always thought it would be your name on that invitation with hers?"

"Yeah."

"Even after everything?"

Rich nodded. Even after everything. It was amazing how much could be encompassed in those three words.

Even after everything. After the affairs. After Juliet's miscarriage. After Juliet had turned to Ethan because Rich hadn't been there when she needed him most. Jesus, that had been seven years ago. He could have married Juliet seven years ago if he hadn't screwed it all up.

He'd tried to reconnect three years ago when Isaac had been born and he'd had an excuse to see her again, but that had been the same time Juliet and Ethan had gotten together. Juliet had fallen in love with *him* instead of getting back together with Rich.

It didn't help that Rich had spent that summer sleeping with Alex.

God, Alex. Rich hadn't thought about her in months. The feisty blonde roommate with golden skin he hadn't seen coming. It had been a mistake to sleep with Juliet's best friend, Rich had known that at the time, but he'd never been very good at making the right decision when sex was involved. Just like his dad.

Toward the end though, he'd thought maybe he and Alex . . . He didn't know, maybe they could have had something, but the second he'd hinted at an actual relationship she'd kicked him out the door and avoided his calls until he'd given up.

Rich had always wondered if Alex had known then that she was pregnant, or if she'd found out later. How long had she kept her secret from him, from Juliet, from everyone?

Even now, the only reason Rich knew Alex had ever carried his child was because Juliet had told him after Alex had terminated the pregnancy.

Another low point in his life, realizing that Alex hadn't cared about him enough to even tell him that she'd been pregnant. If nothing else, Rich would have liked the chance to be there for her. He would have done his best to convince her to keep the baby of course. To make an honest go of it with him. To marry him, even, so they could become a family. It was something he didn't allow himself to think about often. What might have been with Alex. As if maybe if he didn't acknowledge how much he'd been hurt by her actions, it would make the pain less real.

He couldn't help but think that Alex should have known that he would have been there for her, if only she had come to him.

The urge to cry tugged at the back of his throat and pinged at the back of his eyes, but Rich didn't cry.

Even after everything.

"Aren't things going well with Lynnette?" Gina asked.

Lynnette had been Rich's girlfriend for the past year, and things were alright, he supposed, so he shrugged.

"She's not here tonight," Gina said.

Again, Rich shrugged. Lynnette didn't like kids. She'd come to dinner at Gina's a handful of time in the past few months but considering how Rich showed up every week without fail, it was becoming a little too apparent to all of them that Lynnette was staying away on purpose.

"The kids stress her out," Rich said.

Gina snorted. "Kids stress everyone out."

"Yeah, well."

"Aside from the fact that your girlfriend is a monster who hates my kids, how are things going?" Gina's smile was tight, and she spoke through clenched teeth. Rich had known Gina wasn't exactly Lynnette's biggest fan, but he raised his eyebrows at the question.

"What? How can you not like my kids?" Gina asked, even as he could hear Isaac screaming from the next room.

Rich waited to hear Colin comfort the crying preschooler before saying. "Things with Lynnette are fine."

Gina stood and patted him on the shoulder again, "As long as you're happy, little brother, I'm happy, even if she does hate my kids."

Rich wrapped his arms around his sister just before she plunged her hands back into the dishwater. "Thanks, Sis."

Gina kissed him on the cheek then smacked his arm. "Stop being such a sap, I have a deadline."

Chapter Three

When Alex unlocked her door on Friday night, she wished she'd spent the 150 bucks it would have taken to install a heavy bag in the corner, because she was ready to beat shit up.

Ben had canceled their post senior presentation dinner because his paper, or book, or whatever he had to turn in to his advisor wasn't done. Alex understood. She really did, but he'd cancelled on Wednesday night for the same reason and she was starting to wonder if Ben was really busy, or if he was avoiding her.

They'd met in October in the coffee line at the student union, and he'd complimented her glasses, which was a sure way to get her to smile. Alex was never giving up her chunky black frames. Whenever the fashion swung back to ultra-tiny frames, Alex would be that woman who wouldn't change. Hopefully she'd come off as eccentric and zany instead of an outmoded nut with questionable taste.

Alex had been attracted to Ben's glasses too. He wore the 1950s style hornrims that made him look like a nuclear scientist. When he wore them with black slacks and a white button down, Alex had to stop herself from drooling. Maybe it would have been better if he'd been after his PhD in chemistry rather than philosophy, but he still looked good. They chatted over coffee between classes for a few weeks before Alex finally asked him out for a drink. He seemed surprised at first but accepted. She'd spent the night with him that night, and he'd spent the next few months worshipping her while she'd done her best to take care of him. Alex made sure he ate and tidied up around his place when she was there. She'd even picked up groceries for him a couple of times. Ben was smart, but he was the kind of guy who got so absorbed in his work he tended to ignore his setting.

Things had been good for a while, but something shifted after February. Alex's Gran had been ill, and Alex had spent her time coordinating her Gran's care instead of doing Ben's dishes, and he'd grown distant. For most of May she'd been clinging to the hope that, once the semester was over, they could reconnect, but as Alex balanced her purse, school bag, and gym bag along with the last week's worth of mail while she tried to unlock her door, all she wanted was a pizza, a couple shots of tequila and a good lay. Since Ben wasn't coming over, she'd have to settle for the vibrator in her nightstand.

Alex dropped everything inside the door and fell on top of the pile. She lay there for a moment, listening to the sounds of the city. She'd only rest for a minute. Exhaustion weighed heavily at her limbs, but her growling stomach had her leafing through her mail for a coupon as she called in her pizza. Would Dale buy the coupon as an excuse for eating an entire pizza herself? Probably not, but screw Dale and his happy marriage with a man who actually liked him.

How did people even do it?

That's when Alex saw it, in the middle of a heap of bills was a white square envelope with neat handwriting on the front. It had been addressed by Juliet's little sister, Colleen. Alex had been in charge of finding the invitations because

Juliet had almost had a breakdown over the phone, saying that if she had to look at one more piece of lacy burlap she was going to puke. So, Alex had taken that off Juliet's plate, but her handwriting was atrocious. The actual mailing of the invitations had been delegated to Colleen.

Alex missed Juliet with a visceral longing that hadn't waned since Juliet had moved. It hadn't even been sleeping with Rich that had been the problem. That part hadn't been great, but the whole finding out she was pregnant not long after Juliet had broken things off with Ethan hadn't helped. Juliet had been so miserable without Ethan, but her fear of being expelled for dating a mentor had won out, leaving Juliet a raging mess for that entire semester.

Juliet had been expecting a baby once upon a time, and a combination of losing that pregnancy and Rich's infidelity had been what killed their relationship. Juliet had been desperate for that baby, and Alex couldn't bring herself to pile one more hurt on her friend.

So, she made the hardest and yet easiest decision of her life.

Alex talked a big game. Since college she'd told everyone that she didn't want a relationship, didn't want a family or kids because she didn't want to do to a child what her mother had done to her. But deep down, those were exactly the things Alex did want. She wanted a chance to prove that just because you had a crappy mother who abandoned you didn't mean *you* would be a terrible mother. She'd always told herself that if she ever got pregnant, she'd be the best damn mother there ever was. But at the price of destroying her best friend? Alex hadn't been able to do that to Juliet.

She'd asked Ethan to take her to Planned Parenthood. It had perhaps been the loneliest point in her life. She hadn't been able to go to Juliet, or anyone at the Birthing Center where she'd been working at the time, because Juliet also worked there. Her mom had been in California and barely answering Alex's calls—no change there—her Gran would have probably told her she was going to hell. Rich just hadn't been an option. She'd messed up too much as far as he was concerned already.

While Ethan had agreed to take her in Juliet's stead, he'd spent half the time telling Alex she needed to tell Juliet what was going on. And because he was an OB-GYN, he'd spent the rest of the time telling her exactly how the procedure would go and how she needed to approach her recovery, which included letting Juliet, her roommate, know in case something went wrong and she bled to death in her sleep.

When Alex refused again, Ethan had called her in the middle of the night—twice—to make sure she was alright. It had been annoyingly adorable, and Alex understood a little more why Juliet was stuck on him.

Of course, the whole thing had blown up in her face when some busybody from the hospital had recognized them and told Juliet Ethan had taken Alex for an abortion. That's when Alex had officially become the worst best friend in the history of the universe, because in protecting Juliet from a small hurt, Alex had left her thinking that not only did her best friend have a habit of picking up Juliet's leftovers, but that the man she was in love with, wasn't who she thought he was.

When Juliet had thought Alex had slept with Ethan, gotten pregnant by Ethan—that had truly been the lowest point in Alex's life.

They'd worked it all out eventually, but Juliet had moved to Colorado, and Ethan had chased her there. Those two had worked things out together, leaving Alex and Juliet to patch things up piecemeal through phone calls and texts.

Almost three years later things still weren't the same. Alex thought the guilt of it all might never leave her.

She slit the envelop open with her keys.

She'd asked one of her friends from art school to design the invitations. Juliet was right, everything she'd found was mason jars and burlap and lace, and while Juliet was kind of a hippy, she wasn't into burlap. She did have a green thumb though. When Juliet had lived with Alex, the apartment had been covered with broadleaf tropical plants. Alex had given most of them away after Juliet moved since Alex wasn't cut out for anything more complex than spider plants.

Her art school friend had painted watercolor banana leaves and hand-lettered Ethan and Juliet's names beneath. They were simple, minimalist, and modern. And since they were getting married on some ranch in the middle of the Colorado summer, and Ethan was paying a fortune for Juliet to be surrounded by the plants she loved on her wedding day, Alex thought the invitations were appropriate.

Juliet had loved them, and Alex had been glad she could do something nice for her friend from afar. It was small, but since Alex had so much to atone for, she had been happy to do it.

Tears gathered in her eyes as she read the invitation.

Ethan & Juliet

Together with our families we invite you to celebrate our wedding

Then the time and date and address of the ranch they were getting married at was listed with a website to RSVP to at the bottom.

Simple and to the point.

Alex wasn't sure if she was feeling jealousy or exhaustion or just confirmation that her friend was really and truly leaving her behind. In three months, Juliet would be Mrs. Ethan Harvey, and Alex would be doing the same things she had always done: make jewelry and try not to become her mother.

Making jewelry had been the only thing Alex had ever been good at. She'd found her mom's old supplies in one of her grandmother's closets as a teen and started selling bracelets and earring to her friends at school for enough money to keep her in beads. Her grandmother had printed up business cards for her on her sixteenth birthday and Sparkle & Shine had been born. By the time she was eighteen, she'd had pieces on sale in a little boutique in Pittsburgh, Kansas, and another in Frontenac. She'd set up an etsy shop and sold a few pieces the summer after she graduated, but it hadn't made her any real money.

When she'd moved to Kansas City for nursing school, Alex had been determined to concentrate on her studies. Having Juliet as a roommate had been good for her that first year. Juliet had been focused and driven, and the only two things that had mattered to Juliet were being number one in their class and Rich. When they weren't studying, Juliet had been off screwing her older, gorgeous, boyfriend who spoke to her in Italian. Alex had made out with awkward college guys and expanded her necklace selection.

At the beginning of her sophomore year, two things had happened that derailed Alex's nursing aspirations permanently. The first had been that Juliet had moved in with Rich. After that, it had become clear that having a live-in study buddy had been the only reason Alex had passed any of her classes. Second, the buyer for the Kansas Historical Society had emailed Alex on etsy and asked if she sold wholesale, because she wanted to stock Alex's jewelry in her gift shops.

Alex had said, "Yes, of course. I'll get you my line sheet in a couple of days." Alex had to do a quick google of wholesale terms, because she'd only ever sold on consignment before. She'd had no idea how wholesaling worked and hoped she hadn't sounded like an idiot throwing out the words "line sheet" when she'd had no freaking clue what one was.

Instead of studying or attending classes, Alex had parked herself in the school library and read everything she could find about wholesaling. Then, she'd gone back to her dorm room and designed a few sets of easily duplicated pieces in her still developing style. She'd photographed them, wrangled them into a pdf along with some terms and prices and she'd sent the whole package back to the buyer within three days of the initial request. She'd missed two tests and her first clinicals, and Alex had never looked back.

Gran had been livid. She'd ranted to Alex on the phone for an hour about how she was making the same mistakes her mother had made. That Alex was throwing away a good opportunity on a pipe dream. And Alex knew she couldn't live on the 300 dollars she'd received from her first wholesale order, but it was still more than she'd ever made on her jewelry before. So, to appease her grandmother, Alex had found a job—a good job, working as a medical receptionist.

Gran's response had been, "It's not as good as nursing, but it will help keep that jewelry making a hobby and not an obsession."

While Alex had said, "Yes, Gran. It is a good job, and I'm grateful to have it," she'd also been googling boutiques and museum gift shops she could send her sparkly new line sheet to, berating herself the entire time for being just like her mother.

If Alex were to ever list out her lifelong goals, there would be the career success, happy marriage, and successful kids goals that most people would say, but at the very top, it would say:

Avoid becoming my mother.

Vivien Stafford was an artist. Strike one. Alex had never figured out how to not be an artist. It wasn't something she could turn off, even though that was the way Gran always talked about her jewelry, as if it was something she could choose not to do.

Alex supposed it was the same for Vivien. She was in her mid-sixties, but looked younger, despite embracing her gray hair, which she still wore in long waves down her back. The unreal amount of energy she had made her feel like she was barely fifty. She traveled most of the year, attending prestigious art festivals around the country where she sold her pottery, both functional and decorative, and had done since she herself had dropped out of college.

Strike two against Alex. She'd dropped out of school the second her jewelry business had shown promise, and her grandmother had never let her forget it. Alex hadn't put in the last two years of hard work for nothing. Unlike her mother, she would have her degree. That it was in metalsmithing and not nursing like her grandmother had wanted was something Alex tried not to focus on. She liked to think of it as a compromise of sorts.

Strike three against Alex was, just like her mother, she couldn't hold down a relationship. Vivien had always flitted from man to man, living with someone new every time she visited her home. One year, she'd come home to Kansas after art festival season three months pregnant with Alex and never told anyone who the father was. Starting when Alex was five, Vivien came home less and less between shows until she only ever came home at Christmas with new mugs for Gran and Alex as gifts.

Alex had a whole cabinet full of mugs her mother had made.

The problem was that, on the surface, Alex liked her mother. She was outgoing and witty. She was interested in catching up on Alex's life whenever she was around and encouraged her daughter to be confident and independent. But then she didn't call for months at a time, and as independent as she encouraged Alex to be, when she did call, she was usually in the process of having her kiln moved from her old boyfriend's house to the new one's. Once she'd even left a show early because the wife of the guy she'd been sleeping with had found out, and had broken a whole shelf of urns with a baseball bat.

Then there had been the time, when Alex had been getting ready to move to Kansas City and her mom had swung by Gran's "just because" and given Alex a lesson on how important it was to find good birth control by describing for Alex the not one, not two, but three abortions Vivien had after Alex was born.

No. Alex agreed with her Gran that she wanted to be absolutely nothing like her mother.

But at every major crossroads in her life, even when Alex was trying to not make the same decisions her mother did, she wound up looking just like her. She had avoided serious relationships so she wouldn't rely on men the way her mother did. But since she had needs just like any other person, Alex wound up with a string of casual hookups and a reputation for being easy that somehow made it to her grandmother, who called and told Alex she was just like her mother.

Then, when Alex actually tried to keep a boyfriend, nobody wanted her. She was the pretty, petite blonde girl guys only took serious enough to date because her glasses gave her that "smart girl" appearance. When they found out she was a foul-mouthed artist instead, they bolted.

The first person who'd stuck around longer than two months was Ben. Alex tried to convince herself that this was a serious relationship for him, but as time went on, he seemed more focused on his budding academic career, than on building something with her. Until recently, Alex had been willing to give it time. She'd seen, via Juliet, how much work it took Rich to become a well-respected professor at a young age, so Alex tried to be understanding.

Of course, at least some of the time Rich claimed to be working late, he had been sleeping with other women behind Juliet's back.

Asshole.

Alex had hated Rich for a long, long time for breaking Juliet's heart. But when he'd turned his charm on her one night after too much sake, Alex had fallen on her back just like the many, many women before her. She hated herself for it even more than she hated him. Alex had known Juliet hadn't been completely over him when she'd hopped into bed with him. Alex had known it had been hypocritical to sleep with him when she'd told Juliet over and over not to. That Juliet deserved better.

But for Alex? Someone like Rich was right up her alley. He was a known cheater who'd been screwing around with someone else the same day Juliet had been at the doctor's office finding out she'd lost their baby. That was exactly the kind of guy Alex deserved, someone who wouldn't stick around long and someone she could despise just as much as she liked him. Someone who wouldn't be able break her heart.

Alex hadn't even been able to do that right. She'd had to go and get knocked up with fucking Rich Durand's baby and screwed up everyone else's life in the process. She was cursed, doomed to live a life littered with failed relationships, romantic and otherwise.

Maybe that's why, instead of returning Alex's phone calls this month, her mother had only texted that, no surprise, she had an art show in Colorado the day of Alex's graduation, but she'd been coming to Topeka in June for the Mulvane Art Festival. Maybe they could do lunch.

Or maybe that's why Elise, her grandmother's neighbor had told Alex the day before that Gran was too sick to travel, and that going to see Alex graduate might be too much for her. Alex had suspected that was the case rather than her grandmother just not wanting to come, but it didn't make the situation any less disappointing.

Alex might have to resign herself to knowing that the only thing she'd ever succeed at was her jewelry business. Sparkle & Shine had become a well-known brand name in the KC-Metro area, with more buyers calling all the time. She was doing so well, she'd quit her job at the birthing center last year and hired two employees. Janet was her business manager and mostly worked remotely. Avery worked out of the apartment with Alex and helped her organize and brand the orders on top of packaging them and shipping everything. Avery had kept things running while Alex finished school, and Alex made a note to give her a raise. And Janet too.

Since Janet was a genius, it had been she who had talked Alex into planning the high-end line called Alex & Co Jewelry. They already had preorders from ten stores, and the line didn't even launch until mid-June.

Now, if she lived long enough to make it through graduation, and the launch, Alex might be sane enough to enjoy Juliet's wedding.

Chapter Four

It was a fucking gorgeous day. What had been a mild and rainy spring so far had blossomed into a warm and sunny May with flowers in bloom everywhere. Rich might have a skewed sample since he was walking across the University of Kansas campus, and they had it all done up for graduation, but still.

It had been a mistake to walk through campus today. It was too crowded, but Rich hadn't been thinking. He'd needed to escape Lynnette's cluttered apartment, needed just one moment to himself to breathe. Taking Bijou for a walk was his usual excuse, so Rich had taken their normal Sunday afternoon route. Most weeks the campus was empty.

Now Rich's lack of forethought had him navigating through crowds and around barricades while keeping Lynnette's little Bichon Frise from snapping at anybody's ankles.

The commotion didn't leave much time for contemplation, which was why he'd wanted to get away in the first place, to think about his relationship with Lynnette, and why he wanted to escape. It wasn't a good sign when you couldn't stand your girlfriend for an entire weekend.

Really though, Rich was running from the truth. He knew he should have broken up with her months ago, but he had never met someone, aside from his sister, who spoke both French and Italian as fluently as he did. That paired with Lynnette's curves and sassy mouth, had Rich inviting her to his bed the first day of the teaching conference last spring. They'd been dating for real by the time they'd left. That had been just over a year ago, and it was time to end things.

He was not proud of the reason he hadn't.

Rich had wanted to make it one whole year without cheating. He couldn't make it a year if he wasn't in a relationship for a year. And now that he'd made it that year? He wanted out.

Other women were turning his head left and right. The brunette in the yellow heels who smiled at him from beneath her cap as he steered Bijou past her. The blonde standing off to the side up ahead with her long hair blowing out behind her in the breeze. The girl with curly red hair was out. Too much like Juliet.

He sighed and tried to push that damn wedding invitation out of his mind so he didn't have to deal with the pain the sight of it had brought him.

It was his own fault Juliet wasn't marrying him. She would have once upon a time. And Rich had wanted to marry her. He'd only been twenty-six when she'd lost the baby, and he'd been scared out of his mind. He'd wanted that baby. That marriage. That life.

After losing Juliet and the baby all in one day, Rich had thought he might die from the heartbreak and regret. If he hadn't been so afraid of becoming his father, he might not have done the exact things that he hated his father for. He wouldn't have cheated. He wouldn't have abandoned Juliet when she needed him the most. Maybe, if Rich had been less afraid, he might have been able to hang onto Juliet even after they'd lost the baby.

Finding out that he could have been a father again after it was too late to convince Alex to make a go of it with him had driven home how much he wanted the wife and kids thing. It had been almost three years since his affair with Alex, and he'd been searching for someone to fill that role since. It had been part of the reason he'd stayed with Lynnette so long, but when he was honest with himself, he saw no future there.

The blonde's hair was still blowing in the wind as Rich approached her. She was small and wore black pumps that made the little bit of calf he could see beneath her robes look strong and sleek. The urge to run his tongue over her ankle and up her leg hit. He was shaking it off when Bijou decided to dash toward where the pretty blonde stood in the grass, staring at her phone.

"Goddamn mother fucking asshole," she said, sidestepping the yapping, panting dog as if it wasn't there. "You'd think being on time to your fucking girlfriend's fucking graduation would be important, but no, Asshole of the Year missed it, and now he can't find a motherfucking parking place."

She finished her tirade before she'd looked up to meet his face, but Rich had recognized her voice the second she'd started to speak. Alex might be small, but she had a sultry voice that could sound like 900-number operator.

He almost didn't draw her attention. She hadn't seen him, he could walk right on by and not confront the woman he'd avoided for the better part of the last three years, but he surprised him by veering toward her as she continued to curse.

Rich's lips curled into a grin. Strange. He'd expected the first emotion he would feel upon finally confronting Alex would be anger. Or disappointment. Not amusement and curiosity.

When he said, "Hey, Alex," she flinched.

Flinched.

Then she looked anywhere but at his face, choosing instead to focus on the fluffy white dog jumping around her ankles. "Nice dog," she said, before reaching down to pet her. "I never pictured you with a dog."

Bijou rolled on her back. Lynnette would have a fit if he brought her home with grass clippings in her newly groomed coat.

Alex just rubbed the dog's belly and babbled, "I mean, if you were going to have a dog, I always pictured you with something big and sleek like a greyhound, but I figured you as more of a cat person. Definitely not the fluffy lapdog sort."

"She's my girlfriend's," Rich said.

Alex tapped the bow in the middle of Bijou's forehead. "Oh, that is more than obvious."

Rich knelt beside Alex to pet Bijou as well, but his eyes were on the white tassel that hung from her mortarboard. "What's your degree in?"

She met his eyes before answering, looking at him like he was daft. "The only thing I'm good at."

Rich wanted to crack a joke about how he didn't know they offered degrees in fellatio, because damn, the woman gave a hell of a blow job, but knowing Alex, she'd knee him in the balls for saying so.

When he only raised his eyebrows in question, she rolled her eyes. "Metalsmithing. You know, for jewelry making." She stood brushing her palms over her gown. "And a minor in business."

"You're still doing the jewelry thing then?"

She nodded, still regarding him the way a cat might when it's noticed a strange person in the room, cautious, but still curious. "Full time and ever expanding. I'm throwing a swanky party next month to launch a fancy new line and everything."

Rich smiled. "That's great news," he said, and he meant it. He was glad Alex was doing well, even with everything between them. The disappointment from when she'd broken things off, the anger and betrayal of learning she'd terminated her pregnancy and never planned to tell him about it, and the sadness of the knowledge she'd gone through all that alone. Not knowing what else to say, Rich said, "Sounds like you chose the right degree."

Alex snorted and looked up the hill to where crowds of people, mostly dressed in black robes

swelled one second, then contracted the next like a flock of starlings. "Not that anyone was here to see me walk, apparently."

"Nobody?" he asked, furrowing his brow.

But Alex's phone buzzed, and she cursed again. "I swear to God he better have something really fucking good planned for tonight or I am going to kick his ass. The one thing I wanted out of today—the only goddamned thing was to have a nice picture of me all decked out," she motioned to her cap and gown, "to send to Gran, and he wants me to pick me up at the fucking Kwik Shop. I can't send my Gran a photo of me with an advertisement for dollar off Red Bull in the background."

She meant for the words to sound frustrated and annoyed he knew, but all Rich heard was the distress in her voice that bordered on panic.

"I can take your picture, *Piccolina*," he said.

Alex's eyes widened and she took a step away from him. "I don't want to trouble you," she said. Meaning she didn't want to ask him for anything, not even a simple photograph. Not that he blamed her. Not really.

"It's no trouble," he said, holding out his hand for her phone. "You deserve better than a Kwik Shop parking lot."

Alex hesitated, then placed her phone in his hand. The case was black and sparkly, and it made him want to laugh. The only time he'd seen her in something that wasn't black was the one time she'd worn a matching red lace bra and panty set beneath her little black dress. It had been the hottest thing he'd ever seen.

Rich almost dropped the phone in his shock, and he couldn't even pretend it was Bijou pulling on the leash, because the dog was lounging in the grass, panting. He just looked like the stunned clutz he was as fumbled the phone through his fingers until it was upright once more.

Was Alex in red lace the hottest thing he'd ever seen? If anyone had asked him five minutes ago, he would have said that time that Juliet had—but Alex was talking to him and he hadn't heard what she's been saying.

"I'm sorry?" he said.

"Can you get the Campanile in the background or are there too many people?" she asked, enunciating the words slowly.

"Of course. Smile." Rich framed the shot so the bell tower reached into the blue sky and Alex stood, smiling, in the foreground beneath it. He took a few, then focused close on her for a few shots, the hill and the path to Potter's Lake in the background. There were also a few people's butts, but that couldn't be helped with the lawns as crowded as they were.

Alex flipped back through the pictures. "Thanks. Gran might not like what my degree is in, but she'll be glad for the pictures all the same."

"She couldn't come?" Rich asked, remembering that she was the only family Alex had left.

Alex scrunched her nose. "No. She was sick all winter, first with the flu, then with pneumonia. She's been going back and forth to the doctor . . ." Alex trailed off.

"I hope she feels better," Rich said, feeling more shy and awkward than he had since he was a teenager. Teasing, flirting, testy Alex he could handle, but today's Alex seemed fragile, like one more ounce of pressure might break her.

Alex slid her phone back in the neckline of robe. Was she stashing it in her bra? He remembered the way that red lace had wrapped around her breasts, exposing just enough skin to make him want to peel it off to expose the pale peaked nipples he knew he'd find below.

No. He could not be thinking about Alex's nipples right now.

"I better get moving, Ben's probably waiting."

"Can I walk you?"

She shook her head. "It's only a block away." Kneeling again, she patted Bijou on her ridiculously puffy head. "Nice to meet you pup." Then she stood, her fingertips grazing the exposed skin on his forearm as she passed. "See you around, Rich."

"Congratulations!" Rich called after her and watched her walk away until she blended into the sea of other black robes headed off campus. Alex meant that she'd see him again when they ran into each other in another three years, but Rich didn't want to wait that long. Yes, seeing her again had stirred up bad memories and mixed emotions about their past, but there was something else there too. Not just that he couldn't get the picture of Alex in red lace out of his mind. The old Rich would have fixated on that image, but the new Rich wanted to know why Alex looked like she was about to shatter.

"Come on, Bijou. We better head back."

Chapter Five

The damn keys weren't working.

Alex's head hurt. It had pounded the entire drive home from Lawrence. She'd had to drive into the sun. That was the problem with living in a different city than your boyfriend, you had to drive half an hour home—into the sun—more often than not with a hangover. What she wanted was a shower and a burrito with beans and cheese and a flour tortilla.

Finally, Alex examined her key ring and realized she was trying to unlock her apartment key with her building key. She switched to the right one, and let herself in.

God, Dale was going to kick her ass if she was sluggish this evening. And she would be. He could always tell when she'd been eating like crap and drinking too much. Despite Dale's otherwise commendable merits as a trainer, not least of which were that he didn't think she couldn't be a badass just because she was a woman, he had the annoying habit of looking at food solely as fuel. That meant the meal plan he'd written for Alex included a lot of lean meat and vegetables cooked in avocado oil. No gluten. No dairy, and definitely no pizza or burritos. Funnily enough, tequila was approved, but his plan said 1 to 2 ounces a week, not the half a bottle she'd knocked back last night.

She sent Avery a quick text to bring Mexican food when she showed up for work, then started a pot of coffee before hopping in the shower.

Last night had been disappointing. Ben had picked her up at the Kwik Shop and greeted her with a bouquet of roses and daisies. It was a nice gesture, she guessed, if she cared for flowers. Then he'd taken her out to an Italian restaurant, even though she had asked for sushi, because according to Ben, she ate sushi all the time. Italian was special. Which, while technically true because she lived above Tokyo Nights, did not make pasta sound more appetizing. She wasn't used to all the carbs, so pasta tended to give her a stomachache these days. She'd ordered the fried calamari and pretended.

As the night wore on, Ben was not interested in hearing about the launch party she was throwing for Alex & Co. Jewelry. Every time she tried to tell him about the plans she'd been making with Janet and Ichiro, the manager at Tokyo Nights, he changed the subject back to the research he'd been doing for his thesis. While Alex had enjoyed talking about the merits of ontological versus teleological arguments for the existence of God when Ben had first brought it up, he never tired of the subject. Alex resorted to making up outrageous—and unsound—arguments to every point Ben brought up. Which might have finally pushed him over the edge into thinking she was as stupid as her blonde hair made her look. As she'd consumed more and more tequila, she'd found herself more and more hilarious.

At some point, Alex was pretty sure he kissed her just to shut her up, which led to them having mediocre, unsatisfying—for her at least—sex on the sofa. Alex had woken up there an hour ago, with her dress still hiked up to her boobs. Ben had still been passed out in his bed when she'd left. Alex had said a prayer of thanks that he didn't have roommates before letting herself out.

They were supposed to have dinner Tuesday night, but Alex didn't even want to go anymore. She wanted to go to Tokyo Nights and dance and drink sake and eat sushi. She wanted to find a man who knew how to perform oral sex, then get up the next morning and go pound a punching bag with everything she had. As she turned off her shower, she acknowledged that the desire to sleep with another man probably meant she was done with Ben.

On top of everything else, Alex was still pissed off about running into Rich. She knew full well that she had no reason to be angry with him. None of the things she was pissed about were even his fault. Every one of them had to do with the fallout from what they'd decided to do together. They had decided to sleep with each other. They had decided to not use condoms anymore because Alex was on the pill, and because they hadn't been sleeping with anyone else. Alex had still made him get tested. He was a man whore; she wasn't going to be stupid about it. Since she'd had her fair share of one night stands over the past year, she asked one of the midwives at the birthing center to run some tests just in case. They'd even talked about her birth control, which until Rich, had worked just fine.

Alex still wasn't sure how she'd ended up pregnant. She hadn't missed a day on her pill. She hadn't been sick or on any antibiotics. The midwife she talked to about it before she scheduled her appointment at Planned Parenthood had told her that these sorts of things happened sometimes. Ethan had suggested she'd left her pills out in the heat too long. It was possible she supposed. It had been summer, but Alex still couldn't remember if she'd ever left them in her car during the day.

After her abortion, Alex got an IUD, and lived in less fear of another accidental pregnancy, but she was forever on the lookout for sore boobs coinciding with nausea. If she ever did get pregnant again, she wanted it to be one hundred percent on purpose.

Alex groaned and rubbed her eyes, too dry this morning for contacts. She would have loved to run into Rich when he was disheveled and hung over. It would have been so satisfying if he had been wearing a wrinkled shirt that didn't match his pants, or had red eyes and whiskey spilled down his front. But that was the thing about Rich. He always looked put together. Though he dressed the part of the college professor with tidy button downs under sport coats and even the occasional tie, he looked anything but stodgy.

Even on a Sunday he'd been wearing a gray button down with dark jeans. He'd probably taken his fancy pants girlfriend out to a fancy pants brunch where they could bring their fancy pants dog.

The dog was ridiculous. She looked like someone had stuck her tiny little paw into an electrical outlet then plunked a bow on top of her head.

But man, how long had it been since Alex had thought about Rich? Actually thought about *him*. She thought about how much she'd screwed her life up since she'd slept with him that first time, but she hadn't spent much time thinking about Rich the man.

That's because Rich was a dangerous territory where her physical desires warred with her sense of loyalty. Because she loved Juliet like a sister, Alex had broken off her affair with Rich. It was probably the one and only time Alex had ever been the one to initiate a breakup. She was usually the one getting dumped. But holy mother of God, for two and a half months, Alex had had the best sex of her life. The first time, they'd been drinking, and she'd thought it had been a fluke. When she tried him out a second and third time, purely for scientific reasons, it only got better. Alex was no innocent. She liked sex and wasn't shy about it.

For years, Alex had given Juliet shit about sleeping with Rich after they'd broken up. She didn't think any man was tempting enough to put up with that kind of shit. But cheater or not, Rich's practice had paid off, because she totally got it. Sex that good messed with a girl's head.

Alex groaned and squeezed her thighs together as she thought about the last night she'd spent with Rich, when he'd woken her up by nipping his way up her thighs until his mouth was on her core and she was grinding into his face. That had been the standard she'd held all oral to since, and all had fallen short—not that she'd a ton of experiences to compare it with in the last couple of years. Until Ben, she'd been more focused on school or her business.

Of course, the morning of the epic oral was also most likely the morning she'd gotten knocked up, so she almost wished it hadn't happened at all. Almost. God. Rich Durand was a minefield, and Alex needed to stay far, far away from him.

Alex was sipping her second mug of coffee and reviewing the newest wholesale orders when Avery arrived, banging through the apartment door when she came in. Avery was never quiet, and it was one of the things Alex liked most about working with her. The sound of footsteps, the constant humming along to their music, it was good to have signs of life in her apartment. It made it feel less empty when she was alone.

"Got the food boss," she said, rustling the white paper sacks in the studio doorway. "Where do you want it?"

"On the bar," she said, making one last note before she left the studio.

After Juliet had moved to Colorado, Alex had thought about moving to a smaller place or finding another roommate, but the temptation to turn Juliet's old room into her jewelry studio won out. The room that used to be full of jungle plants and Juliet's yoga accessories now housed tools, both large and small, littered over various tables. It wasn't a huge space, but she had a place for cutting sheet metal, a place for soldering, a giant cabinet for storing beads and fittings. She even had a little shipping table for Avery to work at.

Alex followed the click and rattle of dishware out into the living room and to the breakfast bar that separated the living room from the galley kitchen. Avery was filling a purple and blue mug with coffee and had pulled a single plate out of the cabinet.

"What is this?" Alex asked as she pulled a paper wrapped bundle out of the bag and peeked under the wrapping. It looked like meat and cilantro on a tiny tortilla.

"Tacos," Avery said. "Real tacos."

Alex took a bite of one of the tacos and moaned, then said. "I would have been happy with Taco Bell." It was a Taco Bell bean burrito she'd been craving after all.

Avery rolled her eyes as she dug in her purse. "I know." She slapped a receipt down on the counter. "You can thank me later."

Alex started in on a second taco while Avery topped off her coffee. "Now, since those of us who aren't hung over don't feel like eating Mexican food at ten o'clock in the morning, how about you tell me what I'm working on today."

Alex had just finished reviewing the orders they needed to get out over the next week when her phone rang. She glanced at the screen and her heart dropped into her still roiling stomach when she saw it was Elise. While Alex sometimes called and pumped Elise for information on her Gran, they weren't regular gossip buddies or anything. The last time Elise had called Alex had been when Gran had been in the hospital.

Trying to control her panic, Alex answered with an, "Hey, Elise. What's up?"

That Elise opened with, "Alex, honey. It's your grandmother," didn't help matters. "We were supposed to meet for breakfast this morning before my yoga class, but she wasn't answering the door, so I called an ambulance."

"Gran is in the hospital?" Alex asked.

"No, Alex." Elise's voice was quiet and gentle, and Alex forgot how to breathe. "She passed in the night. I'm so sorry honey."

Gray static settled down over the room. Alex couldn't hear or see anything other than a buzzing like TV snow. Gran was dead? How could Gran have died? She was immortal. Immoveable. She was too stubborn to die.

Somehow, Alex made it through the rest of the phone call. When she hung up, the static had cleared enough that she was aware Avery had pulled her chair up right in front of Alex and was resting a hand on her knee.

"I have to go to home," Alex said.

"Yeah." Avery pulled Alex into a hug. "I'm so sorry."

Alex was relieved she didn't have to explain. She didn't have the energy for it now. Her mind was racing with everything she had to do.

When Avery released her, Alex took a deep breath, then launched into what she needed Avery to do to get what orders out they could and let their customers know there was going to be a short delay on somethings.

"Whatever you need us to do. We've got it."

"Can you call Janet? I need to pack."

Avery pulled out her phone and Alex wandered, dazed into her bedroom. She sat down on her bed and stared at the wall. She needed to pack. It was a two and half our drive down to Pittsburgh, the little town in Southeast Kansas where her Gran lived, and she needed to get on the road now. She had a funeral to plan. Gran's house to take care of. Phone calls to make. Find someone to take the cat. Her head was spinning with everything that needed done, even as Alex couldn't quite grasp that her grandmother was gone.

She'd been alive yesterday. They'd talked yesterday. Gran had called Alex on the house phone so Alex could walk her through how to download the picture Alex had sent—one of the ones Rich had taken for her.

Before she even thought about it, Alex dialed Juliet's number. She assumed Juliet would be mid-birth and unable to answer and didn't expect to get her, but even leaving a voicemail might help.

Juliet picked up on the second ring. "Hey, what's up?" The background noise almost overpowered Juliet's voice, like she was in a car.

"You're not on your way to deliver a baby or anything, are you?"

Juliet laughed. "Just got done doing that. Ethan has a surgery this afternoon. We were grabbing a late breakfast so we actually have a chance of seeing each other today. Is everything okay?"

Alex heard Ethan asking the same question in the background.

Guilt hit Alex. With Juliet being a traveling midwife, and Ethan being one of the only obstetric surgeons in a rural part of Colorado, they often worked opposite shifts. Their time together was rare and precious, and Alex was going to interrupt them some more.

"No. Gran died this morning."

Juliet gasped. "Oh, honey. I'm so sorry. Do you know what happened?"

Ethan asked what happened, and Juliet said, "Her grandmother just died. Shh!"

"I don't have all of the details yet. I need to get down there today to start taking care of things."

"Of course. I'll check flights once we get to the restaurant and let you know when I can get in, okay?"

"You don't need to come. You have patients, and Ethan."

Juliet made a sound like a hissing cat. "Ethan is nearly forty years old. He can take care of himself. And someone else can cover my patients for a few days. I'm coming."

Ethan grumbled about how often Juliet brought up that he would be turning forty in the fall, and Alex let out a sad, little laugh.

"I'll text you the address," Alex said.

"Good. I'll see you in a few hours," Juliet said. "Take care of yourself and be safe on your drive, okay?"

"You too. I've gotta get going."

"I understand," Juliet said. "Call me when you get in so I don't worry, will you?"

"I will."

"I love you, honey. I love you, and I'm so sorry this is all falling on your shoulders, but you've got this. And I've got you."

Tears welled in Alex's eyes. Why did Juliet always know the right thing to say? "Thanks. I love you, too."

Alex hung up and let a few tears fall before dashing them from her cheeks with her fingers. She didn't have time for this right now. Maybe once Juliet was with her.

God, Alex did not deserve a friend like Juliet.

After throwing some things into a bag and a quick call to Dale that she would be out for a few days, Alex left Avery to lock up and headed south. It was only as she pulled into her grandmother's driveway that she realized it hadn't even occurred to her call her boyfriend. Worse, someone had to tell her mother.

Chapter Six

Alex went to Elise's house first, leaving her bags in the back of her RAV4. She couldn't bring herself to go into the small, old house, not without her Gran's large presence filling it up.

Elise greeted her with a hug and an egg salad sandwich with apple slices for a late lunch. Alex could barely eat, but thanked her old neighbor, nonetheless. She did learn that Elise didn't have Vivien's phone number, only Alex's, so the burden of calling her mother still rested squarely on her shoulders. She did know who her grandmother's lawyer was, and that he had Gran's funeral preferences in her will. So, after Elise insisted on helping Alex bring her things into Gran's too quiet house, Alex headed to Steve's Sheldon's office.

He was a member of the same church Alex's grandmother went to, which was probably the only criteria Gran had considered when selecting him to draft her will. Alex had always gotten a distinct creeper vibe off the middle-aged man, as if it was only a matter of time before they found the bodies buried in his basement, and she had to suppress a shudder as she pulled up outside his office at a quarter to five.

He was in the process of locking the front door as Alex stepped out of her car. Sure enough, as Alex approached Mr. Sheldon, his eyes took in everything from the top of her light, billowy sweater to the heels of her ankle boots.

"Can I help you, young lady?" he asked, taking his time about dragging his eyes back up her body.

Alex put on the smile she saved for store buyers. The confident, professional one that hid most of her usual snark. "Good afternoon, Mr. Sheldon," she stuck out her hand, "I'm Alex Stafford, Geneva Stafford's granddaughter."

Recognition flashed in his eyes as he grasped her hand in the limp handshake of a man who clearly thought he was dealing with someone delicate and inferior. Why he would think that after dealing with her Gran, Alex had no idea. It was all she could do not to squirm away from him.

"Of course. It's been a long time. How is Geneva? I haven't seen her around much this spring."

Was that because Gran hadn't been getting out, or because Mr. Sheldon hadn't been making it into church? And did he not know? Elise was not exactly known for her discretion. Plus, there would have been the firetruck and ambulance announcing it to the world. And Pittsburgh, Kansas was not that big of a town.

Alex took a deep breath. Here went nothing. "Actually, Gran passed away this morning, and I was hoping I could stop by and see if she left any information with you that might affect how I plan her ceremony. I won't take much of your time."

Mr. Sheldon nodded, an air of passable professionalism washed away the creepy old man vibe, and he turned around to unlock his office door. "Come on in. She didn't leave much, but she came in last year and made a few changes."

It only took about twenty minutes to go over her grandmother's slim file and get a copy to take with her. Mr.

Sheldon was all professionalism until he escorted Alex back out the door, his hand lingering a little too long and little too familiarly at the small of her back. Alex scooted out from under his touch the second there was room to move away and glared at him.

"Thank you for staying late," she said, crossing to her car to put as much distance between them as possible, then turned around at the last second. There were too many other times Alex had let things like that slide. "You know, most people don't like to be touched uninvited, especially by men they don't know."

Mr. Sheldon looked startled. "I was just trying to comfort you. You look so sad, darlin.'"

"I am sad. My Gran just died, but I didn't come here for comfort. I came here for business. And you should respect that."

Mr. Sheldon sputtered about how he'd known her since she was a little girl and how he'd known her Grandmother for years and how he would never, but Alex didn't stick around to hear it. She had what she needed, so she turned her back, hopped into her car, and left.

Anger warred with grief on the drive to the coffee shop she'd frequented in high school. She ordered a sandwich and a latte and sat down to make notes on everything she needed to get done over the next few days. It was too much for her mind to handle, and her brain kept running in circles between calling the minister at the Presbyterian church and figuring out how she was going to get rid of all Gran's stuff, and put the house on the market, and then zipping back to figuring out which funeral home to use and how to afford to pay them until Gran's life insurance check came in.

At six, she got a text from Juliet. *I just touched down in Springfield. I'm on my way, and I have wine.*

Bless you. Alex typed back, then ordered a giant chocolate chip muffin in the hopes that she could while away the time it would take Juliet to drive in from Springfield. Under normal circumstances, she would have snapchatted the chocolate monstrosity at Dale, just to annoy him, but she couldn't muster the energy.

As she picked the chocolate chips off the top of her muffin, she calculated how much longer she'd have linger at the coffee shop before going back to Gran's. She hadn't realized Juliet would be flying into Springfield. It was the closest airport, but Alex didn't even want to think about how much it had cost her friend to get on a last-minute flight from Denver to Springfield's dinky little airport. She definitely was not going to ask. Ethan had money. Alex knew that. She would not let herself feel guilty about this too.

At seven, guilt about not calling her mother finally caught up with her. She hadn't seen Vivien since Christmas, when she'd brought around her most recent boyfriend. Edgar was more straight-laced than Vivien usually chose in that he wore clean clothes and didn't smell like cigarettes. He was a history professor at a small university in Montana and smelled like old leather books. Alex hoped her mom was still with him. But outside a handful of texts, Alex hadn't heard anything from her mother. Maybe they had broken up.

The funny thing was, Alex had liked Edgar, a divorced father of two grown children. He had been courteous to

Geneva and shown an interest in Alex's business, and her stupid gushing praise about Ben, because that relationship had been new at Christmas. Alex had even thought Edgar might be good for her mother. She'd mentioned something about teaching classes at a community art center, which would make her invested in something other than just her own work. But maybe, just like Alex's relationship with Ben, which had seemed so promising at first, things hadn't turned out like they'd hoped.

As her mother's phone clicked over to voicemail, Alex decided that her next call should be to Ben, even as she acknowledged that she probably should have called him before she left town. What did it say about her relationship with him that she'd called her trainer first? Nothing good probably.

"Hey, Mom. It's Alex. I thought you should know I'm in Pittsburgh. Gran passed away this morning. I'm not sure when the funeral will be yet, but I could really use your help going through the house and stuff. Call me back when you can."

Next, she called Ben, who also didn't answer. She left him a similar message, minus the part about needing his help. She didn't want him to come.

When the coffee shop closed at seven-thirty, Alex packed up her things and drove back to her grandmother's house. She waited in the driveway for Juliet to arrive.

It was only a few minutes before a silver sedan pulled into the driveway behind Alex's black RAV4. Juliet's long hair was a blur of red as she jumped out the car and threw her arms around Alex. Unable to hold it in anymore, Alex buried her face in Juliet's gauzy yellow scarf and bawled.

• • • •

RICH HADN'T STOPPED thinking about Alex all day. Most of his reminiscences were x-rated, as had been most of their time together. He remembered the way her breasts turned up on her chest when she arched her back and rode him hard. The way her red-painted lips looked closing around his cock. The way her heat engulfed him when he plunged himself inside her with no barrier between them. She was the only person since Juliet that he'd not used a condom with. Even last night, as he'd tried to rid Alex from his mind by keeping Lynnette in bed for hours, things hadn't ever gotten so out of hand that either one of them had forgotten protection.

Rich sighed and shook his head at the papers he was still grading from his last class. Grades were due Wednesday. In the end, he'd given Lynnette the wrong impression. She'd been acting insecure, saying that they hadn't seen each other enough lately, that he wasn't returning her phone calls as quickly as he used to.

Instead of telling her she was right, that he was thinking about seeing other women—and after running into Alex last week, one woman in particular—Rich had kissed Lynnette and taken her to bed.

Now she'd been texting him all day about how great last night had been and how she couldn't stop thinking about him and she wanted to know when they could schedule a repeat performance.

He should just tell her that she was a little too particular, a little too structured. That it was a problem for him that she didn't want children. That he couldn't handle speaking French all the time like she liked to do. He mainly taught Italian for a reason.

But he wouldn't. Not yet.

The class he should be preparing for but was also avoiding was the one French class he taught. It was an advanced lit class taught entirely in French, and all he had to do was talk about books and grade papers. He liked it enough to think about how in a different life, he probably could have been a literature professor.

Italian was his first love though. The language itself was a poem. It was the language of his mother and his grandmother, and they were the strongest, most genuine, most honest people he knew. Italian represented everything he knew of beauty. Watching students grasp the language for the first time truly was the reason he got out of bed in the morning.

French was his father's language. The language of loss, betrayal, bereavement. Their father had left when Rich was thirteen. For five years he'd made a cursory attempt to keep in touch, but Rich hadn't heard from him since he'd turned eighteen. Rich had given up trying to contact his father by the time he was twenty and too many phone calls and letters had gone unanswered.

Gina had written their father off the moment he'd left. She'd only been fifteen and already didn't have any patience for men wasting her time. Secretly, Rich had always thought she was the smarter one for doing that. Who left their wife and kids for a woman in a different country? Especially when he'd been the one to move his family abroad in the first place?

Rich's mother, Sonia, had met his father, Marius, at a bar on a post-school vacation to Paris. The way his mother told it, it had been a classic love at first sight sort of fairy tale weekend. Then Marius had followed Sonia back to her family's olive oil farm in Tuscany, where, though she'd welcomed him into her bed at night, she'd told him she couldn't marry someone who never did anything for himself. Marius had been doing odd jobs, content before to make just enough money to stay in booze and food, but when Sonia asked him for more, he'd moved to Florence and taken a job teaching French.

Marius and Sonia were married a year later, and conceived Gina almost immediately. Marius was offered a job teaching at an American private school who was looking for a native French speaker, and that's how his family had ended up in the Midwest.

Maybe it was strange that as a half French-Algerian, half Italian man, Rich felt comfortable living on the Missouri River, but it was the truth. As much as he loved visiting his grandmother or marveled at how he could sort of blend in with the crowd whenever he visited Paris, Kansas City was home.

His mother had made the United States her home as well. She'd helped establish a culinary olive oil direct trade between chefs and farms in Italy. She'd moved to Savannah, Georgia a few years ago. There she could not only stay close to the ports, but also stay warm. She hadn't heard from Marius either.

But unlike Gina, who had written their father off as a jerk and an asshole, Rich had never quite been able to let go without knowing what had become of him. Two years ago, after Juliet had moved away and he'd learned that Ethan had followed her to Colorado, Rich had given up on so much. He couldn't compete with that level of romantic gesture, especially because he didn't trust it. His father had followed his mother once, after all. He wished Juliet the best, he truly did, but he'd seen the outcome of that sort of story, and it always ended badly.

That didn't mean he didn't want to know what had become of his father in the last fifteen years. His inquiries had started slowly, trusting consulates and public records offices to take his requests seriously. After waiting months for each reply over and over again, Rich had finally contacted a private investigator in France. The case had been a low priority for the man, but Rich hadn't cared. As long as he received monthly updates on his progress, he would be happy.

In the weeks since Rich had hired the man, there had been precious little information. Marius Durand had returned to Paris in 1998 and taken a job as a translator, but that was all Rich had to go on. The French government was famous for its bureaucracy, and Rich was trying to be patient as the P.I. navigated the forms and permissions and faxed signatures required for information, but Rich was beginning to wonder how much effort it took to track a man down.

Shouldn't the bureaucracy also mean there was a solid paper trail to follow?

The worst part was that Rich didn't even want his father to be a part of his life anymore. It had been twenty years since Marius had left them. Rich didn't think he'd let him be a part of his life even if he could find him. Rich just wanted to know what was so important as to keep his father away from his family for so long. What could he possibly be hiding that was so embarrassing? Didn't he know that even if they didn't like that he'd left, they'd still accept that he'd tried to do the right thing for himself?

Rich wasn't sure.

Part of him wasn't positive he'd ever find his father, because part of him knew the selfishness that drove the desire to disappear. No one liked facing the consequences from when they messed up. Rich especially. And Rich had lived seven years knowing he'd messed up the best relationship he'd ever had. He wasn't sure he'd ever find something to rival what he'd had with Juliet, but he sure wouldn't let fear of failure keep him from trying.

Of course, that meant figuring out how to extricate himself from this relationship with Lynnette. He could avoid her well enough for the next week while they both finished up their end of semester grading, but after that, he'd either have find another excuse or face the music and tell her they were over.

Alex flashed through his mind again. To his surprise, it wasn't a vision of her naked beneath him, but of the one time Alex had let him take her out.

Alex had strict rules about when and how they could see each other to avoid upsetting Juliet. They could only meet at Tokyo Nights if they were going to meet in public, and only for the purposes of having sex later. During those weeks, Alex had often dropped by his apartment and greeted him with a hand on his belt buckle. While hot, the message that he had been nothing more than a good lay had been loud and clear.

But there had been that one Sunday morning. They had stayed out too late and had way too much to drink the night before. He remembered laughing with her as they'd eaten a post-coital bowl of cereal standing naked in her kitchen, then gone to sleep shortly before dawn. He'd woken her by kissing his way from her ankles to the apex of her thighs, and after he'd feasted there, they'd had slow, lazy Sunday morning sex. While they were still in bed together, he'd convinced her to let him take her to breakfast, and they'd walked, hand in hand, the few blocks over to a place that served a late brunch. The image of looking down at their entwined fingers was the one that stole over him. That had stayed with him. It was just about the only indication Alex had ever given him that maybe more than her body was involved in whatever they were doing.

Rich had fun with Alex that day. He'd nearly broached the subject that they try to be something more. He'd understood Alex's hesitancy about Juliet. It hadn't been ideal, Alex living with the woman he'd nearly married, the woman who would have had his child had things turned out differently. And yes, maybe his original motivation in sleeping with Alex had been an immature reaction to seeing Juliet out on a date with another man.

But as of that morning, Rich hadn't seen Juliet for nearly a month. She'd been spending every spare second with Ethan. Rich didn't think her feelings would be all that hurt if Rich and Alex wanted to date for real. It might have made things better, actually. He'd known Juliet and Alex's relationship had been strained because of him, but he hadn't been in any position to do anything about it. He'd been in love with Juliet since he was eighteen, but he'd found himself at some point over that summer not wanting to give Alex up either.

He'd held back though. Something told him Alex wasn't ready for more, and it had nothing to do with Juliet. He'd met Alex when she was a freshman in college, and he'd never seen her in a relationship, and by her own confession she hadn't been in one in the four years since he and Juliet had broken up. Rich had just decided to ease her into the idea. He'd already had her hooked on his body, he just needed to press her gently into more brunches, surprise ice cream dates. Maybe a bouquet of flowers every now and then.

Alex had not given him the chance. Apparently, the brunch had already pushed her too far, because she'd ghosted him for a week after that, then finally told him she couldn't see him anymore. She'd said things were too awkward with Juliet and she had to put that friendship first. Rich had understood, but he thought he'd deserved more than a few text messages.

He'd wondered more than once if she'd already known she was pregnant when she'd sent those texts. If maybe it was the pregnancy that had spooked her. Since he'd had no idea she'd been pregnant until weeks after she'd already terminated, he had no frame of reference.

A knock on his door startled him from his thoughts. A different petite blonde woman leaned against the frame, her arms crossed over an Italian study guide he'd never assigned, but which was available in the school library. She was dressed in short pink running shorts and a matching top that was probably a size too small but showed off her generous cleavage.

Her name was Bethany, and she'd been in Rich's beginning Italian classes for the last two years. She was not a day over twenty, and she had made her interest in *Signor Durand* clear on more than one occasion. Rich had never dated students. Not only did the university have strict, lose your tenure type rules against dating anyone enrolled in your classes, but Rich was repelled by the idea of leveraging grades for sexual favors. As much as Rich was a fan of sex, he was also into pleasure for pleasure's sake. He had no delusions of grandeur, no need to exploit his power. The very idea made him sick. As he got older, getting involved with someone any more than a few years younger than him had lost its appeal. Looking at Bethany now, he knew she thought she was sexy, but all Rich saw was a kid.

Twenty was so far removed from his life experience that he couldn't relate to it anymore. Did she even know what loss was? Rich didn't know much about his students' personal lives, and he liked it that way. Maybe Bethany had suffered in her twenty years, but it didn't change the fact that, to Rich, Bethany looked like a little girl playing dress up rather than a candidate in the search for the woman to love for the rest of his life. Again, a vision of Alex in her cap and gown flashed before his mind's eye. He pushed it away.

"What can I do for you, Bethany?" he asked.

"Well, I was preparing for the trip next month, and I wondered if you had any pointers about traveling in Italy."

Rich nodded to the chair in front of his desk, and Bethany sat down. For the first time in three years, Rich wasn't leading the summer study abroad trip to Italy. One of his colleagues, a professor pursuing tenure had coordinated with one of the art historian professors to create a dual purpose language and art history study track. Rich had settled for teaching Italian 101 over the summer. It would be nice to have a break, and maybe he'd take a quick trip to see his grandmother in August.

"You'd be better off talking to Professor Russo," Rich said. "She can tell you what to expect on your trip."

"But you've been so many times," Bethany said, arching her back so her boobs stuck out. "I'm sure you can tell me so much more than she can."

Rich used his teacher smile, the one that was nice, but not too indulgent. "Find a travel belt and carry your money and your passport inside your clothes, especially when you're in Rome. The pickpockets are bad there."

"Oh, thank you," Bethany said, leaning forward to display the low cut of her tank top more fully. Bile rose in his throat. He wasn't quite sure on her angle. She was either insecure to the extreme, or she was too confident in her ability to attract an older man through sheer perseverance. Either way, Rich wasn't interested.

"I just thought you'd know more about traveling in Italy since you're from there."

"Actually, I'm not," he said quietly. "My mother is. Now, if you'll excuse me," he said, rising, and hoping he could usher Bethany to the door with nothing more than good manners so he wouldn't have to actually touch her. "Practice your basics. Know how to order espresso, ask for a bathroom, that sort of thing."

"But-"

"Thank you for stopping by, Bethany. Have a good trip. I'll see you in August."

Then he shut the door. He knew she was standing on the other side of it, staring at the wood. He locked the door for good measure, then sighed audibly. Usually he kept an open door and encouraged his students to stop by whenever he was available. And if Bethany had wanted to talk about how she still had trouble with masculine nouns, he'd have been much less rude.

Rich circled back around to his desk and pushed aside the notes for next semester's French class. He didn't have the patience for French anymore. Screw the whole lot of them. He'd thought, more than once, when he was younger about replacing Durand with Pieri, his mother's maiden name. It sounded better with his first name, not that anyone but his mother called him Riccardo. But Riccardo Pieri had some poetry to it whereas Riccardo Durand sounded broken to his ears. Of course, to most people, he was Professor Rich Dew-Rand, which he couldn't help but patiently correct to the softer, less grating French pronunciation of Du-Rahn, even if he knew it was annoying.

But as much as he loved his mother's family, and as much as he told himself he despised his father, Rich couldn't bring himself to do away with the name. He wanted to be able to shed the name as easily as Gina had when she'd married Colin and become a Stewart. But it wasn't the same for men. For Gina, it was choosing to go by her husband's name as well as a rejection of her father. For Rich, it would only be a rejection—and he didn't hate his father. For thirteen years he'd been one of the best parts of Rich's life. Gina's too. It was probably why they'd been so hurt by his leaving—and why Rich had missed him so much after he'd gone.

With the investigation all but at a standstill, he barely dared to hope anymore.

Chapter Seven

The first night Juliet stayed with Alex at her grandmother's house they finished two bottles of wine. Alastor, Gran's fat white cat draped himself over Alex's lap and didn't budge as Juliet told Alex about her patients and the births she'd been at, and how exhausting it was to travel all over the mountains to different hospitals and clinics.

"It's worth it," Juliet said, "Even if I only end up driving them to the closest hospital. She ends up giving birth in a place that she feels safe and is safe for her baby and not trapped alone and afraid on a mountain."

Juliet glowed when she spoke about her work, and Alex almost regretted quitting her receptionist job at the Birthing Center back home. Every day there was a birth, the place was filled with joy and awe. Every damn time. Alex missed that. It made working out of her house seem lonely by comparison.

"Your job is so important, and all I do is play with metal and rocks," Alex said, caressing the cat's velvety ears

"That's not true," Juliet said, fingering the necklace resting against her collarbone. It was one of Alex's, a simple piece with a raw yellow crystal hanging from a delicate golden chain. "You make beautiful things. And the world needs more beauty in it."

"You don't think it's frivolous?"

Juliet shook her head. "Not even a little bit. You create things that have meaning to the people who buy it. They incorporate them as part of their identity. You build their confidence, help them to be more authentic and honest. That's one of the most valuable services I can think of."

"You get all of that from a little piece of jewelry?"

Juliet shrugged. "Isn't that why we buy it?"

Alex finished off her glass of wine to try to combat the tears gathering in her eyes and told Juliet about how much her business had expanded in the last year, and how much it was going to expand in the coming year, and how exhausting it all was.

"You need a vacation," Juliet said. "You should take a few days and come stay with us at the lodge."

About a year after he and Juliet had moved to Colorado, Ethan had purchased a big rustic style house halfway up a mountain. Alex hadn't been there yet, but Juliet was an Instagrammer, so Alex had seen plenty of pictures. It looked like the sort of place that was meant to be a timeshare for super rich skiers, but it had apparently always been Ethan's dream to be a mountain man who lived in style, because according to Juliet, he was never moving again.

"Like you two almost newlyweds want me under your feet," Alex said. "You're going to be too busy making babies." Then, because she was stupid, and a little drunk, Alex had to add, "Why aren't you knocked up yet? I thought Ethan wanted to have kids like three years ago."

Juliet's smiled faltered then fell. Juliet had always been tall and willowy, with a lithe strength that came from her years as a yoga teacher, but Alex watched her shrink down to half her size as if she were filling a hole inside herself.

Alex crossed from the armchair to the sofa in a second, wrapping an arm around her friend's shoulder. "Hey now, what happened? What did I just step in there?"

"I had another miscarriage a couple of months ago."

Alex squeezed Juliet tighter, but inside she went numb from a new wave of shock and grief. Juliet had lost another pregnancy? And she hadn't even told Alex she'd been pregnant.

"I'm sorry," was all Alex could say.

Juliet rested her head against Alex's. Her voice was low and tired when she said, "I should have told you. Ethan told me I should. But after the last time, I thought if I could just make it to twenty weeks, I'd be in the clear, you know. So Ethan and I kept it between ourselves. And it was such a special secret."

Alex nodded, and Juliet relaxed into her a little bit more. "We found out on Christmas. I'd been feeling a bit off for a few days, and I was so busy I didn't think about it much. I took a test Christmas morning on a whim and started screeching in the bathroom. Ethan was still in bed and came running in thinking I was dying. But when I calmed him down and showed him the test, I've never seen him so happy.

"Everything was going well too. I felt like crap, but got an early ultrasound, and we found the heartbeat with my doppler at ten weeks, and then the next week, I got up in the middle of the night to go to the bathroom and there was some cramping then so much blood. I screamed and then Ethan was there. I don't even remember most of that night. I know Ethan brought me to the hospital, but all I remember is that his hands were trembling the whole time."

Ethan's hands didn't shake. They couldn't. He was a surgeon *because* he kept his cool in stressful situations. But as an OB-GYN, he also knew everything that could be going wrong with his love, and the at the thought of losing Juliet, he'd trembled.

"He was afraid he was going to lose you," Alex said.

"He keeps saying that he's just glad I'm alright."

God, all Alex wanted in this whole entire world was for someone to love her like that.

"I'm glad too," Alex said.

Juliet shifted, leaning back so she could look Alex in the eye. "What if I can't ever have a baby?" She asked. "What if I'm the midwife who can't give birth?"

"You'll have a baby," Alex said. "Probably lots of them. Lord knows you have the room for them."

Juliet let out a huff of a laugh. "It was Ethan's idea to stop my birth control."

"And do you know anyone else who knows more about pregnant women than Ethan?"

Juliet laughed for real this time, and Alex took that as an assent.

"He'll figure out how to keep you pregnant *and* healthy.

"Thanks," Juliet said, swiping at her tears. "I've missed you."

"I've missed you."

"We should talk about non-wedding stuff more often."

"Well, since your wedding will be here before you know it and I'm not getting married, we'll probably be better at it in the future."

Juliet laughed again, and when they went to bed that night, it almost felt like they were roommates all over again.

Together, they passed the next two days hauling load after load of clothes and knick-knacks to Goodwill, shooing Alastor out of boxes and answering phone calls. Elise kept them in sandwiches and baked goods while Alex finalized plans for the funeral, answered relative's questions, and figured out how to dispose of the rest of Gran's things.

Juliet's phone rang constantly, because even though another midwife was seeing her patients this week, it seemed that she was still indispensable. And she was constantly smiling to herself as she received another text from Ethan.

Alex was envious every time. Not in a jealous way. Yes, she wanted something like that too, something more than what she had going on with Ben, but Alex was happy for Juliet. She'd been looking for this sort of love for a long time, and Alex only wanted to feel a tenth of that sort of contentment.

• • • •

THEY HELD THE FUNERAL Thursday morning. Juliet stood by Alex's side as the guests offered their condolences. The entire time she stood in the greeting line, Alex kept her eyes out for her mother. She'd almost thought Vivien wasn't coming, but as the last of the guests filtered into the church, Vivien emerged from a tan rental car in the parking lot, dressed in a flowing black dress. Her long silver hair had been braided, then coiled on top of her head.

By the time she'd reached Alex's side and given her a kiss on the cheek, Juliet had disappeared inside. As much as Alex could have used a little of Juliet's strength, it was probably for the best that Alex spoke to her mother alone.

"I didn't think you were going to make it," Alex said as her mother pulled her into a hug. She'd left her several voicemails, but Vivien had never answered, not even to just check in and see how her daughter was doing.

"I wasn't sure I would there for a minute either, but Edgar and I made it work last minute. He's setting up my booth for me in Colorado, and I'm flying back out this afternoon for the show tomorrow."

"You're not staying."

It wasn't a question. Alex didn't know why she thought her mother would help them finish cleaning out the house. She'd hoped Vivien would at least want some of the hundreds of paperbacks that were still in her room at Gran's house. Alex had saved packing them up just in case Vivien wanted to take them home with her.

"I can't miss the show," Vivien said like the very thought was preposterous.

"Would it be that big of a deal?" Alex asked.

"I'd lose my vendor fee."

"But your mother just died," Alex said, tears gathering in the corners of her eyes against her will.

Vivien ran a hand down Alex's arm and squeezed her hand. A sincere but sad smile tightened her lips. "I know, but I have to go on living, Alex."

Alex understood that. She really did. She had to go on living too. "I'm only asking you to stay one night," Alex said. "I could use your help." What Alex couldn't bring herself to say was that she just wanted her mother's presence. Alex needed to take comfort in what family she had left, and right now, she was feeling closer to her employees than her own mother.

"You know I can't. Maybe we can plan some time together in the fall. There are some great events in your area before Thanksgiving. We'll set aside a few days then."

Alex wanted to stamp her foot like a child and scream that she needed her mother now—today—not six months from now, but she bit her tongue and nodded instead, blinking to keep her frustrated tears at bay.

Vivien pulled her into a hug then, and said, "I'm so proud of you. Putting this together all on your own. You're all grown up. Gran would be proud of you too." Vivien pulled away and thumbed away the twin tears that streaked down Alex's face. "It's time to put on a brave face, Alex. We're strong, and we can do hard things."

Alex nodded and lead her mother inside. While it was nice to know that her mom was at least aware of her shortcomings, Alex wanted to know why Vivien continually left her to face the hardest parts of life alone. Why did it work out that the hardest thing Vivien ever had to do was show up?

Chapter Eight

It was six o'clock before Alex and Juliet had a break after the funeral. They'd had a small catered lunch provided by the church after the ceremony. Vivien had stayed for half an hour, eaten a tea sandwich, then swooped in to give Alex a hug before vanishing. Alex had been asked by five separate people if her mother had even come.

After lunch, Juliet had helped Alex finalize everything on the post-death to-do. They'd lined up an estate sale company. The house was clean and going on the market after the weekend. Elise, was going to keep an eye on things while the house was for sale, and Mr. Spencer hadn't so much as looked Alex in the eye, let alone touched her again.

Keeping busy had kept Alex's mind off why she'd been doing all of these things, but now that she had time to sit still, every stray emotion she'd blown through over the last few days hit her like a she didn't know how to block a punch. And she did know how. She'd spent a lot of time and money and skipped bread learning how to block a punch. That didn't keep her from feeling as though she was perpetually having the wind knocked out of her.

"I am exhausted," Juliet said from where she lay sprawled on the sofa next to Alex. They'd collapsed there together after the realtor had left.

"Me too," Alex yawned. The tight feeling in her chest was only growing sharper the longer they sat. Alastor had chosen to drape himself over Juliet's lap this evening, so she didn't even have him for comfort, the traitor.

Alex kept running her mother's perfunctory goodbye through her mind. She'd whispered, "Remember how proud I am of you," in Alex's ear as she'd hugged her just before her departure. She supposed her mother meant it as a compliment, but all Alex heard was that her mother was glad for the excuse not to deal with any of it. Just like she couldn't be bothered to deal with Alex growing up or returning her daughter's phone calls. And now with her Gran gone, would Vivien even bother coming home for Christmas?

The entire burden of keeping up a relationship with her mother now rested on Alex's shoulders. She was so tired she didn't even know if it would be worth it. Did she want a relationship with her mother? Yes. She always had. But Vivien had never actively cultivated one with Alex. And losing Gran felt a lot like losing her last connection to her mother too.

Alex's eyes must have glazed over, because Juliet asked, "You want to grab a nap while I figure out dinner?"

Alex shook her head. "I want to hit something."

Juliet looked confused, and Alex raised her fists as if she was wearing her boxing gloves. "You know, like a punching bag."

"Oh, right. I keep forgetting you box now. Have I told you how kickass that is?"

Boxing made Alex feel kickass, but only after she finished a workout. Going in, she felt small and had to fight off the suspicion that she didn't belong in the boxing gym. But she'd screwed up her courage and done it over and over again for a year, and she was starting to actually get good. Somehow, she hoped some of that perseverance might translate over to the rest of her life.

"Come with me," Alex said.

"Where?"

"Boxing."

"Now?"

Alex stood and stretched. "My trainer told me the college gym here has some heavy bags if I felt like a workout. It probably costs a fortune for a day pass, but I don't care. I need to hit something."

Juliet rose as well, Alastor melting on to cushion Juliet had just vacated. "Let's go then. I don't suppose there's a place to get Indian food on the way back?"

Alex laughed. Pittsburgh was way too small a town for that. "We might be able to swing Chinese. Or grocery store sushi."

Juliet scrunched her nose. "I'm googling it. There has to be at least a Thai place or something."

"You find dinner. I'm going to go get changed."

They were almost the only women in the place. A couple of women ran on the treadmills across the room, but the majority of the people were men lifting free weights in their corner of the gym next to the heavy bags. A couple of big college aged guys with the sleeves cut out of their t-shirts, one in black, one in white watched them cross into what was probably considered male-only territory. When Alex reached for the tape and showed Juliet how to wrap her hands, she noticed they'd put down their weights and were staring.

Alex knew they didn't look like typical boxers. Juliet was long and lean, and wearing yoga leggings paired with a pink sports bra, but with the muscles of a ballet dancer. Alex was short and thin and knew she didn't look like much in her red running shorts and black tank top. She employed the same feigned obliviousness she used at her gym and pretended she didn't notice the negative attention as she searched out a pair of gloves for Juliet.

Alex showed Juliet how to hold the bag, then showed her a few punches, and after working through a satisfying series of punches, she switched places with Juliet, and coached her through how to hit without hurting herself. The guys could smell how out of her depth Juliet was and circled the other heavy bag under the guise of gearing up to do a few drills themselves, but Alex could feel their eyes on her.

Alex wished this kind of behavior didn't bother her, but it did. Part of her wanted to be used to it, and another part of her screamed that she shouldn't have to get used to it, that she deserved just as much respect in this sport as any hulking dude did. So, she did what Dale had coached her to do in one of their first training sessions when two seasoned gym-goers had stopped their sparring and just stared, she pretended the bag was these guys and that she was totally kicking their asses—or in this case, teaching Juliet how to kick their asses.

The form and technique that had taken Alex months to learn, Juliet had picked up in minutes, but despite her strength, she had little power behind her punches, and Alex told her so.

Juliet squared up for another hit, and Alex could tell from her red face that she was trying to drum up more force, but her one-two hit the bag like a couple of pebbles dropped into a still pool. Juliet could tell it too, because she dropped her hands to her sides and blew out a frustrated breath. "I'm a nurturer. I don't know how to hurt things."

Alex showed Juliet how to square up to the bag again and how use her whole body. "It's all connected," Alex said. "I always imagine I'm pulling the power up from my toes, and if I need inspiration for things to hit, I pull up Rich's face, or you know," she nodded toward the two college guys who were basically circling them like vultures, "pretend the bag is one of these jokers and then I'm not attacking. I'm defending women everywhere."

Juliet glanced over her shoulder at the leering men who weren't even bothering to pretend they were lifting weights anymore. "That could work," she said.

Juliet's power improved somewhat, but she begged off after a few more drills.

Alex gladly donned her gloves again and dove straight into one of the more complicated combinations Dale had taught her. Alex surrendered herself to feel of blood pumping inside her as sweat gathered on her skin. She felt herself grow into something more as she added in a few kicks. She was more than a scrawny screw up in these moments. She could feel her energy extend outside herself, feel herself grow stronger, more stable.

Alex didn't see anything but the way her gloves connected with the bag. She didn't hear anything but the sound of her breath. But she felt everything. She wasn't picturing Rich, or the stupid guys from her gym. She remembered watching her mother walk away, she felt the cold, powdered paper feel of Gran's forehead against her lips when she'd dipped her head into the casket this morning for her final goodbye. She stood over the pit of yawning emptiness inside her and flipped it the bird. She would not fall down again.

Alex stopped when she'd lost track of how many repetitions she'd done. Juliet, grinning like mad, handed Alex a water bottle. Alex's chest was heaving as she took it between her gloves and drank. It was then that she noticed that the quiet wasn't in her head. The whole place had gone silent.

"What?" she asked.

Juliet nodded behind her and noticed that they'd drawn a crowd. The guys that had been circling had disappeared, but the women who'd been on the treadmills before were standing at the edge of the mats, hovering just beyond the free weights. The men who had ignored them before had stopped to watch Alex as well but turned back to their routine now that Alex had noticed them. She smiled at the women and turned back to Juliet.

"That's a little embarrassing."

Juliet shook her head. "You are a badass."

And apparently, the other women thought so too, because they came over and introduced themselves, then asked for a quick lesson.

Alex looked to Juliet who gave her an encouraging nod. She spent the next hour teaching them the basics before her growling stomach was too loud to ignore.

"I am going to be so sore tomorrow," Juliet said as she stretched her arms overheard on the way out. "I can already feel it in my shoulders."

"Oh yeah," Alex nodded, blotting her neck with the towel she'd brought with her. "You're going to feel it for a week." Then she asked, "Did you ever find a Thai place? I'm starved."

"Pad Thai to go?" Juliet asked.

"And whatever greasy, fried appetizer they have," Alex said.

"Oh my God, yes. Two, because I'm not sharing." Juliet pulled out her phone as they sank into the seats of Alex's SUV and placed the order.

They drove in silence for a few minutes before Juliet asked, "Are you still hanging on to your grudge against Rich?"

"What do you mean?"

"Earlier, you said—"

"I only said that because I thought you—"

"I don't," Juliet said. "I forgave Rich a long time ago. There's no anger there anymore."

Alex kept her eyes on the road. "Oh."

"What about you?"

"I'm like the Hulk," Alex said, going for a joke. "I'm always angry."

Juliet's hand landed on Alex's sweaty knee. She didn't laugh. "I'm serious though. Have you seen him at all these last couple of years?"

"Who? Rich?"

"Who else were we talking about?"

Alex motioned to her back seat. "Hello, I'm Alex, let me introduce you to my emotional baggage." She didn't have to look to know Juliet was rolling her eyes.

"So, that's a no, then."

Obviously, Juliet was not going to let the subject drop, so Alex sighed out through her nose. "I ran into him on Sunday, actually."

Juliet whipped head around so fast, her braid thunked against the window. "What? Where?"

"On campus, after graduation. He was walking his girlfriend's dog."

"I can't believe he's still with her. She's awful."

Alex's mouth dropped open as she pulled into the restaurant parking lot. "How do you even know? Do you guys still talk? Does Ethan know? How is he even okay with that?"

Juliet threw her hands up in surrender, but her smile had grown wicked. "Mostly from Facebook. We've messaged there a couple times here and there, but we don't talk. We haven't really since I told him about your abortion."

Alex cringed. She wasn't sure she wanted to hear about that conversation. But, apparently her not asking about it as she got out of the car wasn't enough of a signal for Juliet to change the subject. She emerged at Alex's side and said, "He was devastated, you know."

Alex continued toward the restaurant, her heart pounding. "It wasn't hit decision to make."

"No." Juliet stopped Alex with a hand on her elbow. "Look at me." Juliet gave her arm a little shake. When Alex met her eyes, Juliet continued. "It was only ever your choice.

I'm not disputing that. But I am saying that once I emerged from my own cloud of hurt and grief, I was able to look back at the situation and see it differently. I know Rich really well, maybe even better than I know Ethan, and he was devastated to lose you. Yes, he would have wanted to keep the baby, but he also wanted you."

Alex shook her head and maneuvered out of Juliet's grip. "I think the boxing made you insane. That or hunger. You're talking nonsense."

Juliet opened the door for Alex and ushered her inside, but she leaned in and said, "You and me, we recovered from all that, but you should talk to Rich and find out that you don't have to be angry."

Alex was going to reply that her anger had nothing to do with Rich, but the words wouldn't come, and then Juliet was paying for their takeout, and Alex stood alone by the door, wondering if maybe it did.

Chapter Nine

For the past thirty minutes, Rich had been chasing his nephews as they sprinted back and forth across the yard. Gina's house didn't have a big yard, but by the time he corralled the kids back inside for dinner, Rich was sweaty and exhausted. He wanted to sit down, have a glass of wine, and eat his weight in the pasta Colin was making. But his nephews were already making plans for him to take them to the park after dinner, so Rich made himself a compromise in his mind. He would only eat half his body weight in pasta so he wouldn't throw up at the park, and in the few minutes he had before dinner was ready, he would steal a couple of beers from the fridge and sneak up the back staircase to Gina's office.

Part of Rich felt guilty for interrupting her when she no doubt had a deadline to meet, but another part of him really needed to talk to his sister.

He knocked on the partially closed door before slipping in and shutting it behind him.

"Just a second. I'm almost done" Gina said in English, not looking up from her computer screen.

"I brought you a beer," Rich said in Italian, and Gina spun around in her chair. Her wavy black hair was pulled back in a ponytail, and there were dark circles under her eyes.

"Oh, thank God." she rolled toward him with an outstretched hand. She took it and threw it back, emptying half the bottle in one long gulp.

"Everything alright, Sis?" he asked.

She nodded and sat back in her chair. "Been up late writing most of the week," she said, brushing off his concern. "It's my own fault, but I refuse to give up my time with Colin after the kids go to bed, no matter how big a story I'm working on."

"Who's this one for?"

Gina took another pull of her beer and said, "Another article for the Guardian on where immigration reform meets racism. It's becoming my niche and I'm not sure how I feel about it."

Rich took his first drink of beer, then checked the label. He hadn't been expecting a sour, but it was nice. Some sort of berry, and not too strong. Colin worked as a rep for a local brewery, and there were always new and unusual beers in his sister's refrigerator.

"It's an important topic," Rich said.

"It's stressful and comes with a lot of hate mail about what does a white woman know about immigration just because her parents are European, because apparently Europe doesn't count as a foreign country."

Rich pursed his lips. "Not entirely white."

Gina pursed hers right back. "I'm not justifying a heritage I don't claim to these bozos."

"Nor should you have to," Rich said, but nobody ever brought up that their father was black, and sometimes that bothered him. Rich thought Gina could maybe mention that her father was actually born of Algerian parents who were refugees in Paris in her articles, but she never did. She was so dead set against recognizing Marius at all that it was like she didn't see how much more it would give her to write about. There was credibility hiding in that history, but he had long ago stopped trying to fight that battle with his sister. Their father had betrayed them both when he'd left, and Rich tried to respect his sister's stance, even if he didn't agree with it.

Gina nodded and finished her beer, dunking the bottle into the bin under her desk.

"What do you need, little brother?"

He stalled by taking another gulp of the sour. He wasn't sure how Gina drank hers so fast. It was too tart for him to do much more than sip. But, because he knew there wasn't anything else to do but start, Rich asked, "Do you ever wonder what Dad's up to?"

Gina sat up straight and narrowed her eyes. "No. I don't."

He ran a hand over the scruff on his chin. He'd been feeling lazy and hadn't shaved that morning, and now he wished he had, like a more formal appearance would make this conversation easier. "You're really never going to forgive him?"

For a second, he saw a flash of resentment in Gina's eyes before she covered it up with the calm indifference she always wore when referencing their father. "He walked out on mom, after she'd forgiven him over and over for cheating on her. And then he left us all for a woman in a different country. That's not something I'm able to forgive."

"Do you know that for sure?" Rich asked. "About the other woman."

Gina shrugged. "Why else? It was his M. O."

"So, you don't know. Not really."

Gina cracked her neck, and Rich knew the conversation was wearing on her. Talk of their dad had to be short with her.

Rich crossed and uncrossed his legs as he stood against the door, searching for the words to express how all of this was making him feel. Not uncomfortable, just uneasy. He didn't like not knowing.

"I want to know," Rich said. "I want to know why he left. I want to know what he's doing now."

"So, what. You're trying to find him?" Gina was barely able to contain her sneer.

"Gee, Sis. Tell me how you really feel about that."

"I think it can only end badly. He left us. He doesn't want anything to do with us."

Rich ran his fingers over his stubble again, searching for the right words to use so his sister understood, but settled on, "Then at least I'll know for sure."

Gina watched him, warily for a minute, then said, "Is this about what happened with Juliet?"

His stomach still dropped when other people said her name. "What?"

"Are you still feeling down about the wedding?"

"No—Yes. I mean, I'm glad she's found what makes her happy, and while part of me still wishes that could be with me, I know she's better off in Colorado." He still didn't really like mentioning Ethan by name. Partially because he'd blamed Ethan for years for ending his relationship with Juliet the first time, and partially because Rich just really didn't like the guy.

"But?" Gina prompted.

"But I'm not better off."

"Ah," Gina leaned back in her chair. "And would that be different if Juliet weren't getting married?"

Rich shook his head. Bouncing from his dad to Juliet had made him dizzy. He had too many emotions tied up in both people to process what he was feeling all at once. All he knew is what he'd been telling himself the last three years. "It has nothing to do with Juliet. Yes, I miss her, but we had our chance. But I also don't want to think I've missed my chance on the kids and marriage thing, and the only person I've ever wanted that with until now was Juliet."

"You see that with Lynnette?" Gina's sneer made her opinion on that clear.

"No," Rich pulled the armchair in the corner over in front of Gina's office chair. "I'm breaking up with her this weekend so I can start over."

His sister's shoulders slumped. "Oh, I'm sorry. I know you were trying hard to make that work." At least she cared about his feelings, even if she didn't care for his soon-to-be-ex-girlfriend.

Rich shrugged. He had been trying to make it work, until he'd known it never would. Running into Alex while he'd been actively avoiding Lynnette had only driven home that he needed that relationship to be over. In the past few days, Rich had found himself grumbling aloud about how Alex's boyfriend wouldn't even drive onto campus to pick her up *after* he'd missed her entire graduation. Rich was not a violent man. He preferred to talk things out rather than use his fists, but the more he thought about it, the more he wanted to sock the guy in the jaw for making her walk to the damn Kwik Shop. Who did that? And more importantly, why was Alex letting him?

"Have you heard anything from Alex lately?" Rich asked. Strictly speaking, he knew Alex and Gina weren't really friends. But they were both close with Juliet, so there was a good chance Gina would know what was going on with her these days.

"No way. Uh-uh. You have done enough damage there."

"Jesus, Gina. Stand down. I ran into her over the weekend and she seemed off balance—not as confident as I remember her, and I was wondering how she was doing. That's all."

"Oh." Gina's shoulders, which had shot up to her ears at his question, relaxed again. "She had a hard time finishing school, I think. Balancing that with her jewelry business made things stressful. And I guess her boyfriend is an ass. And her grandmother died this week, but that wouldn't have happened yet if you saw her over the weekend."

"Her grandmother died?"

Gina nodded. "She's been out of town all week taking care of things, because her mom's a flake and couldn't be bothered to help."

"Shit," Rich said. He remembered a few offhand comments about how she and her mother didn't really talk, that she was raised by her grandmother. A new sort of anger rose up in him, along with regret "She deserves better than that. I wish I'd known." He didn't know what else he could have done, but asking if Gina knew how long Alex would be gone was on the tip of his tongue when Colin popped his head in. "Dinner's ready, baby. Help me wrangle these kids to the table, will ya?"

Gina gave Rich a suspicious sideways look before following her husband downstairs. So maybe Rich was interested in Alex. His sister could throw all the shade she wanted. It wouldn't change that Rich hadn't been able to stop thinking about Alex all week, or the suspicion that there could be potential between the two of them for more. There'd been a glimmer of it once before. Who was to say that Rich couldn't rekindle that potential under the right circumstances?

. . . .

ALEX MADE IT HOME LATE Friday afternoon. She'd stayed in Pittsburgh until Juliet needed to leave for her flight, and Juliet had talked Alex into doing yoga with her as a trade for the boxing. Her friend had to have broken out one her most difficult routines, because Alex's limbs were shaking by the end of it. Alex lay on the floor groaning that she needed breakfast while Juliet hopped up off her mat on light feet saying something about using up the last of the eggs before they left.

The sadness Alex had managed to keep at bay so far settled in as she locked the keys in the little lock box the realtor had provided. She was leaving her Gran's house for the last time—not just her gran's house, but *her* house. Her childhood home. The last real ties Alex had to anything like family were gone. Her mother had made it clear she was on her own. She hadn't even come for her books. Alex had packed a box of her favorites and loaded them in her own trunk, just in case, even though she was still angry with her.

Had her mother's words before the funeral been supposed to make her feel proud? When she knew that the only reason her mother was impressed was because Vivien couldn't handle anything more "grown up" than putting money in the bank and honoring vendor agreements? Was she supposed to feel proud that she'd been able to pull off burying her grandmother because there was literally no one else to do it?

And Alex wasn't a grown up. She could run a business, but the rest of her life was a mess. She probably should have found someone more responsible to take Alastor in. She'd proven what a disaster she was with the whole debacle with Rich three years ago. Alex could hear exactly what her grandmother would say if she knew the truth about why Alex had come to stay all of sudden back then.

Gran had given her an earful about letting a man break her heart, because that's the story Alex had given her. She'd had six separate lectures that you only get into that kind of relationship when you want to get married, not just for shits and giggles. Gran would have probably charged her with ten years hard labor to work off the sin of having had an abortion if she'd known. But at the same time, she'd made Alex biscuits and gravy for breakfast three times that week, and there was never a night that went by without cherry pie, even though cherries hadn't been in season. And Alex's laundry was clean and crisp and folded every day.

Gran had been hard to deal with sometimes, but she'd shown her own type of love. Alex was going to miss having her to lean on. She would even miss her calls that were half telling Alex she wasn't good enough, half telling her that she had no choice but to follow her heart. Alex wasn't sure there was anybody else in her life who had the guts to point it out to her when she was screwing up, and she'd miss that too, even if she and Gran often disagreed about what being a screw up meant.

Alex had called Ben just before she'd left Pittsburgh. She'd gotten his voicemail—again—and asked him to meet her at Tokyo Nights when she got in. She'd claimed she needed a drink—and she did—but she also needed to break up with him.

It was time.

She was unlocking the door to her apartment, looking forward to a shower and a simple dinner when her phone pinged with a voicemail. She must have missed it ringing while she hauled Alastor's carrier and her bags up the stairs.

She waited until she'd set her bags and let Alastor out before she looked at her phone. The call had been from Ben.

"Hey, Alex. I can't make it tonight. It's been a long day, and I can't handle the drive to Kansas City and back. It's too much work. This is too much. Keeping up with you is too much work, and I don't think I can do it anymore, so I guess I'm out. I'm really sorry about your grandmother. Good luck with everything. Bye."

Alex listened to the message twice more before she dropped her phone in her bag so she didn't throw it across the room.

What. The. Fuck.

That's all she got? A whiny voicemail about how she wasn't worth the effort?

Fuck him. He didn't even have the guts to talk to her in person. That fuck.

Then Alex gave in and threw her purse against the wall. "Fuck you, Ben!" she screamed, then picked her purse up and aimed at the refrigerator. It fell short, landing with a jingle and a tink on the kitchen floor. Alastor shot beneath the sofa in a blur of white.

Great. She was already a horrible cat mom.

Screw this.

Alex heaved in a deep breath and forced herself to release it slowly. She was so done feeling sorry for herself. She was going to Tokyo Nights anyway. It may have been a while since she'd gotten dolled up and gone dancing by herself but that was what she was going to do. She was going to take a long bath, shave her legs, paint her toenails, curl her hair, put on her shortest, most scandalous black dress, her tallest heels, and she was going to get laid.

Chapter Ten

R ich knew going after Alex was a bad idea the second he buckled himself into his Jeep, but that wasn't going to stop him. The drive from his midtown flat to Tokyo Nights wouldn't take more than fifteen minutes. He would go in, buy a drink, see if she was around. If not, he'd go outside and call her, because he had never deleted her number. Then he would tell her how sorry he was to hear about her grandmother. Then, he would send her flowers, and then something else that had less to do with her grandmother and more to do with telling her how much he wanted to see her again.

If Alex was in the club, Rich was going to be in trouble. He'd been thinking of her all week. Imagining her sad and alone and bereaved had stirred a restlessness in him that he knew wouldn't be satisfied until she was in his arms. It was a sensation he wasn't entirely comfortable with, like an itch, and not one he could ignore. If he found Alex in the club, and if Alex allowed it, Rich would take her upstairs to her bed, and make sure she had at least one good memory from what had been an otherwise shitty week. And then maybe they could talk about everything else.

There was so much left unsaid between them.

It took a few minutes for his eyes to adjust to the darkness in the club, and for him to tune out the loud music enough to focus on anything other than his manhattan. Since it was a Friday night, the club was crowded, and the bar was full, but as he skirted the dance floor, searching out an empty table or booth, he spotted her.

She was in the middle of the dance floor, her hands in her hair as she danced too close to some guy who had his hands on her hips. Was that the boyfriend? Somehow, Rich had forgotten about him, but it wasn't anything Rich couldn't work around.

The guy looked young, younger than Rich, maybe even younger than Alex. But he had dark brown hair that didn't have Rich's natural wave, and his shoulders were probably broader, but Rich was definitely taller. Alex's hands settled on the guy's shoulders and he pulled her closer so they connected at the hips. Alex pushed off they guy's chest and out of his hold, shaking her head. She said something, then left him as she forsook the dance floor for the bar.

Rich didn't hesitate to follow her, squeezing in to stand next to the lone empty stool she'd found. "The boyfriend piss you off?" he asked before she'd noticed he was there. Her head whipped to her left, then cocked to the side as her eyes slid over his black button down and casual jeans then back up to his face.

"That's not my boyfriend. In fact, I don't have a boyfriend anymore."

"Who's the guy, then?"

"Don't know, don't wanna know."

Rich grinned at her. "Looking for a rebound fuck, Alex?"

"Maybe. And even if I am, I still need to be wooed. I'm not going home with someone who doesn't even buy me a drink before he tries feeling me up."

"I'll remember to tell the next guy," Rich.

Alex offered him a feeble grin. "What are you doing here?" she asked.

He held up his mostly empty manhattan. "Having a drink. Would you like one?"

"Tequila and soda with lime. Double short."

Rich snagged one of the bartenders and ordered her drink, and a second manhattan for himself. Then he downed the rest of his glass and said, "I heard about your grandmother. I'm sorry. And I'm sorry about the boyfriend too. That's shitty timing."

Alex blew out a breath, catching the strand of bangs that sloped over one eyebrow. "Good riddance," she said. "That asshole didn't even have the decency to break up with me in person. He left me a goddamn voicemail saying *I* was too much work. Can you believe that?"

Rich noticed that she didn't mention her grandmother, but he let it go. If she needed to concentrate on the boyfriend for now, he'd let her.

"What a lazy ass," Rich said as their drinks were delivered, and the bartender raised an eyebrow, but Rich didn't pay any attention to him as he turned to face Alex, resting an elbow on the bar.

Alex toasted, "To the end of the Lazy Ass," then scanned the area around and behind Rich as she took a long sip through her straw. "So, the dog doesn't go with you everywhere then?"

For a second Rich wasn't sure what Alex was talking about, but then he remembered he'd been walking Bijou the last time he'd seen her.

"You were right. I'm not really a dog person."

Alex looked again. "And the girl that goes with the dog?"

"No longer in the picture."

Strictly speaking, this wasn't true, even if Rich had spent the last two days dodging Lynnette's phone calls and returning her texts with vague answers, he was technically still with Lynnette. He planned to end things over lunch tomorrow, but tonight was about reconnecting with Alex. He didn't even want to think about Lynnette.

"So, you're on the rebound as well."

"You could call it that."

"And you came looking for me?"

Rich grinned in a way that said yes but spoke the more acceptable answer. "I came to make sure you were okay."

Alex knocked back the rest of her drink and plunked her glass down on the counter. "Well I'm not. Not even close. You think you can do something about it?"

Rich took a slow sip of his still mostly full drink. "Buy you another drink? Be a dance partner that doesn't grope you."

Alex laughed and nodded when the bartender asked if she wanted another.

"My tab," Rich said.

"And what about after a few dances?"

Rich didn't really need to answer the question. He knew from experience that she wouldn't be leading him down this road if she didn't want to sleep with him, so he decided to give her the power.

"That's up to you," he said.

Alex snorted and her response surprised him as much as it turned him on. "I don't believe for a second that you came here because you heard about Gran. You, sir, always only have one thing on your mind, and that's who your cock is going to be inside next."

Alex had always said whatever she thought before, but for some reason, he hadn't expected her crass honesty tonight. Rich leaned in and whispered in Alex's ear, "You have such a dirty mouth. I like it."

"I remember," Alex said as her drink arrived with no hint of flirtation in her voice. She stirred the ice into the tequila with her straw, then sucked the whole thing down in two gulps. "All right, lover boy, let's see if you can make me forget just exactly how awful my week has been."

· · · ·

ALEX WAS AN IDIOT. She knew this was a horrible idea. She'd told Juliet a million times that sleeping with Rich was never a good idea. And once she'd tested the theory for herself, Alex had proved it true.

Sleeping with Rich Durand would be a mistake, but sex with Rich was fucking amazing. With the week she'd had, Alex was going with the sure thing instead of gambling on some guy who may or may not take her pleasure into account.

They'd been dancing for an hour already, and true to his word, Rich hadn't touched her inappropriately once. They hadn't talked much either. The loud music made it hard to hear on the dance floor, and it was more fun to tease and flirt with scant touches as they danced. A touch of his fingertips against her waist, the back of her hand down his arm, fingers clasped briefly when they met by chance, his knuckles over one of her cheekbones when they paused, laughing, to catch their breath between songs.

It had been fun, but if he didn't grab her ass soon, Alex was going to explode. That or throw him over her shoulder and haul him upstairs caveman style.

"Would you like another drink?" he asked, bending down close to her ear to be heard over the music.

"I've had six shots of tequila," she said, and Rich chuckled in her ear.

"So, no."

"No," she agreed. She'd had just enough alcohol to not talk herself out of this, but not so much that she wouldn't remember it come morning.

He pulled her into his arms so their bodies were flush at last. He dipped his head in closer, his nose grazing the shell of her ear. Alex shivered as anticipation gave way to lust. She was really going to do this. With Rich. Again.

He sucked her lobe, earrings and all, between his teeth, and Alex gasped in a breath of air. Just for tonight. She could give herself this one pleasure tonight and get on with the process of putting her life back together in the morning.

Alex circled her hands around Rich's neck and pressed her chest against his. Normally, her chest was approximately level with the bottom of his ribs, the top of her head barely reaching his chin, but in her tallest heels, she could nip at his jaw and play with the hair at the nape of his neck without reaching.

"What are you waiting for?" she asked.

"I don't want to spook you, *Piccolina*."

A little thrill ran through her at the pet name, it was the same one he'd called her before. She'd googled it once, and found out it only meant "small," but the way he said it, small sounded like a precious thing. This, this was why Rich was dangerous. She knew he was a cheater and liar, but in isolation, when it was just him and her, he could make Alex feel like she was the only person in the world that mattered to him—and it was so nice just to be wanted by someone.

Alex would never ever tell him that. Instead, she said, "Your cock doesn't scare me, Dew-Rand," putting as much twang into mispronouncing his last name as she could.

His grin spread wide and his eyes lit up. "Maybe not," he said. Then dropped his lips to hers in a kiss that was not at all urgent and greedy in the usual way of one-night stands, but soft, his lips caressing hers with a familiar confidence and a slow, sure patience. Alex almost hated him for it, because he was acting like a cocky bastard, and he was doing it to get a rise out of her. Then he got his teeth involved, nipping at her lower lip before running his tongue over the bite, across her teeth and over her tongue.

Alex's body woke up as the taste of whiskey invaded her mouth. She pressed up into him, moaning as she parried his tongue with her own, trying to deepen the kiss. Rich tempered her ardor by withdrawing and said, "But I think you are afraid of me," against her lips.

Alex had to reel herself back in enough to figure out what they'd been talking about before the kiss. She leaned back just far enough to see into his eyes. They were dark and intense, and not the least bit amused anymore.

Excitement welled low in Alex's belly, because Rich looked more than just lust-addled. His expression was almost tender, like instead of being a taunt, the kiss had been an intimation of affection. He was right, that scared the shit out of her. She and Rich could not ever be a thing, and if that's what he was thinking, he was going to be disappointed.

Alex lowered her gaze and traced a fingernail down the row of buttons on his shirt. "I don't trust you," Alex said. "But that doesn't matter because this," she grazed over his belt and flattened her hand against the bulge in his jeans, "is all I'm after." Alex found amusement creasing the corners of his eyes when she looked up. Good. "And maybe your mouth." She remembered the last time he'd had his mouth on her and said, "No. Definitely your mouth."

Rich raised his eyebrows, and moved her hand off his erection, wrapping her arms around his waist and picking up the beat of the song they'd stopped dancing to. "And what about my hands?" he asked. "Are they invited to this little party?" He drew his fingers down the length of her spine and traced the spot where her waist dipped in before flattening his palm over the flare of her hip. "Because they'd like to come."

Alex took the opportunity to press her hips to his for just a second. "Only if they're prepared to do naughty, naughty things."

Rich chuckled. "Whatever you want, *Piccolina*. All you have to do is ask."

"Then stop wasting time and take me to bed," Alex said.

Rich placed a quick peck to her lips. "My pleasure."

Alex expected the pace to pick up once they were enclosed in the privacy of her bedroom, but it seemed Rich was determined to take things slow. She'd tried to attack him with kisses when they'd first walked in the door, and while he indulged her for about ten seconds, he quickly pulled out of her arms and walked, without a word, into her bedroom.

"What are you-?" Alex trailed after him, but he held his hand up as she entered the bedroom, and she cut herself off.

"I want to look at you," he said.

Alex frowned. "Well, I want to fuck you, and I'm not going to be very patient about it."

In a move just as bold and possessive as Alex putting her hand on his cock earlier, Rich slipped his hand under her skirt and grabbed her ass, pulling her into him. He ducked his knees so the ridge of his erection ground against her pubic bone.

"And I want to take my time," he said, squeezing her bare cheek as he ground against her again. "I don't want this to be over in ten minutes. I'm going to make you come over and over again until all you can think about it how good you feel. Sound alright?"

Alex moaned as his hips moved again. If he kept this up, he'd get her off right here and now. "I want that," she said. God did she want that. She wanted to forget everything. She needed to step away from the overwhelming tumult of emotions she'd been feeling for so long and just have something—anything—feel good for a change.

Rich kissed her forehead and stepped back. "Then you have to trust me." The tilt of his lips let Alex know he was aware of the irony, so she grinned back at him, standing with her back straight, shoulders back and chin lifted as he circled her, one hand grazing across her stomach, then down her arm as he went. "You've changed."

"It's been three years," Alex said. "Do I get to point out your flaws next? Because I've always thought your nose was a little crooked."

"It is. But it only makes me more handsome."

Alex clicked her tongue, but he was right. He knew exactly how to work those dark, earnest features to his advantage too.

"I was going to say that you've got biceps now," he made another circle, brushing a knuckle over the slight bulge on her upper arm. "And your legs." He whistled. "Fantastic."

"I box now. And if you don't stop circling me like a damn vulture, I'm going to use my new muscles to kick your ass."

Rich stopped behind her, his hands, spread wide, sliding over the curve of her hip and covering her stomach. "Oh, I don't doubt it," he whispered in her ear, then kissed his way down her neck to the strap on her dress. He stole it down her shoulder, kissed his way over the back of her neck to the other strap, brushing it away as well.

Despite the heat of his body at her back, a shiver ran down Alex's spine as one of Rich's hand reached for the hem of her skirt, and the other moved up, cupping her breast over her bra. "Are you wearing panties, Alex?"

She leaned into him, thrusting her hips out in invitation for him to find out for himself. His fingers slid higher, beneath her skirt, up her thigh and over her hip where the strap of her thong rode high. He pushed it over her hips and down and pretended it hadn't been there at all.

"Tsk, tsk, naughty girl."

"Woman," Alex breathed, arching into the hand at her breast. "Naughty woman."

Rich chuckled as his hand rounded back down her hip, drawing slow circles across the top of her leg, edging closer to her center with each little rotation. Alex simultaneously couldn't wait for him to get there and wanted the anticipation to last. Understanding dawned and Alex was all about going slow.

The hand at Alex's breast stopped kneading, then jumped up and pulled the top of her dress down, revealing her black, strapless bra. Rich pushed the cups down, exposing both breasts.

Alex moaned when Rich's hand closed over her bare breast, squeezing, then sliding away until only one finger remained, and he was circling back in toward her nipple at the same agonizing pace as his fingers on her thigh.

He was close, so close to finding out exactly how wet his hands on her made her. Just another inch, and his fingers would slick into the moisture gathering at the tops of her thighs.

He reached her nipple at the same moment his other hand found her wetness, and time stood still for a moment as he pinched her nipple and stroked one finger over her. How was he making a simple brush of his fingers feel so good?

His fingers traced up now, then down again, the pressure increasing just a little bit each time until he was rolling her nipple between his thumb and forefinger and the first finger on his other hand slipped inside her. Alex bucked and moaned.

"Is this naughty enough for you?" he asked.

On an exhale, Alex said, "It's a start."

Rich kissed her neck and pressed his thumb to her clit. "Oh, *Piccolina*, you have no idea."

Chapter Eleven

The pressure of Rich's thumb against her clit was all it took to finish the tumble toward orgasm his fingers had started.

"Oh my God." Alex voice was higher pitched than she expected, but she couldn't control it as her inner muscles fluttered. Then, as Rich rubbed his thumb in a circle and pinched her nipple at the same time, she clamped down on his finger. Her groans grew louder as her legs gave out and Rich caught her around the waist before she crumpled.

"Hold on, *Piccolina*. I've got you."

Alex wouldn't have cared if she fell in a heap on the floor. That orgasm was all she was hoping to get out of her night of decadence, and Rich was only getting started.

"Holy shit."

Rich held her about the waist as he withdrew his hand from between her legs.

"You are amazing," he said, and guided her toward the bed she'd had the foresight to make before going downstairs. "Now let's get these clothes off you."

Alex looked down at herself. Her dress was pulled down at her waist. The strap on the left side pinned her arm and she somehow had managed to pull her right arm free without noticing. Her bra was upside down, and there were wrinkles in the fabric of the skirt where Rich had bunched it up to get between her legs. Naked was better than looking like this.

Alex flung her bra to the side and lay down to shimmy her dress down her hips. Rich loomed over her, fully dressed and looking completely unscathed by their encounter. "What about your clothes?" she asked as he took one of her ankles in hand and unfastened the clasp on her shoe.

"They're coming off soon enough."

He moved to her second shoe.

"I want to do it," Alex said.

Rich tossed the shoe over his shoulder and held out a hand to her. Alex took it and he pulled her to sitting. Her hand immediately went to the top button on his shirt. She could feel his eyes wandering over her chest, down her stomach and up again as she worked her way down to his belt. She undid the buckle and the fly on his jeans before pulling the shirt tail out and shoving the black fabric down his arms.

When her hand slid under his white undershirt to rest against hot skin, he said, "What do you think? Who has a better six pack? You or me?"

Alex giggled. Rich had always been long and lean and trim with some muscle definition. He had always been a runner, but she didn't remember him having a six pack. Then again, three years earlier, neither had she. She'd been lucky if she let Juliet drag her to yoga once a week back then. She let her hand roam further, palm flat, fingers spread. There was some texture under the dusting of hair.

"Probably me," she said, "But let's take a peek and find out."

Alex flipped the undershirt over his head and traced her hands back down his shoulders and chest. "What have you been doing?" she asked, before she could think about it. He didn't have a lot of bulk to him, but Rich's thirties had been good to him so far. He'd filled out a little across his chest and shoulders, and just as promised, his visible abs led down to a V that was obscured by the half-open fly of his jeans and the peek of gray boxer briefs underneath.

"I added some weightlifting after my run," he said.

"I like it." Alex leaned forward and dragged a tongue up the line between his abs and pecks. "But mine's better," she said when she reached the top.

With his hands on her shoulders, Rich knocked her backwards on the bed. He followed close behind and ran his tongue between her breasts and down her stomach, the opposite direction of what she'd just done to him. "I agree," he said. His words were muffled against her belly button as he pressed kisses to her tummy, edging his way toward her center.

"Take off your pants first," Alex said as Rich drew her legs apart.

"No way," he said. "That's the only thing keeping me from pushing inside you." He kissed the inside of her thigh, putting him to close to where she wanted him. So close.

"But that's where I want you," Alex whined.

"And I promised you this first." Rich's tongue flicked against her clit, and Alex groaned.

He didn't give her any more time to argue. His tongue continued to lap at her clit while his thumb slid inside her. Alex writhed, trying to ride his thumb. He spread his free hand over her abdomen to hold her still, then withdrew his thumb to replace it with his tongue. Alex relaxed into the feel of his mouth on her, his tongue fucking her, and latched on to the slow build of pleasure budding again in her core.

He slipped his tongue up to lap at her clit every few strokes, and it drove Alex crazy. She wanted the pressure there.

All of sudden there was pressure somewhere else. His thumb drew a line of moisture from her pussy to her backdoor, and pressed in.

"Holy shit," she gasped. He'd never pulled that move before.

"Good or bad?" he asked, drawing just far enough away to speak.

"Good," she said. "Don't stop."

"Yes, ma'am."

Rich lowered his mouth back to her clit and rotated his hand to slip two fingers back inside her.

"Holy fuck," Alex said and rocked against his mouth as his hand seesawed inside her. It was too many sensations all at once, and she knew she wasn't going to last long. Rich's teeth closed around her clit and Alex fell apart in a stream of curses punctuated by keening moans.

When at last she stilled, the heat of Rich's body disappeared, but she was too weak to follow. She heard jeans hitting the floor and the crinkle of foil before he was back over, his cock nudging her entrance.

He lowered his lips to hers at the same time he sank inside her and she felt so gloriously full.

Rich groaned against her lips, and said, "Fuck, Alex. I've missed you."

Alex chose to believe he meant he missed her in bed, because what else could he mean? She hadn't spoken to him at all since the last time they'd slept together. She'd blown him off after that. Ghosted him. Then told him not to come back. She hadn't told him about the pregnancy, not about the abortion. Nothing. She knew he was aware because Juliet and Gina were close, but he'd never confronted her about it. And now he'd missed her? No, there was nothing more for him to miss than this.

"Shut up and fuck me," Alex said.

"There's that dirty mouth," Rich said, and moved inside her.

. . . .

RICH WAS NOT GOING to last long. He'd known it from the beginning and tried to give Alex as much pleasure as he could beforehand, because he knew once he was inside her, all pretense of going slow would disappear. There was something here that had been missing over the last three years. Maybe it was just that they'd been lovers before, so Alex was comfortable enough to bring her snark into the bedroom, but Rich had a hard time believing she didn't tell all the men she'd taken to her bed to shut up and fuck her if they were taking too long.

Whatever it was, Rich wanted more of it. He'd berate himself for taking three years to find her again, but it was taking all his concentration to keep up the circular motion that kept Alex arching her back and cursing without coming himself.

It became a lost cause when Alex said, "Fuck, Rich. I'm going to—" then she tensed before relaxing into a moan that was more of a scream. His orgasm ripped from him, and he held tight to Alex's hips as he pulsed inside her.

The only noise in the room was the sound of them catching their breath. After her inhalations had evened out, Alex got up from the bed without a word and disappeared into the bathroom. He disposed of the condom in the kitchen trash and washed his hands, then retreated to the room. He heard the water running in the bathroom as he slid his boxer briefs back on.

He debated whether her should pull on the rest of his clothes as he listened to Alex's footsteps in the hall. She rustled around in the kitchen for a moment, then came back to the bedroom. She wore a pale pink cotton robe and carried two glasses of water.

"Here," she said, holding out one glass to where he still stood beside the bed in his underwear.

Rich took a sip, then set it on the bedside table.

"What's wrong, Alex?"

She shook her head but sat beside him on the bed.

"You can talk to me," he said. "I am more than a collection of body parts."

Alex shook her head again. "It's easier to think of you that way. Then I'm not as much of a screw up."

"You're not a screw up," Rich said. He was confused, but he knew sometimes people grieved in strange ways, especially when the hurt was new. "You're a beautiful, successful woman. A little scary to lesser mortals, maybe—"

"My Gran just died."

"I know."

"And what do I do? I get tipsy and screw the guy who knocked me up once upon a time. What kind of granddaughter am I?"

Rich wanted to ask about that pregnancy. He wanted to know about it more than he had ever wanted anything. For three years that missed opportunity had dogged him, but Rich would ask Alex about that later. He'd make sure of it.

"After you spent the whole week tying up her loose ends and planning her funeral. Probably without any help from your mother, I'd say you are a stellar granddaughter who deserved to do something for herself."

Alex nodded, in a way he could tell meant she didn't believe him. She ducked her head and her cheek fell onto his shoulder. "Juliet was there."

The bottom of Rich's stomach dropped out at the name. Of course Juliet had been there. She would do anything for Alex. It dawned on him that possibly the two most important women in his life, outside his mom and sister, were always going to be best friends. He wanted them to be, but it didn't make courting Alex any less compilated. Rich wrapped an arm around her shoulders. "I'm glad you weren't alone, but you shouldn't feel bad about this."

"All I can hear is my Gran telling me off for sleeping with you after you already broke my heart."

Rich's heart might have stopped beating at her words. He hadn't, had he? They hadn't a chance. "Did I?" he asked.

Alex's head rolled against his shoulder. "Of course not. But I went home after my D&C. Juliet was moody, and I couldn't tell her why I was being a bitch, and I just needed to get out of town. Then I couldn't tell Gran that I'd had an abortion because that would break her heart, so I told her you'd broken mine. She ripped me up and down for a week, but she took good care of me."

"Sounds confusing," Rich said.

"She was. She was always afraid I'd turn into my mother. Flighty. Self-absorbed with no empathy toward anyone. I am those things to a certain extent, but I try not to be. Mostly because I have Gran's voice in my head telling me I could be better."

"I don't think you're any of those things," Rich said.

Alex only snorted.

Rich was gathering all her positive attributes to expound upon, but then Alex sniffled. "I just lost my home," she said. "Gran wasn't perfect, but she was home, and if I ever actually do get my heart broken, I have no one to go to."

It started with a single tear dripping onto his shoulder. Then another. Then he reached for the tissues on the nightstand and Alex sobbed and murmured self-recriminations in between apologizing for crying all over him. Rich held her, stroking her hair and telling her to let it out until she eventually fell asleep cradled against his chest.

He tucked Alex into bed, made sure the apartment was locked up, and brushed his teeth with a spare toothbrush he'd found in a dusty basket below the bathroom sink. Then he shooed a big white cat he hadn't seen earlier out of Alex's room and crawled into bed beside her.

Chapter Twelve

Alex wasn't sure what woke her, but she sat up in bed and surveyed her room like there had been a loud sound she had just missed. It was daylight. She had her robe on, but it was twisted to the side and gaping open on the left. Her throat ached, and her mouth was dry. There was a slight headache behind her left eye that was nothing that a cup of coffee wouldn't cure.

The grief settled in as she adjusted her robe. There was an aching hole behind her ribs Alex tried and failed to fill with the long calming breaths Juliet had taught her. It was as she lay there, concentrating on fitting herself and her loneliness in this new post-Gran body that she noticed the soreness between her legs.

Alex groaned as she stretched into the pleasant ache, so different from the anguish in her chest. The warmth and satisfaction in her body rose up to soothe that miserable hollowness as Alex relived how much she'd let herself feel last night. The exquisite luxury of good sex followed by unleashing the mountain of emotion she'd been stockpiling all week just to survive.

Normally, Alex would be mortified that she'd cried all over a man. As far as one-night stands went, it was probably most dude's worst nightmare, but Alex had a feeling Rich could deal.

Alex sat up with a jolt as all the comfort and warmth left her, only to be replaced with panic.

She'd repeated the single stupidest thing she'd ever done. Rich Durand was off limits for so many reasons. Because of Juliet, because of who he was and how he'd broken her friend's heart, but also because Alex was only just now learning how to live with herself after what had happened the last time they'd hooked up. Alex didn't like who she'd become then. She wasn't the kind of person who hurt her best friend on purpose, but that's who hooking up with Rich had made her.

Alex had worked too damn hard for too damn long to make up for it. She wasn't going back now.

She held her breath as she surveyed her room in the soft morning light. The other side of the bed had been mussed, but it looked like Rich had left sometime in the night.

Thank God. She wouldn't have to talk to him about how last night had been a mistake and how it could never, ever, ever happen again.

She padded to the bathroom, which had an adjoining door to her bedroom, and was doubly grateful Rich had gone after she looked in the mirror. Her hair was more Gorgon than human, and she had raccoon eyes from all the smeared eyeliner and mascara. At least her outside finally matched how she felt on the inside.

A long, hot shower later, Alex looked more presentable, even if she didn't feel that way. She left the bathroom in search of any clean and comfy clothes to work in. She'd never catch up if she didn't jump to back on the bench immediately.

Alex was pulling on a pair of black leggings when she imagined she smelled coffee. She dismissed it as her downstairs neighbors. She got cooking smells from them all the time. But as she pulled a black tank over her head, she heard the clank of silverware against a plate and a rustle of paper.

Maybe Avery had decided to work today? She wasn't usually scheduled on Saturdays, but Alex would gladly pay her if she wanted to work.

Alex padded down the hallway. The living room was empty, and the front door was shut. She couldn't see into the kitchen until she turned the corner out of the hall, but she could hear someone moving in there.

Sure enough, when she turned the corner, Rich stood in her kitchen plating up two huge cinnamon rolls. Two large cups of coffee already sat in front of the two stools at the breakfast bar.

"What the fuck are you doing here?" Alex asked.

Rich held up one of the cinnamon rolls, nonplussed by her less than welcoming greeting. He was wearing the same clothes he had the night before. "I got us breakfast."

"I thought you left."

"Just to the bakery down the road. I was only gone twenty minutes."

Alex stared at him. What did he think he was doing staying the night? Providing her breakfast? She'd lived by herself for two and a half years, had been feeding herself for more than ten. When he sat down at the breakfast bar instead of continuing the staring contest, Alex gave in. The food smelled amazing, and she needed the coffee.

"But why?"

"I don't understand why you expected me to leave," Rich said between sips of coffee.

"But we agreed, everything was supposed to be body parts."

"No. You said you were looking for cock and I volunteered mine for two reasons."

Alex waited for him to elaborate. He chewed a large bite of pastry before continuing. "One, I haven't been able to stop thinking about you since last Sunday."

Alex rolled her eyes. That was exactly the sort of thing Rich would usually say to a woman to make her panties disappear.

"Two, I thought you could use a friend. Things can't have been easy for you lately."

Rather than dignify that answer with a response, Alex dug into her breakfast. Rich didn't seem to mind her lack of reaction to either declaration. She was halfway through her cinnamon roll when a thought occurred to her. "Wait, are you proposing a friends with benefits sort of situation?"

Rich dropped his fork onto his empty plate. "I was thinking of more of a girlfriend/boyfriend situation, but I'll take what I can get."

Alex felt her mouth drop open, but she didn't have enough brain power left in her body to close it again, especially with him looking at her all amused and affectionate like. "We can't be together. That's a disaster waiting to happen."

"I disagree, but why do you think so?"

"Because the last time we did the boyfriend/girlfriend thing, I got pregnant and almost ruined my entire life trying to fix it, that's why."

"You could have come to me," Rich said. His voice was low and quiet as he watched his coffee cup revolve between his fingers.

Alex snorted into her coffee, and intended to ignore him until he left, but she couldn't keep her eyes from searching for his when he laid a gentle hand on her thigh.

"You thought of me as your boyfriend?"

It took effort for Alex not to cringe, but she couldn't deny that they'd moved beyond the repeat hookup at some point. "We were sleeping together exclusively. Not using condoms. What would you call it?" Alex asked.

"I wanted to be your boyfriend, but I didn't think you'd go for it."

"And nothing has changed. You still have a way screwed up past with my best friend. You and me being together almost killed my relationship with her, and it's finally recovering from that. I'm not going to jeopardize it again."

"Juliet is beyond caring who I sleep with," Rich said, which did not invoke a lot of confidence in Alex. Sleeping with someone was not the same thing as having a relationship with them. Alex felt like that was a concept Rich didn't quite grasp—and she hadn't even brought up the cheating yet.

"I'm not risking it," Alex said. "And even if I did, you've proven you can't be faithful. Why would I set myself up for heartbreak?"

"I never cheated on Lynnette," Rich said.

"That's one relationship."

"That lasted a year, Alex. If I can commit myself to one woman that I'm not all that serious about for a year, you don't think I can be faithful to the woman I wish I'd had a chance to talk into having a baby with me?"

What was that supposed to mean? That in the middle of all the chaos and turmoil that had been happening when Alex had found out she was pregnant, that Rich would have put a ring on Alex's finger? He would have devoted himself to her and their baby, just like that?

Alex didn't buy it.

"I can't have this conversation. Not now. Not ever."

"Let me ask you one thing before you reject me outright."

"I already have rejected you. Twice."

Rich continued as if she hadn't spoken. "Do you *feel* better this morning?"

"What?"

"Right now, do you hurt as much as you did when you went to Tokyo Nights looking for a hookup?"

Her mouth opened and closed without a sound. The grief, the exhaustion, the loss. They were all still there. Still burning under the surface, and they would be for a long time, but the suffocating weight that had been like an elephant sitting on her chest was lighter. It felt more like a housecat now.

"A little bit," she said. "But that was the point."

"And if you'd gone out and had mediocre sex with some random guy, would you have opened up with him like you did with me, or would you be bottling it all up still?"

The hand on her knee squeezed, then Rich's thumb caressed small circles over her leg. Was he trying to be comforting or manipulative? Alex didn't know.

"By open up, do you mean when I sobbed gibberish at you for two hours and snotted all over your shoulder?"

"Yes."

"That was a breakdown. It could have happened anywhere with anyone."

"Answer the question." More circles over her knee weakened her.

"No, I wouldn't have snotted all over a stranger's shoulder."

A smile stole over Rich's lips. "And I'm honored you chose to do it on mine, *Piccolina*. Honored."

This was why Rich was dangerous, because as his other hand came up to cup her cheek, tears welled in her eyes again, and Alex believed him. She wanted what he was offering, because when Rich was with her, Alex could believe that he cared about only her. She could believe she was the most important person in his life. And just for once, Alex wanted to be the most important person to someone else. To allow herself to become that to Rich was sweet and tempting.

But it wouldn't work. Juliet would always come first for him, even if she was forever out of his reach. Plus, whenever he wasn't with her, Alex would be wondering whether he'd found his new sidepiece yet.

"I want to believe you," she said.

"Then give me a chance." Rich wiped away the single tear that escaped with his thumb, and Alex was on the verge of nodding, of saying yes against her better judgement when Rich's phone buzzed on the counter between them.

Alex glanced down and the notification on his phone displayed the name and the first few words of the text. The words were all in French, so Alex couldn't read them, but the name at the top was loud and clear. Rage and disappointment splashed into Alex's stomach along with a good dose of reality.

"Why is Lynnette texting you?" she asked.

Rich reached for the phone, then tucked it in his pocket with a shrug. "She probably wants to make sure we're still on for lunch. I haven't responded to most of her messages all week."

"Why are you having lunch with her if you broke up with her?"

Alex knew the answer when Rich shifted in his seat, but she waited for him to say it. "I haven't technically broken up with her yet." and he was in the middle of saying, "That's what I'm going to do over lunch." When Alex stood, raised her fist and punched him in the chest, not as hard as she could, but hard enough that the word "lunch" was lost in a *woosh* of forcibly exhaled air.

"Get out," she said.

Rich wheezed out something that sounded like, "Holy shit," as he rubbed the spot over his heart. He sucked in one breath, and then another before looking up at her with shock and hurt in his eyes. "You punched me. Hard."

"And I'll do it again if you don't get out. Now."

"Alex," he still sounded a little out of breath, but Alex didn't care, she pulled back her fist a second time, but this time, Rich was prepared and caught her wrist, then used the momentum to pull her between his legs and pinned her there.

"No way. You said you never cheated on Lynnette. But you just did, with me." Tears were pooling in the back of Alex eyes again, and she wondered if she was going to be a crier now. She never used to cry.

"Checking in on you was more important than tying up loose ends with her."

"Get out," Alex said again, even though he was physically wrapped around her.

Rich stroked the still damp hair over her shoulder, but Alex stood stiff and still, unmoved by his touch. He sighed. "Do you really want me to go?"

"Yes," she said, the word almost strangled as she held back the tears she didn't want him to see her shed.

"This isn't over, Alex," Rich said, releasing her to grab his keys.

Alex backed away until to sofa separated her from Rich. "Enjoy your breakup fuck," she said when his hand was on the doorknob.

"I'm not going to sleep with her. I'm going to buy her a nice lunch and explain as politely as I can that I'm looking for a woman to settle down with. To marry and have kids with, and since she's dead set against having children, we need to go our separate ways. And then I was hoping you and I could make plans for dinner sometime this week."

He was too smooth for his own good. Alex knew exactly what he was doing. But telling her he thought she could be the woman he married and had kids with was not going to sway her. A lifetime with a man who couldn't keep it in his pants was not appealing in the slightest.

Rich took one step toward her. "You have to trust me, *Piccolina*. I would never hurt you."

"You just did," Alex said. "Now get out."

For a split second, Alex was satisfied to see Rich's stooped shoulders as he ducked out of her apartment. But that only lasted until the door closed behind him, and the shock of all that had happened in the last twelve hours washed over her.

Rich wanted to settle down with her? He would have wanted her to have the baby? He wanted to be with her now? To start over with her?

Alex collapsed on the sofa and tried to remember what about their first farcical try at a relationship had made him think that was possible.

Chapter Thirteen

Three Years Ago

If Rich didn't stop staring at Juliet's ass while she danced with Ethan, Alex was going to stab him in the eye with a chopstick.

Instead, she downed another cup of sake and scanned the crowd for any interested looking guys, but of course there were none because everyone thought she was with Rich.

"Who is that guy?" he asked.

Alex knew she shouldn't say it, but she couldn't help herself. "Funny, he didn't recognize you either."

"Why would I recognize him?"

"Maybe if he were naked in your bed again? Minus the beard, of course."

Rich's face screwed up at the idea of another man in his bed, and Alex had to twist the knife in the wound just a little bit. She flipped her hair, because, yeah, that really did distract Rich, and poured herself another cup of sake as she said. "I always wondered, were he and Juliet spooning when you found them?"

Rich's sake cup slammed down onto the table. "What the fuck is he doing here?"

Alex sat up straighter and took notice. She'd never heard Rich growl before. His purr she was well familiar with, but a growl woke up parts of her that weren't appropriate considering who this man had been to her best friend.

She had planned to tease him again, but their food arrived then, and there was an extra roll. "I didn't ask for this," Alex said, tapping the plate.

"I ordered it for Juliet. All the others have fish in them."

"You just can't take a hint, can you? You're stuck with me tonight, *Dew-rand*."

Rich looked down his nose at her, and she could swear he curled his lip. She wanted to make him do that again.

"Jealous?"

"That bastard took advantage of Juliet when she was at her most vulnerable."

Alex downed her sake. "I think it was more like he was there to comfort her when she was falling apart. She told me once that she was pretty sure Ethan was the only reason she didn't break that night."

His lip curled again, and Alex shivered a little. But, since she had to keep him entertained until Ethan and Juliet left, she gave him a consolation. "Look, I'll go see if she wants anything to eat, but you can't hold it against me—or her—if she's happy where she is. She deserves to be happy, Rich. You know that."

When Alex returned from telling Juliet not to come back to the table, Rich had finished the bottle of sake and was ordering another.

"So, what's up with you these days, Alex?" His cheeks were showing a tinge of red, and his words were slightly slurred. "Still making jewelry and fucking any man who talks to you?"

Alex popped a piece of salmon into her mouth, and tried to remain outwardly unaffected, even though she was wincing on the inside. Just because she had a tendency toward one-night stands did not mean she was *that* promiscuous. "Wow. Fuck you, Rich. Who are you cheating on this time?"

"Claws still as sharp as ever, I see."

"Are you comparing me to a cat?" Never mind that she'd just been comparing him to a cat inside her head.

"More like a honey badger."

Alex huffed out a laugh without meaning to. "That's not fair. I have a soft and cuddly side."

Rich looked skeptical and popped a tuna roll into his mouth. Good, hopefully the rice would help soak up the sake. Alex chanced a glance out at the dancefloor just Juliet led Ethan to the door.

Her night just got a whole lot easier.

"I don't think you're ever soft and cuddly," Rich said. "You strike me as wild all the way to the end."

Heat pulsed through Alex's core. Had he just spent the last minute picturing what it would be like to have sex with her? That was so inappropriate on so many levels, but Alex couldn't help her reply. It turned out, it was fun to play with Rich.

"Usually yes, right up until I kick the guy out of my bed and out the front door. But on the rare occasion someone fucks me til I'm satisfied, I'll purr all night long."

Heat and something that looked like possession flared in Rich's eyes. "Oh, *Piccolina*, you have been sleeping with the wrong caliber of man."

And just like that, Alex knew where this night was heading. It both thrilled and terrified her, because this was the last person she should ever, ever have a one-night stand with, but he'd issued her a challenge, and Alex wasn't the kind of woman who back down. Ever.

Her night just got way more complicated.

By the time Rich drained the last of the warmer into their cups, Alex was well beyond drunk, which was good. She could blame her colossal best-friend fuck up on that. No one besides her and Rich would ever need to know this had been premeditated.

Alex dragged him out onto the dance floor. Partially because she didn't want to walk in on Ethan and Juliet doing it on the breakfast bar, and partially because Rich was a fantastic dancer, and she didn't want to waste an opportunity.

They were on the floor for an hour, dancing and laughing and flirting when Rich's hands clamped down on Alex's hips and he pulled her against him. "What are we doing, Alex?" he asked.

She didn't give herself time to think before she said, "Being naughty."

His grip on her hips tightened. "Are you naughty?"

"Only one way to find out, Dew-rand."

His curled lips returned, and Alex giggled as she traced them with her finger. "What will it take to get you to say my name right?" he asked.

Alex pretended to think. "Two—no, three. Three orgasms." It was an outrageous number, she thought. Most of the time she barely even got one. "Deliver on that and I'll call you anything you want."

"Oh, *Piccolina*," he said, dropping a quick kiss to her lips. "Wrong caliber of man."

Alex sneaked Rich upstairs and into her room. The apartment was quiet, and Juliet had either left with Ethan or was asleep. But by silent agreement, neither Alex nor Rich wanted Juliet to know what was going on.

Once the door was shut, and they were lit only in the light that filtered through the blinds from Tokyo Night's big neon sign, Rich made good on his end of the bargain. And boy did he deliver. Between his mouth, hands, and cock, Alex passed out a purring, satisfied, limp-limbed mess before Rich stole out of her room.

"I like it when you purr, *Piccolina*." He said from her door.

Alex raised a hand in the air and flipped him off. "Fuck off, Riccardo," she whispered before lapsing into sleep.

For three days, Alex thought that had been the end of it. But then Rich had started texting her. On the one hand, it kind of pissed her off, because she knew he was texting Juliet at the same time, but the actual texts did nothing but tease her.

He talked about the taste of her on his lips. He told her she was so good he couldn't stop thinking about her. That her dirty talk turned him on.

By Thursday afternoon, she'd made plans to hook up with Rich again while Juliet was out with Ethan. Of course, by the time their rendezvous rolled around, Alex felt so guilty she had to get falling down drunk to go through with it.

Rich wasn't far behind her with the drinks, and they must have lost track of time, because when the made it upstairs for the sex part of the evening, they accidentally burst in on Ethan and Juliet making out on the sofa, then had to wait twenty minutes for an Uber to show up to take them to Rich's apartment.

Alex didn't remember much about their second encounter, but they'd stayed in bed together that night and the sex must have been energetic, because she was barely hungover the next morning when Rich woke her by rolling over on top of her and kissing the crap out of her before slipping inside her.

Alex had stalled on going home, allowing Rich to cook her pancakes for breakfast, so she didn't have to face Juliet right away. She knew she was behaving badly, and she knew she didn't have any good excuses, but Rich had mentioned something about meeting up the next weekend too, and Alex found herself saying yes at the same time she was screaming at herself to tell him no.

It was like he was an addiction. A dirty little secret that she wasn't proud of but couldn't say no to. When the texting and the desire escalated so that she and Rich were spending almost every night together, Alex let it happen. She knew seeing Rich wasn't good for her relationship with Juliet, but Rich made Alex feel good about her for a change.

And she had never felt so guilty about it in her life.

Alex had never been in this position. She knew that every time she was with Rich, she was betraying every ounce of trust Juliet had ever bestowed upon her. That was evidenced by the increasing amount of time Juliet spent at

Ethan's place. That also meant that she and Juliet barely saw one another. Alex knew what Juliet was thinking every time she looked at her. All Juliet saw was the best friend that was fucking the man who broke her entire world, and Alex couldn't even apologize, because she didn't want to stop.

Alex had never felt so alive, and she didn't want to apologize for it. Every time Rich touched her, it felt like more than lust. It felt real, like he cared about her. And after a couple of weeks, when Rich had stopped texting Juliet, Alex thought that maybe Rich had wanted only her. He'd started cooking her dinner as well as breakfast, hinting that maybe they could be more, and Alex wanted to believe him. She let herself believe that Rich was the person he presented himself as when they were alone, and minus the drama with Juliet, those were the best two weeks of Alex's life.

Rich lavished attention on her, hovering over her shoulder, saying the most beautiful things while she finished jewelry orders after dinner was ready. Then, he'd put on a movie while she continued to work until he finally pulled the pliers from her hands and dragged her to bed. That had been so devastatingly domestic that Alex had known she was in a hell of a lot of trouble.

And then, when she'd given herself permission to fall in love with him, to accept that maybe their relationship could be real and that she and Juliet could work something out—because Rich and Alex deserved happiness just as much as Juliet did—Alex got a glimpse of Rich's phone the last morning they were together. It wasn't even a big deal, he'd gotten a text from Gina and unlocked his phone in front of Alex. When he set it down, he left it unlocked, and the background picture was a photo of Rich and Juliet, their heads together, smiling at the camera.

It had been taken that night at Tokyo Nights. The night that kicked off two relationships. A happy, normal one for Ethan and Juliet and this farce of sex, maybe something more she was doing with Rich. Alex's stomach dropped out. And it had to end now.

She might be enamored of him, but she had enough self-respect to not want to be with someone who wished she were her best friend. Who maybe still only hung around in the hopes of seeing Juliet.

Alex would never be that woman.

Chapter Fourteen

Present

After Rich had gone, Alex called Avery. She'd used the excuse that she needed help getting caught up on orders, which was only partially true. Not only had Avery shipped all the finished orders and contacted those still waiting on fulfillment to let them know about the delay, she'd cleaned the studio and cut the chains for their biggest necklace order, then attached the clasps. Alex could have kissed her just for that, but what she really wanted was to not be alone.

Alastor tried to console her by hopping up into her lap, but the fat old cat slipped and dug his claws into Alex's leg so hard she jumped and cursed. The cat hid under the sofa until Avery arrived with a bag full of Indian takeout. While Avery baby talked to her Gran's cat, Alex sent a picture to Dale of herself munching on a piece of naan loaded with rice and lamb vindaloo. His return text said that he expected her to run ten kilometers that evening to put those carbs to good use. Alex had responded by telling him she didn't speak metric.

As Alex wrapped crystals in wire and slid them on chains between bites and caught up with Avery, Alex felt herself slipping back into her routine. Gossiping and working with Avery was comforting. Teasing Dale was fun and familiar. Alastor snoozed in a patch of sunlight on the floor, and it was like having a piece of home there with her. Alex could do this, she could pick up her everyday activities again and her life would keep going, just like it should. It might even be easier now because she didn't have to drive to Lawrence three days a week for school. Now all her creative energy could go into her business.

Alex had been aching for that freedom. She had been waiting to savor living only by her own deadlines since the previous summer. Now it felt like such a hollow victory, especially when the urge to call and check in on Gran struck early that afternoon. Yes, she was living her dream, and she'd worked hard over the last eight years to turn her jewelry hobby into a sustainable business, but she didn't want the business to take over her life. She needed more, some connection to people who weren't employees, dear as Avery and Janet were to her. Gran and Ben had been that for her. Now what?

Alex fired off a text to Colleen, Juliet's little sister, to see if she'd made her dress fitting—which had already been rescheduled twice due to Colleen's work schedule.

Juliet had been worried about Colleen the week before. Apparently, her sister had lost her roommate slash most recent live-in kind-of-boyfriend and was back working at the coffee shop in addition to her marketing job just to keep up her rent. Since Colleen refused to accept money and Juliet's house was a two-hour drive from Denver, Juliet couldn't do much to help her sister outside of taking her to lunch a couple times a month.

Alex understood Colleen's desire to make things work on her own. It's where Alex had always been, proving that she could take care of herself without any help from anyone. She thought maybe she should warn Colleen that it turned into a lonely road after a while. It was probably *why* Alex's employees were her closest friends.

In the spirit of keeping those friends, Alex asked for the latest gossip about Avery's roommates, who were either having sex constantly or yelling at each other so loudly that the neighbors called the cops. Avery's newest story included Ellie slapping Rose for flirting with another girl at a party then backing her into the living room wall and doing things Avery had tried not to see.

Alex was still congratulating herself on her love life not being that dramatic when Avery returned from a bathroom break and ruined all of Alex's pretensions to a drama-free life.

"So, uh, not to be nosy, but I'm totally being nosy. I thought you said Ben broke up with you in a voicemail."

"He did."

"No breakup sex?"

Alex snorted. "Definitely not."

"Then what's up with the condom wrapper in the bathroom?" Avery shifted in her seat, like she didn't want to ask, but couldn't keep her curiosity in. "I mean, I wasn't trying to see it, but it was just sitting on the top of the trash and that blue wrapper next to all of those white tissues kind of stands out, you know."

"Don't worry about it," Alex said, waving at Avery to sit and get back to work.

Avery sat, but instead of resuming the chore of attaching the necklaces Alex had finished to their display cards, she clasped her hands in her lap and leaned forward. "So," she waited for Alex to meet her eye. "Who was the guy?"

"Just a guy from downstairs," Alex said. "Rebound sex, you know."

Avery rolled her eyes. "No way. How many times have to you told me how dangerous it is to screw some rando? You had to know the guy."

Despite it making her a hypocrite, since Alex spent a good portion of her twenties having sex with guys she'd just met, Alex had warned Avery against doing the same thing. Alex knew how to handle herself, but Avery seemed more innocent than Alex had been at the same age. More naive. She didn't want her to trust the wrong guy.

"It was a guy I had a thing with a few years ago. He happened to be at the club last night, and he's good in bed, so you know."

"You banged his brains out?" Avery asked with a waggle of her eyebrows.

Alex gave her a sly grin. "Something like that."

When Alex turned back to her work, she'd hoped Avery would do the same, but no such luck.

"Tell me about him. When did you meet him? Are you guys starting something? Why did you break up if he's so good in bed?"

"It was nothing," Alex said.

"Come on, I have zero prospects. I need to hear it's possible for a man to be worth a second chance. Give me his name, at least."

Alex could do that much. "Rich Durand," she pronounced his name correctly, and felt her stomach clench when Avery's mouth dropped open.

"You had a thing with Professor Durand?"

"Oh shit." She'd forgotten Avery had gone to the same small Catholic university Rich taught at. She remembered noting that when she'd read Avery's application, but Avery had been in the art department, and Alex didn't think of it beyond that. "You took Italian?"

Avery laughed. "No, but stalking Professor Durand is practically an unofficial minor at that school. Did you know that he runs on the track in the school gym in the winter? I'd never been so skinny as I was my junior year when Frankie and I showed up every morning just to stare at his ass when he lapped us."

"That is awful," Alex said through a giggle.

"Oh my God, Frankie is going to be so jealous. She took Italian 101 one year just to be near him, but he didn't even look twice at her."

"Rich doesn't date students," Alex said.

"He doesn't fucking need to," Avery said. "Not when he's got a badass boxing boss babe like you to come home to."

Alex raised her eyebrows at Avery. It was nice to be idolized, she guessed. Alex certainly didn't think of herself that way. "It was a one time thing. Don't expect to start seeing him around here."

Avery deflated, and Alex found herself wanting to parade Rich around, just for her assistant's amusement, until she asked, "Why not?"

That was all it took for the pain of seeing Lynnette's name on Rich's phone to hit her square in the chest. Because maybe, it would have been nice if it could have been more than a one time thing, but with Rich, it was too much of a gamble. "I really don't want to talk about it," Alex said and turned back to her work.

Avery left it alone after that, but Alex felt her employee watching her with assessing eyes the rest of the day.

• • • •

ALEX WOULDN'T RETURN his calls or his texts. Well, she'd returned his first text, but she'd texted, *Fuck off, Riccardo.* Alex had said that to him only once, when he'd been on his way out the door after the first time they'd slept together—and it had been as much of an invitation as it was a "go the hell away and let me sleep."

And now?

Rich had no idea what she wanted from him. He hadn't missed the look of longing that had passed over her when he'd dropped the wife and kids line. Rich had been well familiar with the front Alex put on during his entire relationship with Juliet. She'd always claimed she hadn't wanted a relationship, that a man would just hold her back. But he'd also noticed the way she'd watched Juliet and he with longing. She hadn't been jealous, just afraid to admit that she'd wanted someone of her own to love.

Now that she was willing to admit she wanted a family, Rich wanted a shot at doing that with her, but he'd never get the chance if he couldn't convince Alex that he'd changed.

Maybe he hadn't handled the Lynnette thing with the most delicacy. Rich had known he couldn't just show up at Lynnette's house and tell her it was over on a weeknight. She'd flip the fuck out. There would be yelling and crying, and later, her trying to seduce him in a ploy to convince him that they could work things out. But if he did it in public, during the day, she'd have no choice but to stay calm.

And she had.

Rich wouldn't be surprised if she'd gone home and made a voodoo doll of him with the way rage had burned in her eyes, but she'd listened to him, and told him she respected him enough to let him go after what he needed.

What he needed was Alex, and for two weeks all he'd gotten from her was a *Fuck off, Ricardo.* He'd developed an annoying heel tapping habit while at his desk, the physical manifestation of the nerves from not knowing what Alex was thinking, and how she was dealing with her loss. The guilt that he'd added hurt on top of that kept him awake at night. The dark circles under his eyes and the new twitching habit had him feeling like a neurotic mess.

When he opened the door to his apartment, he tossed his keys on the floor and headed straight for the coffee maker. He had grading to do, and he was going to need coffee to get through it. Summer classes were always fast paced and since all the graduate students had either graduated or were on the Italy trip, Rich was stuck doing his own grading through the beginning of July when the course ended. Then he'd have a month off before he had to be back in the office preparing for the fall. Sometimes that month didn't seem like long enough to recover. And this year, he didn't have any plans other than maybe seeing if his mom was going to be around the weekend of Juliet's wedding. As much as he didn't want to go anywhere near Georgia in August, it would be good to see his mom and let her distract him for what was happening in Colorado that same weekend.

Rich sighed. He liked his life. He had made a successful career out of the only thing that he'd ever wanted to do. To teach, to be immersed in the languages that had formed him. But at the same time, he felt stuck. He'd built this life with the intention of sharing it with Juliet. And while he wouldn't trade his job or give up his tenure, Rich wondered what else he could change to be able to share his life with somebody.

He eyed the two stacks of paper on his breakfast bar. The day's quizzes or yesterday's mail? Would either one distract him from the twinge of regret he felt every time he thought about Juliet's wedding? Or the anxiety over screwing things up with Alex again? Probably not, but he went with the mail anyway. There were only two things that weren't bills. The first, in a big envelope was a hard copy of the latest report from the P.I. on his work to narrow down the possible leads on his dad from the long list of Marius Durands they'd found. Durand was too common of a name, and even if he thought of Marius as old fashioned, there were apparently enough other people in France that didn't, because the list of Marius Durand's around the country was longer than he'd expected. And since Rich didn't have any of his dad's paperwork, he didn't even have any photographs, and was too chicken to ask his mother for one, the P. I. was having to narrow it down the old fashioned way.

Rich just hoped that he wasn't blowing a good chunk of his savings on a wild goose chase.

Rich almost ruled the second envelope as junk mail, but when he opened it, he was not expecting what looked like a press pass with a yellow lanyard to fall out.

On the pass were the details of a private party at Tokyo Nights for Saturday night. A party Alex was throwing to launch the newest branch of her business.

She had invited him to a cocktail party? One where she was courting buyers and shop owners?

This was a major life event for her. It said something that she wanted him there. Hope swelled as he imagined Alex strutting around his kitchen, sassing off as they prepared dinner together. Teasing his ear with her tongue as she set a glass of wine down in front of him. Then she would tell him to buzz off when he did the same to her when she sat down to her own work after dinner. Alex could slide into his life so effortlessly, and everything would just be perfect.

Rich texted his RSVP to the number on the pass, a number that wasn't Alex's, probably the event coordinator, and pushed the rest of the mail out of the way to make room for the papers he needed to grade.

Rich shook his head again as he poured his coffee. No word for two weeks and then she invited him to a party. She was the most confusing woman he'd ever met. That didn't stop him from taking a detour to his bedroom to make sure his blue suit was clean before he sat down to grade.

Chapter Fifteen

Three weeks after returning from her Gran's, three weeks after Rich, some of the grief fogging Alex's mind had eased into a light mist as she found comfort in her new routine. She went to the gym and teased Dale for an hour four days a week while he tried to coax her into sparring. Then she grabbed coffee on the way home and worked at her bench most of the day with the stereo blaring. Trying to keep the cat from eating her beads had become its own sport, half game, half desperate attempt not to have to comb through the litter box for semi-precious stones.

Avery worked six days a week to help Alex get ahead, which Alex appreciated, since it meant she was only at the apartment alone long enough to collapse into bed. Even Janet had spent most afternoons working from Alex's apartment as they prepared for the launch of the Alex & Co. line. It meant they both spent less time on the phone as they put the finishing touches on the launch party and the online store while building hype.

Alex had spent one day doing interviews with local magazines while Janet had sweet talked some journalists into attending the launch party.

The party was the next night and nerves had Alex's fingertips going numb as she placed the last set of earrings on their stand. Surely, she was imagining the shake in her hand as she positioned the stand on the black tablecloth.

Avery directed Janet and Alex as they put together a mockup of the display table that would show off the new line at the party. Janet swapped out two neck forms and Alex fiddled with the exact height at which she wanted the pendant of her signature piece to rest against the display when Janet's phone chimed. She crossed to Avery and they both looked down at the screen, whispering to one another.

"No secrets," Alex called out, not taking her eyes off the display. Something wasn't quite right yet.

"It's not secrets," Avery said. "It's an updated RSVP list from the event coordinator. We need to call and see if we can get more chocolate boxes than we planned. We've had a few late acceptances."

"Anyone good?" Alex asked.

"The buyer from TIVOL is coming after all, and Simone from Vinca will be there," Janet said.

Alex rubbed her hands together. "Perfect." She could see the zeroes accumulating in her bank account already. That wasn't why she did what she did, but it was the point of the party. She needed a successful launch, otherwise Alex & Co. was dead before it even got started. "Anyone else?"

"Well there's—" Janet started to say but Avery elbowed her in the ribs.

"Just a few other stragglers. Smaller buyers. The reporters from the Star you wanted."

Alex looked up just in time to see her employees share a conspiratorial look. Great. They had something up their sleeves but try as she might Alex couldn't get them to divulge. It wasn't until the next night, when Rich sidled up to her wearing a slim-cut navy suit and carrying a manhattan in one hand and a tequila and soda in the other that Alex realized what Janet and Avery had done.

They'd played matchmaker.

• • • •

ALEX WAS GORGEOUS. She wore a form fitting strapless black dress that cut off just above her knees. The high slit had attracted Rich's attention from across the room. The real star of the show though was the jewelry she wore. A large green stone surrounded by a halo of silver wire rested above the neckline of her dress. From her ears dangled two lines of flashing silver strands. And around her wrist she wore a crush of silver bangles. All pieces from her new collection.

Rich had been at the party for fifteen minutes already. He'd wandered the perimeter, perused her display table, and circled back around to the bar. Her work was stunning. The pieces were bold and edgy and still carried her usual boho flair while at the same time maintaining a timeless look. The woman was a genius with metal and stone.

And now her attention was fixed on him as he closed the last few feet separating them. The woman beside her was elegant with her silver hair pulled in a twist at the back of her head, and Alex looked like she wanted to be paying attention to what the other woman was saying but couldn't take her eyes off Rich.

He smiled when the other woman turned her attention to him. He handed Alex her drink then leaned in to place a kiss on each of her cheeks. "You look lovely," he said, before stepping back.

Alex took a long sip of her drink before introducing him to her friend, and her smile looked a little strained. "Simone this is Riccardo Durand—Rich to us mere mortals. Rich, this is Simone, she's a jewelry designer like me."

Rich wondered if she was like Prince and only had one name.

Simone extended a thin, elegant hand. "How pleasant, are you also in the business?"

Instead of shaking Simone's hand, Rich grasped her fingers and brought her knuckles to his lips. "It's my pleasure," he said as he released her hand. "And no, I'm just a fan of Alex's."

"More than a fan, I would guess." Simone motioned to the drink in Alex's hand.

"Only marginally, I assure you," Rich said. "Alex would probably prefer to see the back of me."

Rich could have sworn he heard Simone say, "So would I dear," before Alex talked over her.

"And yet here you are. I'm guessing Janet sent you an invitation?"

"If Janet oversaw sending the invitations, then I suppose so. Someone did."

Alex pursed her mouth in a sideways pucker that almost always meant she was displeased.

Simone's hand landed on Alex's elbow. "I'll have Nina call to hash out the details of those custom pieces this week. You look like you have something to work out here." Then she leaned in and said just loud enough for Rich to hear, "You should take this one home with you tonight, darling."

Simone winked at Rich before she stalked away, and Alex watched her disappear behind him. Her vague smile turned to outrage for a second, before a genuine smile spread across her lips. "She totally just checked out your ass."

Rich couldn't help the bark of a laugh that escaped him. "At least someone appreciates it."

"Oh, I appreciate your ass," Alex said. "I'm just wondering what the hell it's doing at my party."

Rich had missed Alex. He'd missed that mouth, that voice, those eyes. His hands itched to touch her, to smooth back the curl that was snagged on the corner of her glasses but settled for a sip of his drink instead. "I was invited."

"Why did you come though?" A little of her veneer cracked and Alex allowed a little of her vulnerability show through, like his presence actually distressed her.

Rich leaned in a little closer and ducked his head so he could speak close to her ear. "I thought the invitation was from you."

"No." Alex backed up a step, and her mouth was a straight line, her body rigid. "I didn't invite you."

"Would you rather I left?" he asked.

Alex chewed her lip and gave a barely perceptible nod.

"I'm sorry then," he said, and meant it as the bottom dropped out of his stomach. Coming to the party had been a mistake. He had let his desire to see Alex overwhelm his better judgement. If Rich wanted to start a relationship with her, he needed to address their issues in private first. He should have known she hadn't invited him herself.

Alex lifted one shoulder, and let it drop in what was meant to be a casual brush off. But Rich could see beneath it. He could see the fear and the doubt draped around her that had to do with so much more than just him, but Rich understood. It hurt, because he only wanted good things for Alex, but he wouldn't press himself where he wasn't wanted. This was Alex's night, and he wouldn't give her another excuse to despise him.

"Thank you for the opportunity to see your work. You're talented, Alex. Truly." Then he pushed his luck and pressed a quick kiss to her lips. She didn't stop him, only blinked up at him in surprise as he whispered, "Good luck," and turned to leave. Rich deposited his drink on a shelf by the coat check on his way out the door. Halfway to his car a thought occurred to him.

He and Alex did have a lot to talk about, and she wasn't the only one who had grievances. So far, Rich had been apologetic and penitent, but he'd also been crushing down his own resentment about how she'd handled her pregnancy. How she'd never told him, how she'd dismissed his involvement entirely. He'd been leashing his anger over finding out from Juliet, of all people, that Alex had been pregnant at all. And maybe he shouldn't anymore.

Rich turned on his heel and walked straight back toward Alex's building. He'd known the keycode for the door up to the apartments once upon a time. He tried the six-digit code Alex had given him three years ago, and it still worked. The back door unlatched, and Rich climbed the two flights of stairs up to the third floor. He hefted the armchair from the landing and deposited it in front of Alex's door. He draped his suit jacket over the back and settled in the for the long wait in the stuffy hallway.

His mind reeled like it had the night he'd found out he could have been a father–again–but had missed out–again.

He hadn't even been able to process the information at first. Juliet had told him, then gone on about how it related to her own problems. Since Rich had been trying to prove to Juliet that he was better for her than Ethan he'd pushed aside his shock and complete devastation to focus on her.

But he'd sat up for hours after Juliet had gone to bed. He'd finished the bottle of wine they'd opened and watched the moon track across the sky. He'd pulled his phone out to text Alex over and over.

How could you?

What the fuck were you thinking?

You should have told me.

How dare you.

He hadn't been able to send any of them. Rich wasn't that kind of guy, and he hadn't wanted to become that kind of guy. He'd known, even in that moment, that it couldn't have been an easy decision for her. And with her ongoing fight with Juliet, Alex had gone through enough turmoil. He hadn't needed to add his hysteria to the mix.

He'd decided that maybe someday, when he could talk about it rationally, he'd confront her about it, but calling her in the middle of his shock and outrage would have only made everything worse. So, Rich had put away his phone and sat on his disappointment and his resentment.

It had been two and a half years since that night, and though the resentment had lessened over time, the outrage still lingered, along with a heavy dose of disappointment. None of it changed the way he felt about Alex now, but it needed to be addressed, because these were the kinds of feelings that could fester. With that in mind, Rich nestled back into the armchair and tried to relax.

An hour into the mystery novel he had on his phone, he received a text from Alex that said, *Thanks for coming.*

Rich smiled to himself. He wondered if she'd be saying that in another hour or two.

• • • •

ALEX WAS EXHAUSTED and a little tipsy. Not drunk. Just pleasantly buzzed and possibly wearing heels that were a little bit too tall. But she looked damn hot in them, and she had rocked her business woman persona hard tonight, so she wasn't about to complain. She wobbled at the top of the stairs and reached for the armchair that normally sat on the landing, missed, and toppled to the floor.

Giggling, Alex hauled herself back to her feet. At least that hadn't happened in front of everyone downstairs. Nope, downstairs she had been the queen of her own empire tonight, and she had owned that shit. Janet had taken a whole clipboard full of orders, and Alex had seen Avery sweet talking a journalist. What they were doing with this new line, it was going to be big. Alex could feel it coming.

She was hauling herself back to her feet when Rich appeared from around the corner. "Was that you falling just now? Are you alright?"

Alex finished dusting off her ass and tried not to slur her words, "Why are you always where you're not supposed to be? Wait," she looked behind her to where the ugly blue armchair should have been. "Did you steal the chair?"

"I figured it would be a long wait." He reached out a hand to help her up the last two steps. Alex took it on reflex.

"But why?"

"Why did I wait for you?"

Alex nodded, and noted that maybe she was more drunk than she'd estimated, because her head wobbled more than nodded.

"I wanted to apologize."

Alex halted, tugging at their still clasped hands. "For what?"

"For not being transparent about what was going on with Lynnette. I should have broken up with her months ago, but I was trying to prove something to myself, and I ended up screwing it all up in the end anyway."

Alex wasn't entirely following what he was saying, but she wasn't sure she was supposed to. "Wait, so you're apologizing for making me the excuse you needed to break up with your girlfriend?"

"No, *Piccolina*." Rich turned her so her back was against the wall outside her door. "You were never part of that. I'm sorry I didn't tell you it wasn't officially over. You deserve better than that from me."

"I deserve a hell of a lot more than you've ever given me, which is why you need to just go away." Alex tried to free her hand, but he held on.

"Tell me what to do," he said. "Tell me how I can prove to you that I can be better. Be more."

Alex stared at him. He'd lost his suit jacket, and rolled up his sleeves, and he still looked like he should be between the pages of a magazine instead of standing in her hot, dusty hallway. There was a wrinkle between his eyebrows as he met her gaze with a determined apprehension. The sincerity she saw there broke her heart, but could she trust it?

"Why is this so important to you?" she asked.

"Because I need to be better than the man you couldn't come to when you were pregnant. I need to be better than the man who was so angry for years that I'd had no say in that pregnancy that I wouldn't let myself call you even though I wanted to. I need to be better so the next time you're pregnant—."

"Whoa. Whoa. Whoa," Alex held up a hand and use the wall for support. "You are getting too far ahead of yourself here."

"Too bad." Rich crowded her, his hands on either side of her head as he stared directly at her. "I need to talk about the future. I need to tell you what I want, and who I want to be for you, because otherwise I'll give in to the fear."

The panic and devastation in Rich's dark eyes, had Alex softening toward him. After she'd told him to go earlier, she'd felt bad for kicking him out. He hadn't exactly left stoop-shouldered, but that wasn't Rich's style. He didn't wear defeat easily. He was more likely to go on the defensive, which she guessed that's what this was. After a sideways comment from Avery, Alex had recognized that he'd only been there to support her, but Alex hadn't been able to face him down there. Too many negative thoughts had bubbled up in her as he'd approached, and it had been all she could do to stay unaffected in his presence. Having him trail her all night as she spoke to buyers, having him watch her work while there was still so much unsaid between the two of them? Alex hadn't thought she could do it.

"What are you afraid of?" Alex asked. Rich had always struck her as the kind of man who was never afraid of anything. He saw what he wanted and went after it, and if that was banging two women at the same time, so be it. But the Rich standing in front of her, searching for words looked so anguished and apprehensive, it broke her heart.

. . . .

RICH BROKE OFF FROM the wall and ran his hands through his hair. Putting words to his fears had never been easy for him. He'd spent the last two hours searching for them, and still had nothing eloquent to say but the bare, honest truth. "I'm afraid of being too happy. I'm afraid I'll create the perfect life and turn into my father. Then I'll let everyone I love down when it really counts."

"Like you did with Juliet?" Alex asked.

She still pressed herself against the wall, but he felt like she'd punched him in the chest all over again. Rich couldn't face her when she looked like nothing would atone for how he'd wronged Juliet. Maybe nothing would, so he stepped out of her line of sight, turned his back to the wall and slid down it. "Yes. Just like that. I don't want those to be the actions that define me anymore. I want to do better. I have to prove that I can be better."

Alex kicked off her shoes and joined him on the floor. "And you want me to volunteer to be your test subject?" He didn't like her words, or the bitterness he heard in them.

"I want you to let me love you," he said. He hoped the frank words would snag her attention, but all it did was pull a derisive laugh out of her mouth.

"And now you love me? We didn't speak for almost three years, spent one night together, and now you love me? Are you insane?"

"I said I wanted the opportunity to love you." He wanted to reach for her hand, to kiss her knuckles, but he didn't.

Alex sighed and threw her head back against the wall. "I don't know if I can do that."

"I'm not going to give up," Rich said, as a steely resolve settled over him. She hadn't said no. If he could just get her to give him a chance, he could prove to her that there was something between them.

"Why me?" she asked, her voice sounded so small.

Rich knew he had to word his answer carefully, but he didn't know if there was a way to put it delicately enough for Alex right now. "Because you are one of the only women I've ever seen myself starting a family with."

Alex's face turned red and her shoe hit the opposite wall. "And that's where we're always going to have a problem, Dew-Rand. Because you would always be my first choice, and I'm always going to come after Juliet for you. I'm always going to be the party girl you accidentally knocked up and had to think about starting a family with. Don't come to me now with big promises when you and I both know I'm not who you really want."

Part of Rich's brain knew he needed to defend against the charge that Alex came second to Juliet, because that was a hell of an obstacle they had to overcome if he was going to be with Alex. He knew he should tell her it wasn't true, but his attention snagged and held on the words, *You would be my first choice.*

As he opened his mouth to respond, his mind screamed at him to come up with something smooth to say about how Alex was second to no one, but instead, what came out was, "If I'm your first choice, that means you do want me."

And then he flinched as Alex's other shoe hit the wall. The heel embedded itself in the drywall so the toe swung, dangling toward the ground.

"Fuck you, Rich," Alex said as teetered onto her bare feet. "Just, fuck you." And then she slammed her apartment door shut behind her. The sound of the deadbolt clicking into place was too loud in the quiet hall.

Rich buried his head in his hands. That was not the ending he'd been hoping for, and he cursed as he heard Alex's door shut on him over and over in his mind.

He heard a door click open and glanced up, but it wasn't Alex's door, it was the one across the hall that belonged to the other apartment on this floor. A rumpled looking man with graying hair stuck his head out the door and said, "Hey man, can you keep it down? The wife and I are trying to sleep."

"Sure thing. Sorry," Rich said. He hauled himself up off the floor as they guy retreated. He'd screwed up. Bad. Now he just had to figure out how to fix it.

Chapter Sixteen

The gifts started the day after her party. Two dozen white roses landed on her desk while Alex was in the middle of soldering. Rich apologized for being a bastard on a tiny rectangular piece of cardboard. Not wanting to think about Rich or how much of a bastard he was, Alex asked the hostess at Tokyo Nights if she wanted flowers for her coat check window that night.

The next day a gigantic bouquet of yellow tulips and purple irises was delivered. The note read, "You're not my second choice, *Piccolina*. You're my second chance."

Alex tore the note into teeny, tiny, miniscule shreds but kept the flowers. They were too beautiful to pitch.

And today. Today the worst of the lot had arrived. A big brown teddy bear with a white t-shirt that had, "You're #1 Champ" written across the front in red letters, with a pair of boxing gloves that dangled off the "1."

He was ridiculous. The least he could do would be to send along a bottle of tequila if he was going to keep pulling stupid shit like this.

But he didn't, so Alex was doing something equally ridiculous. She walked into her boxing gym with a giant teddy bear tucked under her arm, because she didn't get enough strange looks and taunting gestures already.

When she met Dale at the heavy bags after her usual warm up, Dale shook his head and said, "Girl, what the fuck is that?"

Alex held it out to him. "I brought you a present."

He looked at her like she had three heads. "There is no way in hell I'm taking that bear."

Alex gave it a shake. "Oh, come on. Just because it's soft and cuddly doesn't mean it has to threaten your masculinity. You're a big, tough guy. You can take it."

"Not happening, Stafford. Put the bear down and tape up."

"It was worth a try, I guess." Alex blew at the strand of hair that had already worked its way loose from her braid and drop kicked the bear into the corner.

"So, who's the guy?" Dale asked as she wrapped the tape around her hands and wrists.

"It's a long story," Alex said.

"Then give me the short version."

"You know my friend who's getting married in a few weeks?"

Dale nodded.

"It's her college boyfriend. We hooked up a few years ago, but I couldn't handle the way it affected my relationship with Juliet, so I broke it off. Then found out I was pregnant. After the abortion, he finds out I was pregnant, and its crickets for three years and now he's suddenly trying to convince me I'm the true love of his life, not Juliet, which is a big fucking lie, because the only reason he's interested is because Juliet's marrying someone else and he's being forced to move on."

Dale couldn't hold back a chuckle as he held the gloves out for Alex to slip her hands into. "Goddamn I'm glad I'm married."

"Don't rub it in," Alex said and punched her gloves together.

Dale laughed again and wrapped one arm around the heavy bag from behind. "Alright, here's what we're gonna do. Which part do you want to do more damage to, Lover Boy's face or his junk?"

"His face. I like the other part."

"This is why you're my favorite client," Dale said, trying and failing to hold back even more laughter. When he'd reined himself in, he tapped the front of the bag at Alex's eye level. "Aim right here then three rounds, thirty one-twos. And if you decide you want a good junk shot," he tapped lower on the bag, "You can throw in one of those sloppy kicks of yours just for fun."

"This is so much better than therapy," Alex grinned, and whaled on the bag.

• • • •

A FULL TWO WEEKS LATER, the gifts had kept coming. There were flowers almost daily, along with some fancy chocolates, a gift certificate to her favorite jewelry supplier for 100 dollars, a bottle of Tres Agaves Blanco along with a note about how all of his gifts were probably driving her to drink.

Alex relented and texted him after that one, because it was like he had read her mind.

Alex: *How long are you going to keep this up?*

His response took a while, and Alex guessed he must still be teaching.

Rich: *As long as it takes to get you to take me seriously.*

Alex: *You may go broke.*

Rich: *So be it.*

Alex took a selfie of herself drinking from the bottle of tequila. And Rich responded with a selfie of himself and his flirtatious grin.

Alex found herself staring at the way his wavy hair fell in his eyes and the way he looked like he hadn't shaved in days. She liked how his lower lip bowed in a way that made Alex want to suck it between her teeth. Alex sighed out a breath and tossed her phone to the other side of her work table. She hadn't meant to flirt, and she really hadn't meant to ogle him.

This whole thing was turning a little bit dangerous. Alex couldn't let that happen.

Alex hid her phone and lost herself in the custom order she was doing for Simone's shop on the Plaza. Rings were one of the more underrepresented items in her new line. She'd made a couple designs, but most of the boutiques she sold in didn't have a lot of luck with rings. Simone, on the other hand, couldn't keep up with demand for her handmade rings, and had started showcasing rings made by other local designers to give herself a little bit of breathing space. She'd commissioned Alex to make her a collection of one of a kind engagement rings.

Her designs rarely did anything with gemstones since she preferred to work more with stones that had the appearance of rock or crystal, but Simone's offer was too much of a challenge to pass up.

In front of her on the work table was her new collection of certified cruelty free raw diamond, the single most expensive order she'd ever placed. Alex spent the next eight hours absorbed in grouping the diamonds into different combinations with each other and other more colorful, less valuable stones. Then she sketched out the possible designs.

It was consuming work, fulfilling work. The kind of work that made all the hours and hard work over the past few years worth it. Alex vaguely remembered Avery packing up for the day but couldn't remember what she'd said in farewell. It wasn't until her cell phone alarm interrupted Malcolm McLaren's "Algernon is Simply Awfully Good at Algebra" hours later that she realized how much time had passed.

It was after ten. Alex's stomach growled and her bladder was full. She stood and stretched. After a trip to the bathroom, she pulled some turkey and spinach from her refrigerator, eating the meat and greens wrapped around avocado and slices of tomatoes from the farmers market. She'd been doing better about sticking to the meal plan Dale had given her. While she thought it was probably mostly the not drinking so much thing, she did notice a difference in her energy levels. And of course, she'd wasted her one to two ounces of tequila a week on flirting with Rich.

That had shown a lamentable lack of foresight on her part. She shouldn't be flirting with Rich. He wasn't good for her.

Even if on the days when no gift arrived, like yesterday, she felt a little sad, and wondered if he'd finally given up. She'd been relieved to see the bottle of tequila show up that afternoon. And it would be a lie if she didn't admit she hadn't enjoyed the flirting, hadn't enjoyed Avery's telling her to give it up already, because Avery was going to go out with him soon if Alex didn't.

Alex settled on the sofa with the last of her turkey rolls and pulled up Netflix. It wasn't the best idea, because she was probably going to get sucked in and try to finish the last three episodes of the series she was watching before going to bed. Staying up too late wouldn't do her any good when she was supposed to be at the gym at eight and she and Janet had an appointment with a new buyer over lunch. After that it was back to the workbench for a few hours before she started on the favors for Juliet's wedding—if the delivery arrived like it was supposed to.

Ethan and Juliet were giving all their guests a mini succulent garden, and while Alex thought it was a cute idea, and fitting for Juliet's green thumb, placing Alex in charge of plants did not show brilliance on their part. They wanted to give the gardens a couple of weeks to fill out, and Juliet didn't have time to do it. Colleen had no way to deliver them to the wedding, so Alex had volunteered to make it happen. She'd even devised a way to transport each of the mini gardens in her jewelry cases for safety. Somehow, Alex didn't think the project would be nearly as engaging as designing rings, but she'd get through it.

Her grandmother's cat settled onto the top of the sofa behind Alex's head as the show drew her in. When she woke a couple hours later, there were nibbles out of the leftover turkey rolls on her plate and the blue light from Netflix's *Are you still watching* screen filled her dark living room.

She had to move the cat off her pillow before she crawled into bed and wondered what Rich's next gift would be.

Chapter Seventeen

Avery's bag lay slumped on the breakfast bar when Alex returned from a sushi lunch and a promise of a large opening order from a local department store. It was possible, if things kept up, that Alex was going to have to hire another person to help Avery and herself fulfill orders on time. Alex didn't want to think about that, because she didn't have room for another person to work in her apartment. Janet mostly worked from home. The second bedroom had just enough room for Alex and Avery and all of the equipment. If she added another person, she'd have to find a studio space somewhere—and while she liked the idea of going somewhere to work again and just relaxing at home, she wasn't quite ready to make that leap. Maybe in a year if this new line really took off and Alex had just a little bit more capital coming in. A small part of her nagged at the back of her mind that if she made the shift now, she'd be able to fulfill that many more orders, and maybe things would be less harried, less stressful. But the "maybe" part of the equation always tripped Alex up. She had no way of knowing for sure if another gamble right now would pay off. Alex & Co. was too new. It was safer to wait and see if her buyers put in second and third orders before making those kinds of changes.

"I let two delivery guys in," Avery said, appearing out of the hallway as Alex kicked her flats off and dropped her sample bag onto the wicker armchair by the door.

"The plants?"

Avery nodded. "And the biggest bouquet of roses I've ever seen. I swear, if there's not a ring in that envelope, I'm gonna be so disappointed."

"Rich is ridiculous," Alex said, "but not that ridiculous. I'm gonna go change into something more comfortable."

Alex had gone straight from the gym to her lunch meeting. A woman in shorts and a sports bra was uncommon enough, but one in business attire was apparently cause for the whole damn place to gape and comment about how good her ass looked in her skinny black ankle pants.

They didn't need to tell her. Alex already knew. She'd flipped off more than a few of the beefier ones on her way to the door. It had only made them laugh, but she didn't have time to school them in harassment. Her lunch meeting had been a thirty-minute drive away.

And while she did look like a badass in her skinny black suit, she much preferred yoga pants and an old t-shirt for the fiddly metalwork she had on the agenda for the day.

"You don't want to see the roses?" Avery asked. "They're in the studio."

Alex waved her off. The apartment was already covered in flower arrangements, what interested Alex was what the note said this time. After the note about second chances, he'd sent some article clippings about her new line with congratulations, and a few notes written in Italian that according to google translate were mostly unintelligible sap. Alex expected more of the same, but when she strolled into the studio a few minutes later, she stopped dead. That really was the biggest bouquet of roses she'd ever seen. Sitting on

Alex's workbench was a sphere of roses in red, pink, orange, and yellow. It was stunning.

"That's got to be at least a hundred roses," she said.

Avery raised a hand like she was still in school. "It is. I asked."

"Holy shit," Alex said. She stalked closer and caressed one of the velvety soft petals. "What the hell is he thinking?" She said it to herself, but Avery answered anyway.

"I bet if you opened up that envelope you'd find out. I'm crossing my fingers for more Italian."

The white envelope lay propped against the giant globe vase that left her no room for her to work. Where was she going to put all these flowers? She was going to have to be Lorelai Gilmore with her yellow daisies and give one to everyone in town.

As Alex turned the envelope over, she hesitated to break the seal. What in the hell was Rich up to? Avery had been right, this was the sort of flower arrangement that usually came along with a marriage proposal.

Alex hoped that Rich wasn't that stupid.

With a deep breath Alex sliced into the paper with one of her knives. Inside were several slips of cardstock. Alex shuffled them, looking for a note from Rich, but there was none. She didn't suppose he needed one. His intent was clear.

"What is it?" Avery asked, trying to get a glimpse of what Alex held around the giant flower globe.

Alex held up the first slip. "Dinner reservations at Novel for two."

Avery whistled. Novel was a tiny, intimate restaurant just a few minutes away from where Alex lived. Meals there easily topped seventy-five dollars a plate. Alex didn't buy herself things that expensive, so she'd never eaten there. But she'd wanted to.

When Alex only stared at the rest of what Rich included, Avery asked. "Is there more?"

She held the two slips of paper up for Avery to see. "Two tickets to Perfume Genius for the same night."

Avery's eyes grew wide. Alex had introduced her to all sorts of what Avery called "weird music" since they started working together, and while she'd passed on Brian Eno's *Music for Airports*, she'd loved Perfume Genius from the beginning. "I am so jealous."

Alex had almost given into temptation and bought tickets for herself and Avery to go see the show, but then Avery had plans with her parents that weekend, and Alex couldn't justify the expense for just herself. It was how she'd made it on her own with just her jewelry business supporting her for the last couple of years. Just like she didn't let herself buy top shelf tequila, she also didn't allow herself many purchases outside the bare necessities, her boxing lessons being the one exception. She had resigned herself to finding a concert video on YouTube that night and playing it while she worked.

"You're going right?" Avery asked.

Alex nodded, then shook her head, then said, "Give me a minute."

She pulled her phone out of her waistband on her way back to her bedroom and pulled up Rich's number. "I swear if you're still in class, I'm going to kill you, because I need to talk to you, you monumental asshole."

Rich answered on the fourth ring. "*Incantanta*, Alex. Did you receive today's delivery?"

"How are you not dead ass broke yet? That tiny university you work at can't pay you that much."

Rich chuckled. "I do alright, but definitely won't be going to Italy before school starts like I'd planned."

Alex ignored his easy access to international travel. She'd probably go to Europe twice a year too if she had a free place to stay. "And what the hell is all of this?" she waved the concert tickets even though he couldn't see her.

"I thought you could use a night out. I know you haven't taken a night off since you got back from your grandmother's."

A pang of grief strummed through Alex's chest. She hadn't given herself much time to think about how much she was missing Gran's phone calls, putting up with the cat had been reminder enough over the last five weeks.

God, had it been that long already?

"And how would you know that?"

"I know you, Alex. You're hardworking and dedicated, and if your party went as well as it looked like it did, you have a ton of orders to fill."

He was right, but Alex wasn't going to tell him that.

"Do you even know who Perfume Genius is?"

"Colin said you probably did."

Alex had spent a little bit of time with Rich's sister through Juliet, but she didn't know Gina's husband at all. "And what does Colin know about my taste in music?"

"Nothing, probably, but since he's the rep to all the local theaters and their bars, his assistant keeps a list of shows so they know what booze to market to what crowds. I asked him if he knew of anything coming up that someone who liked eclectic music would enjoy."

Alex had a feeling Rich had used this move before. "YouTube the 'Slip Away' video. Now."

Alex heard the clatter of a keyboard.

"Where are you?" She'd been expecting him to minimize their call and use his phone.

"At my desk. I just got out of class. Want to know what I'm wearing, *Piccolina?*"

Alex didn't need to answer, because he'd pressed play on the video, and she could hear the opening chords through the phone.

She hummed along, only just stopping herself from singing so she didn't distract Rich.

"So?" she asked when the music faded.

"That was . . . theatrical."

"I haven't been able to stop listening to that album since it came out," Alex said. "I've been dying to go to this show."

"Then you'll go with me?" Rich asked.

Alex hesitated, more for dramatic purposes than anything else. "On two conditions."

"Name them."

"You knock it off with the gifts. As fun as your fawning has been, I don't have room for anymore flower arrangements."

"Done. What else?"

"You let me do your makeup."

Chapter Eighteen

When his phone had flashed Alex's number across the screen, Rich had known he'd broken through with today's gift. He'd thought he might. When Rich had asked her to tell him what he could do to prove to her that she could trust him, that he was worth giving a shot, wearing makeup in public had not entered his reckoning.

"You want me to wear makeup."

"Yes," Alex said.

"No."

"Then no deal, Dew-rand. You'll have to take someone else to the weird music concert."

Rich's stomach flipped. This was not working out how he hoped. "Choose something else."

"But this is what I want."

"Why?"

Alex didn't even have to hesitate to gather her thoughts. "You asked what you could do to prove to me you could be better? This is it."

"By parading around in public looking like a drag queen?"

"I'm sorry. What's wrong with drag queens?" Alex asked.

"Nothing. I'm just not one."

"But you said you were sick of being afraid. What better way to prove to me that you can overcome your fears than by placing your very masculinity in my hands."

Rich's mind raced with excuses. Because he was vain and liked the way he looked now. Because he was a cis man who didn't feel the need to wear makeup. Because he didn't want to. Because people would make fun of him. Because people would assume he was gay.

Rich also knew that not even one of those excuses would stand up to Alex's scrutiny.

"You're sure there's not anything else?" he asked.

"It's this or nothing," Alex said. "Take it or leave it, Dew-rand. It's your last chance."

He sucked in a breath of air through his nose and sighed it out. "Fine. You can put makeup on me."

Alex's cheer and subsequent, "Yes!" only made him cringe. After seeing the video, at least he could take consolation that he wouldn't be the only man there with makeup on. He hoped.

• • • •

THE WEEK BETWEEN ALEX'S acceptance and the actual date was long. No matter how many times he asked, she wouldn't see him before, but she persisted in sending him teasing texts.

Are you a more of a summer or a fall do you think?

I think this eyeshadow would really bring out the brown in your eyes.

That accompanying photo had been of a shocking electric blue powder.

I just found the best shade of cherry red lipstick. You're gonna love it.

Is your skin tone more medium pink or medium yellow? I can't decide from memory.

She sent another picture of two different bottles of foundation.

What are your thoughts on glitter? Glam fabulous or totally trashy?

The sanest question she'd asked had been, *Are you going to go clean shaven, or rock that 2 day stubble look you've had going on lately?*

When Rich replied that he didn't shave on the weekends if he didn't have to, Alex's next text just read, *Excellent.*

Rich had to pause grading his class's finals and rub his temples at that one. This was going to be the most humiliating night of his life.

He buoyed himself by remembering that it was only one night. What was one night versus the rest of his life?

When Rich arrived at Alex's apartment an hour earlier than he would have, his stomach knotted in trepidation. One night of humiliation seemed a lot more formidable now that it was here. He was dreading how ridiculous Alex was going to make him look so much, that he'd almost forgotten he was going to be spending the night with Alex.

He was reminded when she answered the door. She wore a billowy black dress with a neckline so wide, it slipped over the side of one shoulder. The short loose sleeves stopped at her elbows, and the hemline was sinfully high. That paired with the thigh high black boots had Rich's more primitive instincts kicking in. He wanted to wrap those booted legs around his waist. And that skirt was so short he'd barely have to push it out of the way.

Traveling up, he took in the artfully wavy hair, cherry red lips and dark eye makeup. Silver earrings sparkled at her lobes, and a thick pink crystal dangled on a chain so long the necklace almost reached her navel.

"You are stunning."

Alex cocked her head to the side and smiled as she evaluated his outfit.

He'd gone casual, but not too casual for the restaurant pairing a grey button down with rolled sleeves and dark jeans with a pair of blue chucks. He didn't look nearly as glamorous as Alex, but the bottom dropped out of his stomach as he realized he was probably going to be the one people stared at tonight, not Alex's fantastic legs.

Alex surprised him then by stepping up to him and placing a quick peck to his lips. "This is going to be so much fun," she said, then pulled him inside. She knocked him into a chair beside the breakfast bar before grabbing a pink apron off a hook in the kitchen.

Rich hadn't missed the assortment of bottles and tubes and colors laid out on the breakfast bar, nor the handful of brushes.

"I don't suppose it's too late to ask you to take pity on me?" He asked.

"Not a chance, lover boy."

Rich would have asked her to go easy on him, but from the gleam of mischief in her eye, he was afraid that would make her go even more over the top.

She reached for something on the counter and came back with tweezers, and Rich stiffened. How far was she going to take this?

She knelt in front of him, the apron regretfully covering just how far her skirt rode up. Just close your eyes, relax and trust me, okay?" Then she planted another kiss on his lips, this one soft and supple and tender, and while it had him itching to get his hands on her, it didn't quite erase the feeling that she might as well be tying him to this chair for some illegal form of torture.

"Let's just get this over with, please."

Alex giggled, and said, "Close your eyes. I'm starting with your eyebrows."

Rich did what she said, and she thankfully spent little time on his eyebrows, so at least he knew they weren't going to be barely there when he looked in the mirror. Then she sprayed something on his face and rubbed in something she called a primer. The she had him open his eyes and look up so she could curl his eyelashes, and the nerves in Rich's stomach began to boil up again just as the cat she'd brought home from her grandmother's jumped into his lap.

Rich pet the purring cat as things started to get ridiculous.

Next Alex pulled out a concealer stick with "concealer for men" written on the side, and he was barely able to keep his groan on the inside. She really had gone all out.

"Close your eyes," she said again, and Rich let her work.

If it weren't for his absolute terror, the process would have been almost relaxing, like having his hair cut. Then he felt a brush on his eyelids, and something sharp at his lower lashes, and it took all his concentration to let her keep going. If he ran into anyone he knew, he was never going to live this down.

A few minutes after that, Alex snapped the lid to something shut and said, "Okay. I'm done." Then he heard the click of her phone camera. Great. Photographic evidence.

Rich blinked his eyes open. "Can I see?"

"Absolutely not." Alex's eyes sparkled as she scanned his face, then brushed a lock of hair out of his eyes. "You'll just have to trust me that you look absolutely gorgeous."

"I'm finding that difficult at the moment," he said.

Alex's smile shifted and fell. "Then maybe, by the end of the night, you'll understand the magnitude of what you're asking me to do."

Right. The reason he was doing this was important. Not just to himself, but to Alex. If he couldn't give her this, how could he deliver on the rest of his promises?

He took a deep breath and told himself to relax. He'd shoo the cat away, take Alex's hand, pull out her chair at dinner, pour her a glass of wine and pretend that he didn't look like he was about to take the stage at a drag show.

• • • •

IF ALEX HAD EVER DOUBTED whether she was vindictive and mean, she now had her answer. Rich looked like he was trying not to puke as he led her up the front steps and into the restaurant. He tensed when the hostess smiled at him, then relaxed. He seemed more acutely aware of people watching him than usual. Poor guy didn't realize that he almost always caught the casual attention of the people around him. He was tall and gorgeous. People noticed him.

Only now he noticed them staring—and he thought they were staring because she'd made him think he wore bright blue eyeshadow, cat eye eyeliner, and lips that matched hers. God, she was mean. And while his self-consciousness was almost painful, Alex couldn't help but delight in her deception.

Because she'd pulled a fast one on him big time.

He was wearing makeup. And she had curled his eyelashes, because why the hell not, but the only things she'd put on his face were toner, moisturizer, concealer and a super light foundation. Everything else had just been her dabbing at his face with clean brushes and the blunt end of her eye pencil. There was no way you could tell he was wearing makeup unless you knew what his face looked like without it.

Alex thought he looked pretty good. Like the TV version of himself.

But Alex wasn't going to tell him that for at least an hour.

Thankfully, the longer they sat at the table, the more Rich seemed to relax. And when their server barely spared him a glance in favor of staring at the exposed skin of Alex's shoulder, he almost seemed like his usual charming self as they traded stories, his summer course shenanigans for her stories about Dale and learning to box.

Rich had just emptied the last of their bottle of red into her glass and their plates were nearly empty when a gentlemen passed them did a double take, then backpedaled to stop at their table. Rich stiffened as he sat up straight, and Alex could feel the panic rolling off him

The tall, balding man held out his hand, and Rich stood to shake it.

"Durand," he said. "Out celebrating the end of summer term as well?"

"No, actually." He motioned toward Alex. "One of Alex's favorite bands is in town. We're having dinner before the show."

Clever. Rich was trying to hedge his bets. He could explain his makeup off as a costume, like they were going to a KISS concert or something.

Alex took it as her cue to stand when the man turned her direction. "Forgive me," He said as he took her hand. "Roland Calgary, Dean of Modern Languages."

Oh shit. Did that mean this was Rich's boss? No wonder he was panicking. She had to stifle a giggle.

"Alex Stafford, Rich's occasional evening escort."

She felt Rich's eyes narrow on her, but she flashed him a bright smile. She wasn't going to claim to be his girlfriend, and the guy had only named his profession because it told Alex how he knew Rich. If Rich's boss thought he was on a date with a hooker, that was his mistake. At least she looked like a high-class whore.

"Alex Stafford," he said like he recognized her name. "Were you in the paper a few weeks ago? Something to do with a necklace my wife wants for her birthday."

Alex laughed, genuinely surprised that he'd remembered her. She would bet five bucks his wife had taped that article on the fridge with a circle around the necklace Alex had worn to her party.

She adjusted her glasses and straightened her posture from possible prostitute to bad ass business woman. "That was me. My company launched a new jewelry line a few weeks ago, and I was lucky enough to tempt the business and art editors with sushi, good booze and expensive chocolate to come to do a write up. There might have also been some under the table jewelry swapping that, if asked, I will totally vow they paid for."

Roland Calgary laughed at her joke. Not polite laughter either, but real, delighted laughter. Then he slapped Rich on the shoulder and said. "It looks like you're in good hands, Durand. I'll leave you and your lady friend to it."

"Thank you. Give Serena my love."

"Will do." Then to Alex he said, "Enjoy your show." And left them.

Rich collapsed into his chair the second Roland Calgary had disappeared around the corner. "I am so toast."

"Why?" Alex asked, smothering her giggles in her wine.

He gestured to his face. "It's a Catholic university. This sort of shit could get me disciplined."

Alex grinned at Rich. "Oh, I don't know. He didn't seem too phased. Maybe it's a more accepting place than you thought."

Rich's expression was skeptical and unimpressed, but Alex only shrugged and took another sip of her wine.

"If he calls me into his office on Monday, you're showing up to explain everything. And making it perfectly clear that you neither bribe people nor sell yourself for money."

"Oooh, bossy. I like it."

Alex's flirtation didn't distract him.

"I'm serious, Alex."

She held her hands up in surrender, it would have been more convincing if one hand wasn't still wrapped around her wine glass, but still, she gave up on teasing him. In a sincere tone, she said, "I'm sorry. If you get in trouble at work, I promise I'll come and explain how all of this was my idea." She paused and searched his worried eyes. "I really appreciate you doing this for me, Rich. I know it hasn't been easy for you, so thank you."

Before he had a chance to respond, Alex stood. "I'm headed to the restroom. You should go before we head to the concert, I'm not letting you out of my sight once we get there, gorgeous." She ran her knuckles over his stubbled chin as she passed him and wondered if she pulled off masculine possessiveness with enough irony for Rich to get the joke.

Rich was signing for the bill when she returned. Unable to resist one last jab, she held out her tube of red lipstick. "In case you need a touch up?"

Rich shook his head. "I'm fine thanks."

As she watched him walk away, she wondered how pissed he was going to be when he came back.

Chapter Nineteen

Rich had avoided glancing in the mirror on the way to the urinal, and again as he'd washed his hands. Part of him didn't want to know how bad it was. Maybe if he didn't know, he could go on pretending he didn't look ridiculous. Pretending hadn't helped him escape the dread as he dried his hands, but he knew he had to look. If only so he knew what he was in for with Calgary.

Slowly, he raised his eyes to the mirror, prepared for the bright colors on his face to clash with the skin beneath his stubble. He was prepared for an overly dramatic smoky eye and lips brighter than Alex's. He was prepared to see a grotesque parody of himself. But that's not what he saw.

Rich blinked, then stared.

Relief washed over him when he saw himself looking back at him in the mirror, just with softer edges.

Then he chuckled.

Then he laughed.

Alex was leaning back in her chair when he finally emerged from the bathroom, still fighting the laughter bubbling up inside him.

Her smile was smug when she asked, "Well, what do you think? As fabulous as you thought?"

Rich leaned over the table, his hands on either corner, looming over the spot where Alex sat. "I don't know if I love you or hate you right now." The taunt came out huskier than he intended, but he was leaning more toward the love side.

Alex's amused smile dropped, and she leaned into him. "I would never do something I thought would hurt or humiliate you. And I expect the same from you, Riccardo. Don't betray my trust."

• • • •

ALEX LEFT RICH GAPING inside the restaurant as she stalked outside. She needed the fresh air, even if it was muggy as hell and tinged with car exhaust and cigarette smoke. Now that her stunt was over, she didn't find it nearly so amusing. She was trembling, and she didn't completely understand why. She knew she didn't have time to analyze it right now, because Rich would be coming out that door any second, and Alex would have to be okay.

She wanted to be okay. She wanted to enjoy the concert, but Rich had passed her test. He'd trusted her. He'd let her take him out assuming she'd mismatched his appearance to his identity. And maybe the implications of that sort of trust weren't lost on her. Could she trust Rich with the most intimate parts of herself too? She wasn't sure she could. And it wasn't just because of Rich's history, but because Alex had never done that before. Ben had been the closest she'd come to a real relationship, probably ever, and despite a cozy beginning, the passion and patience had flamed out quickly.

Then there was the whole situation with Juliet to consider. How did you tell your best friend that you were dating the man who had broken her heart?

She wished she could ask Gran for advice—not that she knew how she'd explain the situation to her grandmother—but having the option would have been nice.

In a moment of weakness, Alex fired off a text to her mother. She didn't expect an answer, but just doing something helped calm the fear that welled in her when Rich had passed her test.

As she heard his footsteps behind her, Alex inhaled deeply through her nose and out through her mouth like Juliet had taught her to do. She was going to see Perfume Genius, and it was going to be a fantastic night.

• • • •

RICH STOOD, STUNNED for almost a full minute as the implications of what Alex had said and done sunk in. She was an evil genius.

If she felt half as much trepidation about trusting him with her heart as he had about trusting her with his face, she should be running for the hills.

He caught up with her on the front porch, where she stood watching traffic.

"You okay?" he asked, his hand settling on her bare shoulder.

Her smile was weak when she glanced back at him. "This is big, you know?" she said.

Rich squeezed her shoulder. "I know."

Alex faced him with a mischievous grin in place again. "I mean, now that you know how good you can look with just a little bit of concealer, you have a whole new world opened up to you. Have you ever tried a French green clay mask?"

"No, and I'm not going to. This," Rich motioned to his face, "Is never happening again."

Alex rolled her eyes and dragged him down the stairs toward his Jeep. "But I got a sample when I ordered all your makeup. I was hoping we could do facials and watch *Dirty Dancing* tomorrow night."

Rich stopped, forcing Alex to a halt in the middle of the sidewalk. "Tomorrow night?"

"I thought maybe we could have a quiet night in," she shrugged. "If you're free."

"I'm free."

Contentment and pride rushed into Rich's chest, taking the place that had so recently been filled by apprehension and fear. Alex wanted a second date. With him. Tomorrow.

It wasn't forever. Not yet. But it was a start.

Chapter Twenty

Alex stretched before she opened her eyes. Her bed was warm, and the sun was high. Her hand glanced over something fuzzy, and the cat meowed at her for disturbing his sleep, then hopped off the bed. Alex popped open one eye just in time to see an annoyed flick of his white tail.

"Glad to know you're still rude," Alex said. "I was starting to think you were getting soft after you purred all over Rich last night."

The cat didn't bother to answer, and Alex closed her eyes again, trying to recapture everything she'd felt the night before.

After the concert, they'd gone out to a speakeasy Alex had never heard of and probably would have never found on her own. She'd thought Rich had been crazy when he'd pulled her into an alley and past a pile of trash to knock on an unmarked door. Once they were inside and the smell of anise and whiskey replaced the smell of dumpster, Alex had appreciated the authenticity.

After a cocktail made of liqueurs Alex had never heard of, an appetizer, an hour of general teasing and flirtation, Alex hadn't wanted to the night to end. Rich hadn't been able to keep his hands off the skin exposed between the top of her boots and the hem of her skirt, allowing the tips of his fingers graze over her skin at every discrete opportunity, and it had driven Alex crazy.

Which was why, when Rich had walked Alex up to her door and hesitated as she'd unlocked it, Alex had been confused. When she'd turned around to ask what was wrong, he'd said, "I should go."

"But-"

"Thank you for doing my makeup," he'd said, then leaned in and placed a long, slow, lingering kiss on her lips. A kiss of promises and intention and desire. It had been a soft, open kiss, that had made Alex want to push up into him and get a better taste of the whiskey on his breath, but Rich's hand on her hips held her in place.

When he'd stepped away, Alex's hands had fisted into his shirt. "Stay," she'd said.

He'd rested his forehead against hers and shaken his head. "I'm trying to prove to you that this is different. More than just good sex."

"You did that already."

"No, I haven't. Not well enough. Not yet."

Alex had played with the tip of his collar and snuggled into him. "You don't have to punish yourself. If we're going to give this a go, I'd rather we be honest about what we want." Alex guided one of his hands to the back of her exposed thigh. Without coaxing, his fingers caressed, drawing a series of small circles. "And I know you want me."

His fingers slid up toward the curve of her ass. "Of course I want you, but I also want you to know I *can* control myself." And to emphasize his words, Rich skimmed his hand back down her thigh, then slid it away.

Alex whined. Him playing with her legs had aroused an ache deep within her that she knew her vibrator wouldn't even touch.

"Sleep. I'll see you tomorrow, *Piccolina.*" Then he kissed her forehead and walked off down the hallway.

Alex called after him, "I don't know how you expect me to just fall asleep after that kiss a minute ago."

"Think of me," he said over his shoulder. "And I'll think of you thinking of me."

A bolt of pure desire struck straight to Alex's core. "Don't you dare walk away if you're going to talk dirty to me," she said, but Rich had already disappeared around the corner to the stairwell.

It was a pleasant surprise to wake up and have memories of an evening with Rich that she didn't feel guilty or apologetic about. Rich had given Alex her perfect date. She wasn't even that disappointed that he hadn't stayed the night. She could respect him wanting to wait.

Alex still felt an uneasiness at her core that she couldn't quite name, but she blamed it on the defeat she felt every time she looked at her phone and she still hadn't heard from her mother. When the art festival her mom had mentioned at the funeral had come and gone a few weeks ago and Vivien had never called, Alex hadn't been surprised. But Alex had asked her mother a serious question, and she couldn't even be bothered to return a perfunctory answer.

Rather than calling her mother to face further disappointment, Alex texted her question to Juliet.

How do you know when to trust someone with your heart?

Juliet's reply, that if Alex hadn't reached a point where she couldn't keep her heart to herself any longer, then she shouldn't try giving it, was absolutely no help. She liked Rich. She like his reserved sincerity, his concentrated intensity, his soft voice, and how he always vaguely smelled of coffee. Alex wanted to give him her heart. When they were alone together, Alex could forget everything, even that he'd once been in a serious relationship with her best friend. But when they were apart, that one fact dropped like a steal wall around Alex. Nothing short of an atomic blast was getting through it.

Not sure what to do about the impasse and annoyed by Juliet's incessant texts badgering her about who the guy was, Alex took her frustration out in the way she normally did, by pummeling a heavy bag, and learning new moves from Dale.

The only thing that pushed her out of bed the morning after the concert was her midday training appointment. Alex always scheduled her Saturday sessions with Dale for noon or later because the gym's standing sparring class was from ten to noon. Even though it was free to members who paid to work directly with a trainer like Alex, she'd never worked up the guts attend.

It wasn't so much that she was afraid to go up against the guys who cat called her all the time—even if she knew it would be the little guys—it was more that she was afraid she'd lose her temper and end up looking like a lunatic as she took wild swings at dudes who were determined not to lose to a girl. Just her luck, when Alex arrived that day, the sparring was still going on and in one of the rings there were two women sparring—neither of them much bigger than Alex.

They were both good. Better than Alex. But as she watched them, she could see which blocks each one threw up in response to the other's punches. She found herself recognizing some of the sequences Dale had taught her on the heavy bag in the brunette's assaults on the blonde.

"There is absolutely no reason you're not in that ring," Dale said, as he joined Alex at the side of the ring. Most of the other spectators were watching two middleweight guys on the other side of the gym.

"Are they both your clients too?" Alex asked.

"Come on, I can't take on all the women." Dale shifted from one foot to the other and re-crossed his arms. "Let your fairy trainer have some street cred."

Alex flinched a step back and pinched Dale's bicep. "They don't call you that, do they?"

Dale shrugged and brushed her off. "Not to my face, no."

"So why do you say it?" Alex asked.

She and Dale had never really talked about the fact that he was married to a man before. The first time he'd mentioned Chris, Alex had just run with it like it was no big deal. Her trainer was married. So what? She hadn't been interested anyway. She had assumed Chris was a woman until Dale had started using pronouns, and that's when she knew she and Dale were going to be friends. They'd clicked in a way that Alex didn't with many people. She'd gone out to dinner with them a couple of times, and liked Chis. Where Dale was beefy and probably about five foot nine with strawberry blonde hair and wore gym shorts everywhere, Chris was tall, and slim and wore his dark hair slicked back. Alex had never seen him in anything less formal than business wear. Now that Alex thought about it though, working in a gym like this, with a bunch of men who probably had some major insecurities they were trying to compensate for by being ultra-masculine and learning to box had probably not been easy for Dale.

Alex tried to give most of the guys credit—the ones who didn't embarrass her on the regular anyway—she tried to assume they were just wanted to learn to hit shit without hurting themselves like she did. But she wouldn't put it past most of them to be intimidated by gay man who could also kick their ass.

Dale shrugged her off. "It was a joke, Alex. Forget I said anything."

Alex didn't believe him but left it alone. "The brunette is yours, isn't she?"

Dale snorted. "Evelyn's a client, yes. How can you tell?"

"She's better," Alex said, as indeed, Evelyn had backed the blonde into a corner, and wasn't giving her any opening.

"What else?" Dale asked.

"I recognize the moves."

The trainer overseeing the match called Evelyn off, and she immediately backed off and gave the blonde a chance to drop her gloves from in front of her face. The two women were covered in sweat, but they were both beaming as they bumped gloves and chatted for a second. Alex was standing too far away to hear what they said, but only until Dale pulled her toward the ring by the elbow and pretty much forced her between the ropes.

"Dude, I still have street shoes on," she said, but he ignored her.

"Evelyn, Sarah, have you met Alex?" Dale said as the two women turned to them.

"Yeah, I've seen you around," Evelyn said, and held out her glove. Alex bumped it with her bare fist. "How come you never come to sparring?"

Alex instantly felt small and weak, and it wasn't helped when Dale threw his arm around Alex's shoulders and said, "Yeah, Alex. How come you never come to sparring?"

Both Sarah and Evelyn were watching her, and Alex didn't appreciate the knowing gleam in their eyes as Alex said. "I'm not good enough yet."

Dale coughed something that Alex thought sounded like "Bullshit," and Evelyn cocked her head to the side while Sarah let out a dry, "Ha!"

"I've seen you working with Dale. If you can hold your own against him, you could totally spar with us."

Alex elbowed Dale in the ribs, and he flinched away, rubbing where she'd hit him. "The big softie likes to go easy on me," Alex said, but when everyone frowned at her, it occurred to her for the first time that maybe Dale didn't go easy on her. Maybe he did, in fact, push her exactly the same way he pushed his other students.

She remembered the women she'd given rudimentary lessons to at the gym in Pittsburgh. At the time she hadn't thought much of it. She'd had a little bit of practice and a lot of tension to work off, and it had looked badass to people who didn't know any better. But maybe she really was good at boxing?

"The best way to get better is to get in the ring," Evelyn said, and Sarah nodded.

"And we need more women to spar with," Sarah said. "We're the only two here most Saturdays."

Evelyn looked to Dale. "Do we have time for one more round?"

He grinned. "Rings not reserved until one. If Alex can get changed sometime this century, you probably have time to show her a thing or two."

Alex shot Dale a glare but headed for the changing rooms all the same.

Chapter Twenty-One

Alex: *How jealous would you be if I told you I was in love with my trainer?*

Rich had been skyping with his private investigator on his laptop when the text came in, and he'd had to look at it twice, before firing back a quick, *I didn't realize I had competition* before setting the phone aside, apologizing and asking the man to repeat what he'd just said.

The investigator scowled, and said, "I might have found a photograph. He rummaged in a file folder. "But I was waiting to file the paperwork for copies of his records until you confirmed." Rich had wondered why the man had wanted to Skype. They'd always communicated over the phone or through email before.

A photograph of a blonde, blue-eyed man appeared on Rich's screen, as the investigator asked, "Is this your father?"

Rich snorted. "No."

The investigator huffed. "I wondered after I saw you, but you could take after your Italian mother."

"My sister does," Rich said, trying to sound casual even though tension knotted in his shoulders. Was it possible he had never mentioned his father's ethnicity?

"But my father is Algerian."

The investigator frowned. "You said he was born in Paris."

"He was, to Algerian parents."

"He's black then."

Rich shrugged, then nodded. "He looks like me but add twenty-five years."

Rich wasn't sure he liked the assessing gaze his private investigator was giving him, but he didn't say anything.

"I wish I would have had this information sooner. It would have narrowed down my search considerably."

"I'm sorry," Rich said, uncowed by the older man's frustration. He was sure he'd mentioned his father's heritage during their initial phone meeting. Perhaps the P. I. had misunderstood and assumed his father's family had been among the many of European decent that had lived in Algeria during the French rule.

Undoubtedly there was some French blood mixed in with his father's line, because they had been Durands for a century, but Rich had never known his father to talk about that part of their history.

"I'll get back to you within next week," the P. I. said, then disconnected. Rich sat back in his desk chair and stretched his arms over his head as he stared at the exposed beams on his ceiling. He hated how tense talking about his father had made him. He also hated how nobody knew what his ethnicity was. He was mistaken for Mexican often, though he had been told to go back to Iraq one day on the street when he was sixteen, just after 9-11. But explaining it to people? It wasn't worth his energy.

His phone buzzed in his pocket, and he remembered he'd been texting Alex. He'd seen her twice more over the last week. He'd gone over to her place for the movie night she'd promised him. To his relief, she'd left the cosmetics alone, and instead had done her best to coax him out of his clothes. Instead, he'd pulled her down on top of him on the sofa and they'd made out like teenagers for almost the entire length of a superhero movie they'd both seen before. Then on Tuesday, he'd taken her out dinner and watched as she'd eaten a gigantic steak along with a salad with no croutons or cheese, and she'd skipped the wine. She'd talked a lot about her trainer that night too, which he supposed was natural since she'd just come from the gym. She'd complained that she'd accused him of going easy on her, and now he was turning up the heat, so she was trying to stick to his crazy meal plan just in case it helped her keep up.

When Rich had kissed her goodnight at her door, he hadn't thought twice about the trainer, but now he wondered. He unlocked his phone to see what else she'd said, but her response, *He does take great pride in getting me sweaty and breathless,* didn't reassure him, beyond the fact that Alex wouldn't tease him if there was really something going on there.

He would see her in a few hours. Rich planned to take her out dancing for the night. As far as he could tell, she'd been working almost non-stop this summer, and he wanted to see her relax. He wanted to watch her come undone and wake up to her satisfied and languid in the morning.

And maybe then, the missing piece between them would magically fall into place.

• • • •

ALEX WAS SO DISTRACTED by her deadlines, both for her business and for Juliet's wedding, that she was having trouble finding the motivation to slog through any of them.

Juliet's wedding was in a week, and Alex was leaving for Colorado on Wednesday morning, so she prioritized wedding projects. She picked her dress up from the shop, finished the necklace she was making for Juliet to wear during the ceremony, and of course put together all the damn mini gardens. It was a miracle she'd kept the succulents alive long enough to plant them properly. The instructions said that they shouldn't be kept in their shipping planters more than a few days, but Alex had been working on them in her spare time for weeks, and she still had forty more to go when Rich showed up on Friday night.

He'd been cagey about what he had planned, and Alex was still wearing yoga pants and had potting soil under her fingernails. He was wearing a crisp navy button down and nice jeans. She needed to change.

"Here to tease me into distraction again?" she asked.

Rich didn't try to hide the way his eyes roamed over her body, and Alex suddenly became very conscious that she wasn't wearing a bra when his gazed stopped at her chest.

"If you play your cards right, I'll let you suck on them later," Alex said, and watched Rich's eyes heat. "Oh, so you do want to?" she teased. "I was beginning to wonder."

Rich reached out and wrapped Alex in his arms, pulling her against him so her breasts flattened against his chest. "Don't ever wonder," he said in her ear then ground his hips against hers so she could feel his erection. "Know. Always."

Alex turned her head to catch his lips, and she had so much pent up sexual energy that she felt like she attacked him. Her kiss was full of teeth and tongue and passion. Rich didn't hold her back this time but tilted her head back with one hand and catching her under her ass as she braced herself on his shoulders and wrapped her legs around his waist. He turned and pressed her back into the wall next to her open door as he ravaged her mouth with this tongue.

"Shut the door," Alex managed to moan after she'd begun to grind herself against the ridge in his jeans, and the door slammed shut next to them. "Now take me to bed."

Rich strode straight to Alex's room and collapsed on top of her on the bed. His lips, never having left her skin travelled down her neck, over her collarbone down the exposed skin of her chest until her met the tank's neckline. Then he jumped down to cover one peaked nipple with his mouth through the fabric. The warm, wet heat soaked through her shirt and Alex moaned as Rich sucked and nipped lightly.

When he switched sides, the chill from the air-conditioner cooled the wet spot on her shirt, making the abandoned nipple pucker even more. Rich's fingers closed over it, teasing and squeezing as Alex writhed underneath him.

Her hips rose, seeking out whatever friction she could find, but there was none to be found. She whimpered.

Both of Rich's hands replaced his mouth as his weight settled over her middle. "What do you need?" he asked.

Alex tried to lift her hips again, but Rich's weight pinned her down as he kneaded her breasts. "You," her voice was almost A whisper, coming out on the exhale. "Your mouth."

"Where do you want my mouth?" Rich asked.

Alex didn't hesitate. "On my pussy. Then your cock inside me."

Rich shifted his hips and the ridge of his erection pressed into the apex of Alex's thighs.

"Oh my god," she said.

Rich smiled and said, "You've been thinking about this."

"Now, Dew-rand."

He rocked into her again and she groaned. "So bossy," he said. "And impatient."

Alex rocked her hips against him this time, and Rich sucked in a breath through his teeth. "Don't tell me you haven't been dying to fuck me."

"Such a dirty mouth," Rich said, and pushed her white tank top up and over her head.

"Shut up," Alex said with a glare in her eye.

Rich smirked at her, then trailed kisses over her exposed breastbone and down a line to her navel as two fingers skimmed under the waistline of her yoga pants. He swiped back and forth over her skin there before pulling the fabric down and off. Rich spread her legs and settled between them. Alex was wishing she'd remembered to get his shirt off at least before he was out of reach, but then his tongue licked her from bottom to top, and she forgot about anything else but the feel of his hands and mouth on her.

After two long swipes with his tongue, Rich latched onto her clit and sucked, causing Alex to buck and moan. He said something that Alex couldn't make out, but the vibrations against her clit made her shiver. He chuckled, then licked as he slid two fingers inside her.

"Holy fuck," she said, and Rich chuckled again.

"Stop. Laughing. At me," Alex said through her panting breaths.

"I'm not laughing at you, *Piccolina.* I'm loving how responsive you are tonight."

Alex wanted to tell him it was because he'd been holding out on her all week. Then, Rich increased the pace of his fingers and resumed sucking and licking at her clit, and Alex found she couldn't form any more words as her orgasm built deep inside her. It was as if her body recognized that she wasn't doing this to herself, because the sensations built more slowly, but with more power too.

"Oh shit. Oh God. Oh fuck." Alex's orgasm broke the surface, and it broke her like seafoam against the shore. Rich's fingers didn't still until her orgasm crested and Alex's body began to relax back into the bed.

"I love watching you come," he said. "It's the most beautiful thing I've ever seen."

Alex felt a pang in her chest at his words. She knew it was the right thing to say in the moment, but she also knew he'd said them before and didn't mean them. He'd said them to her before, even while he'd still been pining after Juliet. God. She'd heard him say them to Juliet before, and Alex wished she were sea foam on the beach, because then she could dissolve into the sand and not feel the pain of jealousy and mistrust swell inside her. She'd wanted this last week to be real so badly.

To distract herself, Alex forced herself up and to her knees, meeting Rich where he still knelt at the end of her bed. She didn't even bother with his shirt, she just went straight for the fly of his jeans, pulling and tearing at the fabric to get him free as soon as possible.

"Take off your shirt," she said. "I need you naked now."

Rich chuckled and obliged. "I was hoping I could be the bossy one tonight."

"Maybe later," Alex said, pushing his jeans and boxer briefs down to free his cock. Her mouth closed around him the second she had him free. Rich sucked in a breath and cursed, even as his hands tangled in Alex's hair.

"This wasn't on your list," he teased, his words punctuated by heavy breaths. It sounded like he had to concentrate to speak. Alex hummed in response. And Rich cursed again.

"Shit, Alex. I need to be inside you."

Alex met his eyes in the fading light coming in through her bedroom window. She gave one last final suck and backed off him with a pop. As much fun as it would be to make him come with her mouth, Alex had wanted this for too many days to delay it any further.

She tipped backward onto the bed and shimmied up far enough for Rich to join her while he shucked the last of his clothes to the floor. Rich practically dove on top of Alex, smothering her with kisses, one hand in her hair while the other guided himself toward her center.

"You better be clean," Alex said against his lips as he sank inside her.

"With the test results to prove it," he said, pulling out and sinking back even as his lips descended again to her breasts.

"God, you're perfect," Alex said, hoping he'd catch on to the double meaning and be distracted by the reason she'd said anything in the first in place, but she was certain he hadn't missed it. She'd appreciated he'd taken the time to get tested, but it didn't change the fact that, despite the makeup incident, Alex was still having trouble trusting him.

As one hand closed around one of her nipples and his mouth closed around the other, all ability to think or panic escaped her.

Rich didn't slow his pace, and with his mouth on her breast and his pubic bone hitting her clit on every upward thrust, Alex was going to be done way too quickly.

"This is going too fast," Rich said, echoing Alex's thoughts.

"Warm up. More later."

"Good," was all Rich said as he stepped up his pace even more and Alex's orgasm caught up to her.

"Rich, fuck."

He silenced her screams with a kiss, moaning his own release into her mouth as warmth flooded Alex's womb. She squirmed against him as she rode out the last of the aftershocks of her orgasm as Rich peppered her collarbone with kisses.

In an almost dizzy state of bliss, Alex asked, "So if that was the warm up, what are we going to do later?"

Rich laughed into her shoulder. "Whatever you want, *Picollina*. But it's going to take a lot of sushi to build my energy back up.

That got Alex's attention. "Sushi?"

"I *was* going to take you downstairs and ply you with sushi and sake and dancing until you couldn't keep your hands off me. I wasn't prepared for such an enthusiastic welcome."

"I could kill some sushi. But lighter on the sake? I've got training in the morning. Dale will probably literally kill me if I'm hungover."

Alex had been mentioning Dale more and more all week on purpose, and she never missed the skeptical glint in Rich's eye every time she did. He was jealous of how much time Alex spent at the gym, and she liked the hint of possessiveness that sprang into his eyes whenever she said Dale's name. It was probably not the healthiest relationship move she could make, and maybe they'd have to go out on a double date with Dale and Chris soon, but for now, Alex was taking comfort in any sign that this thing with Rich was real.

"We don't have to have any sake," Rich said. "But I'm insisting on the sushi and the dancing."

"Give me a chance to shower, and we'll go down."

Rich nodded, sitting up and disconnecting their bodies. "I'll be waiting."

Alex took the fastest shower of her life, and only nominally blow dried her hair so that she wouldn't look like a drowned rat when they went downstairs. It was going to dry frizzy, but really, when didn't it this time of year? With a swipe of mascara and a dab of lip gloss, Alex threw on the same black dress she'd worn in May when Rich had unexpectedly sought her out at Tokyo Nights, and she was ready to go.

Rich waited in the living room. Only his slightly mussed hair hinted at what they'd been doing only half an hour ago. He stood over the extra work table Alex had shoved under the bank of windows on the far wall, taking in all the mini gardens.

"What's this?" he asked, spreading his hand out over the expanse of tiny succulents.

"Favors for Juliet's wedding. I'm behind. I was supposed to have them all planted two weeks ago so they could fill out a little bit, but work deadlines, you know." Alex did her best to sound casual, but trepidation filled her any time Juliet came up. It didn't help when Rich went oddly quiet like did just now.

She didn't want things to be like this. She wanted to put Juliet and Rich's relationship in the past, but there would always be that unspoken truth between them, that Juliet would always be Rich's first choice. And even if Rich did want to be with Alex now, there was still the possibility that being with him would make things too weird with Juliet.

Alex had been tempted to tell her. She'd been texting constantly, wanting to know more about the guy Alex was thinking of giving her heart too, but Alex didn't know where to start. She was in enough denial now that she could tell herself she was waiting a few weeks to see how all of this was going. Never mind that she was going to spend the next few days with Juliet and have to pretend that she wasn't banging her best friend's ex—again.

"I see," Rich said, putting an end to the awkward silence. He scanned the work station for another few, quiet, taut seconds, then he held out his hand and offered her a forced smile. "Let's go."

• • • •

DOWNSTAIRS, ALEX ORDERED a pitcher of sake to go along with their sushi. Dread had filled her belly already, and she wanted to wash it away until she couldn't feel it. She threw back two cups before she took her first bite of food. Rich didn't say anything. Instead he directed the conversation toward his upcoming trip to Savannah to see his mother. Outside of mini gardens, Alex hadn't brought up Juliet's wedding, and Rich hadn't asked about it. She hadn't even let him know when she was going to be gone. Even now, neither one of them mentioned how he was visiting his mother instead of going to the wedding. She was doing her best to outrun it, but Alex's growing realization that this relationship was doomed before it had even begun was threatening to swallow her whole.

He wore makeup for you, Alex kept telling herself, but when she compared that against Rich and Juliet's years long relationship, how they'd been planning to get married, how they'd tried to start a family together, Alex again felt like a little peasant girl playing dress up to Juliet's princess.

Why did Alex have to go and keep falling for the guy that had loved her perfect best friend for so long? He still probably loved her. How could he ever love Alex back after that?

To stop that line of thoughts in its tracks, Alex threw back a third cup of sake followed by a whole slice of California Roll as she zeroed back in on Sonia Durand's plans to finally drag her son to every tourist destination in Savannah.

Alex got the feeling he was trying to distract her from where her mind kept wandering back to as well. And, God, she wanted to be distracted.

As if Rich read hear mind, he covered the hand that was reaching for sake warmer, capturing it between his palm and the table. "Did I tell you I hired a P. I.?"

"What? Why?"

Rich shrugged and didn't quite meet her eye. "To find my dad," he paused for a second to eat a piece of sushi, then continued. "I haven't heard much from him since he left, and aside from some nominal contact with my mom to finalize the divorce and child support checks until I turned eighteen, no one else has heard from him either. It's like he moved back to France and disappeared off the face of the earth."

Alex had never known much about Rich's dad beyond the fact that he'd left, and that it was a sore spot.

"I didn't realize you had zero contact."

"I vaguely remember hearing that he'd gotten remarried in the early 2000s. I'm not sure how or why my mom knew that. Or maybe she didn't, and I dreamed it. I really don't know."

"You never asked your mom about it?"

Rich shrugged again, twirling his sake cup in his fingers. "It seemed rude to ask, you know? I thought, maybe, if we're still not making any headway on the search, I can see if she has any of his old addresses."

"Surely there's something you can track," Alex said. "His immigration records?"

Rich shook his head. "French bureaucracy is dense, and Durand is a common name. We've hit a couple of dead ends already."

In all the years Alex had known Rich, he'd always been cocky. Confident. He'd always known exactly where he was going and what he was doing, and no one could tell him any differently. Not Juliet. Not his sister. But he wasn't bullheaded about it. His arrogance was disarming rather than abrasive, just enough on the right side of attractive to be called charming.

This Rich looked lost and scared. He looked younger than thirty-three years old. He looked like a little boy who didn't understand why his father had left him, like the last twenty years had never happened.

"What are you going to do when you find him?" Alex asked.

Rich let a humorless laugh break through his lips. "I've had fantasies about showing up at his job or his house—just knocking on the door and asking for him. Not giving my name to see if he recognizes me. To see if—if I have any brothers or sisters I don't know—maybe he'll introduce me to them. To my step-mother. To see if he's the proud father of a grown son that looks just like him or if he'll pretend he doesn't know who I am."

Alex flipped her palm so she could squeeze Rich' s hand. "You should go," Alex said. "You deserve answers. But maybe . . ."

"Maybe what?" Rich asked when Alex trailed off.

"Take someone with you," Alex said. "Don't head into the unknown without support."

Rich looked bemused. "I'll think about it. If the time comes." Things were quiet for a moment at their table. Then Rich asked, "Have you ever thought about trying to find your father?"

Alex gave him a watery smile and took her hands back, wringing them in her lap.

"That's actually kind of a funny story."

He cocked his head to side as if to say that she didn't look like she found it funny, and asked, "Why's that?"

"I asked my mom three separate times growing up who my father was. Each time, she gave me a different answer. The first one was a cowboy who ran a sheep ranch on the west coast. The second was a fireman from some little nowhere town in Northern California. The third, and this one was my favorite, was a large animal vet from San Fransico."

"Why was he your favorite?" Rich asked.

"Because I thought once he found out about me, he might buy me a pony."

Rich laughed, genuinely this time, and Alex joined him.

"So, which one is it?"

"None of them. They are all one hundred percent completely made up."

"Your mom made them up instead of telling you the truth?"

Alex shook her head. "She didn't even give me that. When I was a teenager, and I still thought there was a possibility one of them could be my father, I asked Gran if maybe she could help me track them down. She said she would try if that's what I wanted, but as I told her more and more about each one, her face grew redder and redder until she just stood up and dragged me by the wrist into the room where my mom stayed whenever she was home. She walked straight up to the bookshelf, plucked three tattered paperbacks from the shelf and tossed them on the bed.

"There are your fathers. The product of some trashy writer's imagination. Don't listen to your mama. She either doesn't know who your daddy is, or he's someone she's better off away from and so are you."

Alex shrugged. "Since then, I figured he probably wasn't worth knowing, you know."

"Wait," Rich was trying to get his laughter under control, "Your mom stole characters from romance novels for your stand-in dads?"

"Yup."

"That's brilliant." He was still laughing.

Alex rolled her eyes. "Yeah, well, that's my mom, always finding brilliantly creative solutions to problems she doesn't want to be in."

Wiping tears from his eyes, Rich said, "She shouldn't have lied to you, at least."

"It makes me sad for her, you know. Like, what has she been looking for all this time, some idealized hero instead of someone who makes her happy?"

"Maybe that's what kind of father she wanted for you," Rich said.

Alex appreciated his charity toward her mother, but since she still hadn't responded to Alex's texts, Alex only snorted. "I would have been happy with someone who stuck around. He didn't have to be perfect. He just needed to love me."

Rich's eyes met hers, full of significance, and she didn't miss his meaning. *I'm not perfect. I've screwed up, but if you let me, I will love you. I will be there for you.*

Alex looked away. Emotion for everything she didn't have welling up along with the keen sense of loss she hadn't let herself feel about her grandmother since she'd cried on Rich's shoulder two months ago.

She felt tears welling again, but she couldn't do this here. Not now.

"Can we dance?" she asked. "I've had way too much to drink, and I need to work it off."

"Of course," Rich said, holding his hand out to her. "Let's dance."

Chapter Twenty-Two

As Rich lead Alex onto the dance floor, he knew she was spooked. They'd been riding high for a week on the makeup stunt, but one mention of Juliet and Alex was looking like her world had been crushed all over again.

Rich hadn't meant to do that to her.

Did it make him sad that Juliet was marrying someone else? Yes. Of course, it did. But not for the reasons Alex thought. He missed Juliet. He'd never not miss Juliet. For eight years she consumed almost every waking thought. She'd been his first real love, and it had been a good, intense love. So good and intense that he'd sabotaged it every way he knew how.

The first affair started a couple months after they'd moved in together. He had still been in grad school, and he'd been commuting back and forth to the University of Kansas. There had been a girl who was in another TA's class that had hung around the department with a lot of questions. He'd taken her out to coffee after his office hours one day and she'd invited him back to her place. He didn't know why he'd gone, except that a woman had never asked *him* before, and he'd said yes before giving it any thought.

It had been dangerous and different, and it had made him feel powerful to be wanted by two women. The affair had lasted a few weeks before the novelty of it had worn off and guilt had overcome him. He'd liked where he was with Juliet. She'd cooked. She'd filled the apartment with plants and the scent of incense. She argued with him when she thought he was ridiculous, and she snuggled into him in the night. More than once he'd woken up to her climbing on top of him. Living with Juliet had been everything he'd hoped it would be for years. Ninety percent of him loved every minute of it, but ten percent of him secretly thought that it had all come too easily.

The next affair hadn't happened for a year, and was much the same as the first, though it had been with a fellow TA from the English department. She'd known about Juliet and hadn't cared. She hadn't believed in monogamy, and had told Rich it was his right to seek sexual fulfillment where he needed it. If Juliet wasn't always enough for him, that was fine.

For four months, almost the entire fall semester, Rich had told himself the same thing. Only, he did think Juliet was enough. She'd been more than enough. He'd been the one who wasn't good enough for her, but he hadn't known how to tell that to Juliet or Winnie, the English TA. When Juliet had a pregnancy scare in December, Rich realized that he and Juliet could be a real family if he put in the effort—and for more than a year, he'd been faithful. He'd given her everything he had to help make up for his past indiscretions.

And she'd seemed happy. School had kept her busy. Her advisor had pushed her to go for her ARNP, but Juliet had wanted to do her practicum in the OB department before she made any decisions. He remembered the night she'd come home from her first birth. She'd been glowing. Joy had been radiating off her.

"This is it," she'd told him. "This is what I want to do. This is where I belong."

So, Rich had encouraged her to start looking for labor and delivery positions.

Two things happened then. Her advisor started sending her possible positions from all over the country, and they found out Juliet was pregnant. Rich had just started his current job, and was on tenure track, being one of the youngest PhD professors who was also a native speaker. He wasn't going anywhere else, possibly ever, and Juliet had been at the top of her class and so well-liked at the hospital, it seemed like she'd have her pick of jobs once she graduated. Rich hadn't thought he was enough to keep her in Kansas City on his own.

When she'd gotten pregnant, and they'd talked about getting married to make their little family official, Rich had been relieved. She would be staying with him.

There had been a few good weeks early that year when Rich thought his life had been just about perfect. They'd decided to put off wedding talk until Juliet had graduated and his semester was over. Maybe they'd have a small, late summer wedding before the baby was due and before Rich had to get back for the start of the semester. They had both been working hard and Juliet had been sick a lot of time, so it made sense to not finalize anything.

Then, sometime in March, the panic had set in. Juliet had been nearing the end of her first trimester, and the pregnancy had seemed to be sticking around. Reality settled in that he was going to be a father and he was going to have the life he'd wanted since his father had left him.

Rich was afraid that he was going to fail just as miserably at being a family man as his father had.

When he'd called his mom to tell her she was going to be a grandmother, she'd cried on the phone. But she'd also said, "I'm so glad you're settling down. I always knew you were nothing like your father. You've been so good and faithful to Juliet. You're going to be such a good dad, Riccardo."

She'd gushed on for a few more minutes, and when Rich had hung up the phone, he'd wept. He was already failing. He'd been unfaithful to Juliet twice, and he wasn't entirely certain he wouldn't be again. She'd been so sick and so tired with the pregnancy, and he could do nothing to help her, and she'd spent so much time at the hospital, Rich felt it was only natural when he'd drifted into bed with Rachel one night.

She hadn't been anything special, necessarily, a barista at the coffee shop where he graded papers. She'd been cute. A curvy brunette with long, wavy hair and a sassy mouth she'd kept painted bright red. She'd offered to go down on him one day, and he'd let her, delighting in the look of her red lips around his cock. The image made his stomach roil now, but he'd kept going back for more and more and more that spring.

He'd been hiding in his fear, seeking physical pleasure to avoid the pain of knowing that he'd already failed Juliet. That he would always fail her.

Then that night happened. It had been an awful day at work. He'd unexpectedly had to cover a French class and had missed Juliet's call. Then he had grading deadlines to get in, and Rachel, who'd been pushing to see Rich more often, had invited herself over to his apartment after work. He'd known it was a bad idea, but he'd also known Juliet was going straight from her doctor's appointment to her last day at the hospital to hanging out with Alex and some nursing school friends. To get Rachel off his back, he'd promised they could finally spend the night together—at her place. He wouldn't invite another woman into Juliet's bed, but she'd come over, made out with him on the sofa, then they'd had a cup of coffee before heading out for dinner and drinks.

Rich hadn't checked his phone all day. He hadn't had the guts to. If he had to talk to Juliet, he thought the guilt at what he'd been planning—something he didn't really want to do, but had been going through with because a small, dark part of himself that he wasn't proud of, hadn't been ready to give Rachel up yet either.

He should have fucking checked his phone. Anger and shame overcame him every single time the memory washed over him. It had been seven goddam years, and Rich knew that not checking his phone. Not calling Juliet and telling her everything, not being there for her was the single greatest mistake of his life.

Until recently, Rich had thought that if he'd been there for Juliet the night she'd had the miscarriage, they could have salvaged everything. With enough time and enough hard work Rich had believed he and Juliet would have been able to make something even better than they'd had before.

He'd believed a little less after Juliet hightailed it to Colorado, and when he'd heard that Ethan had followed her, he'd admitted to himself that it wasn't going to happen. Though it hadn't been until Rich had seen that invitation on Gina's fridge that he'd known there was no going back. It had been the moment he'd finally given himself permission to move on. If Juliet could find happiness after the mess they made, maybe he should allow himself some too.

When Rich had run into Alex that same week, it had been like he'd been walking around in a fog for years, and when he'd stepped out of it, there she was, the partner he'd been looking for. Rich had the career thing figured out. He was happy and secure in his position, and if he could travel on breaks, he had no desire to live anywhere but Kansas City. What he wanted a was a partner—not just to prove that he could be a better husband and father than his own—but because he wanted to be that for someone. Maybe he'd failed Juliet not because of some fatal flaw of his own, but because they never would have been able to make it work.

Rich knew a relationship with Alex would work. He could feel it at the very bottom of his soul. He wanted her smile and her laughter and her pleasure and her tears. He wanted to work through whatever it was that was bothering her because she was more than a means to an end for him. He knew she didn't think she was good enough, but Rich would convince her that he loved her mouth, her stubbornness, her resilience. He loved her. Only her, even if he had no idea how to make her see that.

After she'd had a front row seat to every single mistake Rich had made with Juliet. It was a miracle she was even dancing with him right now. There had to be something Rich could do to convince her to leave the past behind them, large and ominous though it was.

Alex's mood seemed lighter after an hour, but her body was still tense underneath his touch, and when she smiled, the usual light mischievousness he'd grown used to finding in her eyes wasn't there.

Rich stopped moving, and Alex stilled immediately, staring up at him.

"What?" she asked.

"You're not okay," he said.

Alex shrugged and looked at his shoulder. "I'll be fine," she said.

Rich placed a finger under her chin, forcing her to meet his eyes. "Let's go upstairs," he said. "You can tell me what's bothering you."

Alex nodded and headed straight for the door and was outside and back into the apartment without even sparing a glance at Rich. When she unlocked the apartment door, she didn't stop in the living room like he expected her to but headed straight for her bedroom. Once inside, she collapsed backward onto the bed.

"What's wrong, *Picollina*?" He reached out to stroke a lock of hair out of her face, but she flinched away, so Rich let his hand drop back to his side.

Staring at the opposite wall, Alex said, "Do you really think this is going to work?"

"You know I do. I have zero doubts. I spent a small fortune trying to make sure you knew how serious I was. I wore makeup in public."

Alex faced him. "And I will always remember that and love you for the gesture, but I can't be in a relationship that makes me constantly feel inferior to my best friend."

"I don't want to be in a relationship with Juliet. I want to be with you." Rich hadn't missed that she'd said she loved him, even if she hadn't said that she was in love with him. If they had been having a different conversation, he'd push for more, but for now he would tuck it away for another time.

"Because you can't *have* Juliet," Alex said.

Rich's frustration tipped into anger. Why couldn't she just believe him? He'd just said he didn't want Juliet. "What part of me saying I want to be in a relationship with you is so hard for you to believe?"

"I believe you," she said, meeting his eye. "But I can't compete with Juliet. I won't compete with her."

"I'm not asking you to."

"And I can't keep imagining how much you'd rather be fucking her than me."

Rich reared back as if she'd slapped him. "Do you even like me? Or is it still all about my dick for you?" It was the wrong thing to say and he knew it, but he wanted her to hurt as much as he did right now.

And it worked. Alex shot to sitting on the bed. "How dare you," she said through clenched teeth.

"Well, that's all you seem to think I'm interested in you for."

"No. I think you're interested in whatever pussy gets you closer to Juliet. Why else didn't you call for three years?"

If he'd felt like she'd slapped him a moment ago, this was her reaching her fist inside his chest, pulling his heart out and setting it on fire. He rose from the bed, about to walk out the door, but he stopped just short.

"I didn't call, because I didn't have anything nice to say to you."

Alex snorted. She sat on the bed, her skirt pushed up indecently high.

Rich's temper flared into a mix of rage and frustration he'd never felt before. "You think it's funny? To learn about what you did from Juliet of all people?"

"What was the worst part, Rich? Not having a baby or having to hear about it from Juliet?" Alex's voice was a sneer he'd only heard from her once before—the day she'd come to retrieve Juliet's things from his apartment. She'd called him every filthy name under the sun when he'd let her in, and Rich hadn't been able to muster any words in retaliation. He'd deserved them.

But now? He had more words than he could say at one time. "Both. Do you know how much it hurt that you hadn't even told me about the pregnancy?"

Alex swiped at her face, but it was too dark for Rich to see her tears. "I don't know, probably about as much as knowing you had betrayed your best friend in the worst way possible and had absolutely no one to turn to."

"You could have come to me," Rich said, desperate that she understand.

Alex stood and smoothed her skirt down over her thighs. "Why? So you could convince me to have a baby with you while you were constantly trying to seduce my best friend? I don't think so."

Rich surged forward. He had the urge to shake her but curbed it when she shrank away. He took a deep breath buried both hands in his hair instead.

"There was a time when I was confused about what I wanted, and I'm sorry that overlapped with you and me. I really am, but I figured out how much I liked you pretty damn quick. And it wasn't just because Juliet wasn't available. I liked you, Alex. I enjoyed spending time with *you*. Then you broke things off, and I tried to respect that. But when I found out you'd been pregnant, and you'd made the decision to get a goddamn abortion without feeling the need to tell me first, I was gutted. Devastated that I hadn't mattered enough to you to merit a text. I've spent most of the last three years furious with you for that. Because I would have been there, for everything. So, don't act like you're the only one who's been hurt in this situation."

Alex stared back at him with hard eyes and set jaw "That was the darkest period in my life," she said. "There was no way I could have had your baby. Not after Juliet lost hers."

"Because Juliet and I lost our child, I never get a second chance?" Rich hated the way his voice croaked and broke. He could see exactly where this was heading, and he felt like he was watching a train careening out of control. But he couldn't stop himself from saying those words, because maybe he hadn't deserved her trust back then, but he'd have loved her through all of it if only she'd given him the chance, and he needed to say it whether she wanted to hear it or not.

"Not with me. Not ever. Not when she just had another miscarriage. I'm not going to do that to her."

Rich gritted his teeth. Did he want Juliet to go through that again? No. Of course not. But Juliet was living her own, separate life by her choice, and her miscarriage was none of

Rich's business. No, this had nothing to do with Juliet and everything to do with Alex hiding behind *her* fear.

"I'm sorry to hear that," Rich said. "But that has no bearing on who we are to each other."

Alex's face screwed up, like she didn't want to say what was getting ready to come out of her mouth. When she spoke, her voice was strained by the weight of her tears. "I'm never going to be Mrs. Riccardo Durand, the mother of your children, so if that's what you hope to get out of this, it's time to start looking elsewhere."

Rich felt the blood drain from his face. These were the words he'd been waiting for. The ones that stopped them in their tracks, because Alex knew very well that's what he was after. He'd made it clear from the beginning.

"Then I guess we're done here," he said, even as inside his heart was screaming at him that he didn't want anybody else. Only Alex.

When he looked to her, she held her chin higher and said, "I guess so."

He heard the tears in her voice, felt them burn in the back of his own throat, but he couldn't stay, not when Alex was using Juliet as a shield. He didn't know how to begin to break that particular wall down. And with her shoving it in his face, with her refusing to believe that he'd been hurt too, maybe he didn't want to right now.

Rich turned on his heel and left Alex alone in her dark apartment.

• • • •

HE DIDN'T KNOW HOW far he'd driven before he found himself pulling into Gina's driveway. It was well after midnight, but he needed Gina to still be up writing.

He texted before he knocked on the door just in case.

Rich*: You still up?*

Gina*: Unfortunately. What's up?*

Rich: *I'm in your driveway.*

Gina: *I'll meet you at the door.*

Gina let Rich in, and then tiptoed through the living and dining rooms into Gina's kitchen. "Are we gonna need beers for this?"

"Beer would be good, yeah."

Gina fished in the fridge, popped the tops off two bottles and nodded toward the back staircase. Rich tried to make as little noise as possible going up the ancient wooden stairs, but his feet were heavy, and he was too tired to hold his body upright.

Once shut in Gina's office, she motioned for Rich to take his usual armchair, and swiveled her desk chair around to face him. "So, don't leave me in suspense. What's got you looking like you're about to lose your cookies?"

He hadn't thought about it before, but Rich did feel a little seasick, like if he moved too quickly, he might throw up all over Gina's green flowered rug. He took a swig of his beer anyway, this time thankfully not a sour, and said, "I think I just broke up with Alex."

Gina stared at him in confusion for a minute, then leaned forward in her chair so her elbows rested on her knees. "Wait. You mean Alex Stafford Alex? Juliet's Alex?"

"Yeah."

The chair creaked as Gina slammed back into the backrest, then took a long pull from her bottle of beer. "Wow. I didn't even know you guys were a thing. I mean, just wow. Does Juliet know? When did this start? And most importantly, have you lost your damn mind? You don't think you've played with that girl enough?"

Whatever hold Rich had on his emotions up until this point disappeared, and tears spilled over despite his best efforts to hold them back. "Is that what you think of me?" he asked as he swiped at his eyes. "That I toy with women? That I'm some sort of predator?"

Gina cocked her head, as if not quite sure what to make of her crying little brother, and said, "I think you've never had to work very hard to get a woman's attention." She paused, tapping a finger on the lip of her bottle, "And I think you're a lot like Dad."

Rich let out a humorless laugh that was almost a sob. "You think I'm a good for nothing two-timing asshole?"

With a squeak, Gina launched her chair across the room and settled in front of him. "That's not what I meant. I think everything you feel, you feel keenly and deeply. And that maybe all that charming, casual arrogance you throw out is really a mask you wear because you don't think people will like you without it."

With a sniff, Rich nodded and took another pull on his beer. But Gina didn't stop.

"And I think that whatever was going on must have been serious, even though you hadn't bothered to tell me, otherwise you wouldn't be here. So spill. Let me see if I can help."

Rich started with running into Alex on graduation day and told her everything, minus the gory details, about Tokyo Nights, about the fight about Lynnette, about the launch party and the gifts. He told her about going into Novel wearing makeup and about the ensuing week of courting, ending in that night's fight.

"Huh."

Rich, who'd been hunched into a slouch sat up at her reaction. "What do you mean, 'Huh?'"

Gina, who was still directly in front of him pinned him with a glare. "You're telling me that you want to start a family with Alex. Like, buy a house, settle down, get married and have kids style."

"Yes."

"Why?"

"Why did you want to marry Colin?"

"Because he was the most fun, most sincere, most attractive man I'd ever met, and I love him."

Rich nodded.

And Gina sat at attention. "Oh. I didn't realize. You're in love with her."

Again, Rich nodded. "And she wants fuck all to do with me, because I've screwed up too many times for me to be worth her while."

Gina shrugged. "Maybe not."

Rich buried his head in his hands. "She made it pretty clear she didn't want me around tonight."

Gina finished her beer and set the empty bottle at her feet, "I'm not sure that's true."

Rich's neck popped, he looked up so fast. "What do you mean?"

"I mean," Gina said, "And I don't know Alex all that well, so take this with a grain of salt, but from what you told me, it sounds like she has a lot of issues of her own. Juliet has said over and over again how her friendship with Alex was never quite the same after you and Alex got together, and she always thought it was because Alex fell for you then but wouldn't admit to it. Then you throw the pregnancy in there, and everything's all distorted."

When Rich didn't say anything, Gina asked, "Have you forgiven her for that?"

"What?"

"For not talking to you about the pregnancy? For terminating it without telling you about it?"

Rich let out a long sigh as he searched through his racing thoughts. He'd been going over and over their words on the drive here. "I one hundred percent understand where she was coming from when she made her decision."

"But?"

"But she should have told me. Even if it wasn't what she wanted, I deserved the chance to be there for her. But instead, I find out a month after the fact through a third party, and I have to act like I'm not completely devastated."

Gina nodded. "I knew that would crush you."

After a deep breath, Rich asked, "But I can't hold it against her. I don't want to. I just want the chance to start over with her, but I keep screwing that up too. I told her how angry I had been, because I wanted her to know she hurt me, not because I'm still angry about it."

"You should tell her that, but you're not the only one in this, you know. She needs time to get where you are."

He shrugged. "Then what do I do?"

"Go visit Mom. Give Alex a few days to get the wedding behind her. I'll see if I can't work a little magic while we're in Colorado, and when you get back from Savannah, we'll figure it out from there. Okay?"

Rich agreed, but he couldn't shake the trepidation that had rooted deep in his belly, telling him he had messed this one up beyond repair—again.

Chapter Twenty-Three

It was an eleven-hour drive from Alex's apartment to Ethan and Juliet's remote as fuck cabin. Alex had half watched all the succulents in her rearview mirror as she wound around the twisty mountain roads, afraid the trays she'd stored them in would topple, but both she and the wedding favors arrived at Juliet's intact. Juliet and Camille, their teacup toy poodle, met Alex in the wooded driveway. Juliet, almost as bouncy and excited as the tiny, fluffy, white dog, threw her arms around Alex as soon as she was out of the car.

"Hey there, Bride-lady," Alex said, not used to anyone but Rich putting their hands on her.

"I'm so glad you're here," Juliet said. Then pulled back to take Alex in. She knew her friend saw the rings under her eyes and the pale skin that came along with the churning stomach Alex had been carrying around with her for the last four days, but she smiled anyway. It was good to see Juliet, and Alex's smile was genuine, despite how miserable she had been.

"I've missed you so much," Alex said, feeling tears come to her eyes again. She'd cried more over the last few days than she had since just after her abortion.

"Oh, honey, what's wrong?"

Alex sniffed and wiped her eyes with Julie's hands still in her shoulders and Camille still jumping around her feet. "Don't mind me. It's finally really hitting me that Gran's gone and I'm crying at everything."

It wasn't a lie. Alex had finally given herself time to grieve in the days since Rich walked out of her life. It was like she'd hit a wall that night and she couldn't move forward until she processed all of the emotions she'd been shoving aside all summer. It wasn't just that she was upset at losing Gran, but the kind of life she knew Gran had wanted for her, the kind of life Rich claimed to want *with* her. Alex had also had to come terms with not deserving that kind of life. The domestic stuff was for people like Juliet, kind, gentle, serene, not the queen of one-night stands who wasn't good at anything but making jewelry.

"I'm so sorry," Juliet said, pulling Alex back into a hug. "I know how sometimes the grief just hits you out of nowhere."

And Juliet would know. Alex squeezed Juliet tighter. "I'm just really happy to see you."

Juliet made a squealing noise, "Me too."

A door opened and closed. Alex peered over Juliet's shoulder to see Ethan striding down the wooden porch steps. He hadn't aged a day in the three years since Alex had last seen him. He didn't even have any gray hairs that she could see. Perhaps he was leaner than he had been before. Not thin, Ethan had always been broad, but his muscles looked closer to the surface.

"Hey, Alex," he said when he reached the driveway. "Bags in the back?"

"Yeah," she said, without releasing Juliet, "But you might want to get the plants first."

Ethan grunted and circled around to the back of the RAV4. Both Alex and Juliet adjusted their embrace to watch

Ethan unlatch the frame and lift the entire case of trays out of the back of Alex's car with another grunt.

"That's impressive," Alex said, as he wheeled the whole thing toward their garage.

"Are you ogling my fiancé?" Juliet asked.

"Maybe a little," Alex said with a shrug. "I had to load the thing one tray at a time."

Juliet hummed as her eyes tracked Ethan as he opened the garage door and disappeared into the house, presumably taking the plants somewhere safe. "He has always been a bit of a show off." She stared off into the garage as if she could still see her fiancé, and Alex wondered what she was remembering. Juliet shook herself out of her Ethan-induced stupor. "Anyway, come see the house. It's ridiculous."

The outside was already ridiculous. It was a tall, soaring building of dark wood and huge windows. There was a deck that overhung the driveway, and a long flight of stairs that curved around from a long front porch that looked out over the wooded valley. Tall pine trees kept most of the house in shadow, but an assortment of evergreen bushes and what Alex thought must be herbs and wildflowers lined every walkway around the house. They had no yard per se, just rocky mountain outcroppings and pine litter.

Alex could hear birds and squirrels clamoring about in the trees overhead, and she could hear water rushing somewhere in the distance, probably the stream she'd spied on her way up the mountain.

The interior was impressive, and just as expansive as Alex had guessed based on the photos. The main part of the house had high, exposed-beam ceilings in the same dark wood as the exterior. What walls there were around the floor to ceiling windows had been painted white. A huge stone fireplace lined one whole wall, and what little furniture there was had been grouped around it.

The living room melted into the kitchen, all overlooked by a balcony on the next floor where a line of doors implied spare bedrooms. Ethan and Juliet's bedroom sat through a discreet doorway off the living room. The massive master suite was almost the size of the living room and had a mirroring fireplace covering the wall nearest the neatly made bed. On the far side of the room, near a long line of windows sat two yoga mats overlooking a drop on the mountain side, with the stream peeking through. A treadmill and a rowing machine flanked the yoga mats. Various weights and yoga blocks were stacked on a shelf in the corner.

"This place is frickin' enormous," Alex said, turning in a circle to take in the high ceiling. A potted vine had started climbing the wall near the doorway to the bathroom, and Juliet's usual tropical plants added an airiness to what might otherwise have been an isolatingly large room.

"Let me show you your room," Juliet said, pulling Alex out of the master suite by the hand.

"Are you okay with all this?" Alex asked. Juliet had never wanted much in the way of material possessions, and a house like this, with this much privacy, had to cost a fortune, not just to purchase, but to maintain. "I mean, I know you've lived here for a while, but holy shit."

Juliet giggled and pulled Alex toward the stairs. "I was skeptical at first, but Ethan bought it in foreclosure, so we got it for a steal. Plus, Ethan's love for it is contagious."

Alex grinned. She could see that. The room Alex was staying in had similarly high ceilings as the rest of the house, with hand blown light fixtures hanging from a heavy beam over a large, plush white bed. A line of ferns and split leaf trees sat in front of the tall windows that overlooked the same view as Ethan and Juliet's exercise area. A large, red striped area rug sat beneath the bed, adding warmth to the space.

"Did you decorate every room like this?" Alex asked.

"Ethan insisted," Juliet said. "Once we moved in, it was like he had to make up for all those years of not giving a shit about his condo, so yeah."

Alex flopped backward onto the bed and sank into the down comforter. "You guys could run a bed and breakfast in this place and charge like, five hundred bucks a night."

"Believe me, I've thought about it, but Ethan doesn't want strangers in his house. And really, we don't have time to play host."

Alex knew that was true. "I might just move in and run it myself. This place is so big, you'd barely even notice us."

Juliet giggled again and flopped down next to Alex. "I'd love it if you were here. Ethan would be annoyed at not being able to walk around naked, but he'd deal."

Alex waggled her eyebrows at Juliet. "That something you two do often?"

"Why else do you think he wanted to live in the middle of nowhere?"

They laughed together like they were sixteen again. "You look happy," Alex said as the laughter died down.

"I am happy." She met Alex's gaze with light shining in her green eyes, a wide grin on her face. Then gestured, to the room, "This place, this job, this man," Juliet's other hand moved to rest over her belly and Alex pretended not to notice. "It's all exactly what I wanted and better than I could ever imagine."

"I feel like you moved to heaven."

"This is a nice bed," Juliet said as she snuggled down into the white comforter. "And while I'm happy, it's not perfect. Ethan and I argue. The politics in being attached to three hospitals can make my head spin and clearing out of here in the snow is no joke—but for all of that, I wouldn't change a thing."

"Then I guess this getting married thing is probably for the best," Alex said, then jumped as Camille hopped up onto the bed next to her head.

The dog curled up next to Juliet's chest. Each of them scratched her behind one ear and Juliet's voice softened. "How have you been doing? Really?"

Alex sighed. "I've been sad. I miss Gran, but work has kept me busy. The new line has really taken off, so that's good. I'm thinking about expanding. Renting a studio space and hiring another assistant."

"That's amazing," Juliet said. And while Alex knew Juliet meant it, she also knew that Juliet had not been asking about her business. When she moved to scratching Camille under her tiny chin, Juliet said, "I worry about you, working out of the house so much."

"I'm okay," Alex added. "Avery's there and I have Dale."

"What about the guy you were thinking about giving your heart too?"

Now was not the moment to tell Juliet that she'd been dating Rich. Alex shrugged. "It never got to the point where I couldn't keep my heart to myself." She could tell Juliet recognized it for the lie it was by the way her friend's eyes softened, but Alex couldn't bring herself to care over the way the ugly blackness in her heart twisted.

Juliet scooted close on the bed and wrapped her arms around Alex. "Do you want to talk about it?"

Alex shook her head. She didn't have any words for it yet. When she'd picked the fight with Rich, it had felt like the right thing to do. She'd needed to end things before he got too attached to the idea of them in a committed relationship, because when they'd been talking about their fathers, Alex had felt it. Despite the fear that had been roiling inside her, she'd felt how easily they could slip into forever. It was right there, waiting for them to step into it, and that was too close. Too much. And it could never happen, not for Alex, and definitely not with Rich, but seeing Juliet here, seeing her glow with excitement about her wedding and her future, Alex saw exactly what it was she'd just given up.

Juliet's life made Alex's look that much lonelier.

And she missed Rich. She wanted the quiet, soft steadiness of him, the naughty teasing, the way his smile made her feel strong and worthy. She wanted to be worthy of the sort of love he wanted.

Alex hadn't heard from him in almost five days, so she guessed she wasn't.

She'd expected some blow back from him. Rich had never taken rejection easily and had always tried to plead his case with Juliet. This was the second time Alex had told Rich they couldn't have a real relationship, and the second time he'd respected her decision.

Alex wanted Rich to fight for her, but he wasn't. Would it be so much trouble to text and see how she was doing? She could really use a friend, and he was the only one she wanted to confide in. It didn't make any sense because she wanted to complain about him to himself, but it's what she wanted. That's how much she missed him.

Juliet was frowning at Alex when she emerged from inside her own head, so Alex didn't expect it when Juliet asked, "Was the sex good at least?"

A laugh ripped from Alex's chest, startling her with its lack of restraint. "Uh-mazing"

"A lot can be said for the healing powers of good sex."

Alex tightened her arms around Juliet in thanks for not pursuing the topic. She took one long, deep breath, reveling comforting lemongrass and sandalwood that was Juliet, then scooted back on the bed. She pulled up her naughtiest smile and raised a hand into the air. "Can I get an Amen!"

Juliet's answering "Amen," came with a high-five and they descended into giggles, and Alex tried to concentrate on the joy of spending time with her friend.

· · · ·

ALEX ONLY STAYED ONE night at Juliet's house. They left early the next morning for the resort, that was a good four-hour drive even from Juliet's home. It took all three vehicles, Alex's RAV4, Ethan's old Cruiser and Juliet's little hybrid SUV to move all the supplies and clothes they were going to need. Juliet's sister, Colleen, was bringing more, and her parents were bringing a load of decorations as well.

Alex tried not to think about the work that was ahead of them over the next few days and kept her mind on the things she had to keep track of for Juliet instead—when the flowers and plants were going to be delivered. What time most of the guests were arriving. How she needed to convene with Henry, Ethan's best man, about what the men's plans were for the groom the night before the wedding.

It was a lot to keep track of, but if they pulled it off, the weekend would be one long celebration, and that's exactly what Juliet deserved. Alex only had to keep from breaking down in the middle of it. And she could do that. She was strong. She was good at being a friend, being supportive of other people. It was taking care of herself she wasn't so good at.

Alex checked her reflection in the rearview mirror as she pulled into a toll booth lane. She had brown eyes, where her mother's and grandmother's eyes were blue. She'd gotten those eyes from whoever her father was, and they were what she looked at now, imagining, despite everything, that large animal vet as her father. He was a strong, steady man who didn't let anyone walk all over him. And that's what she would be. Not afraid and flighty like her mother.

She'd texted her mother a few more times over the last week. Alex had told her where she would be in Colorado, in case her mother was close by and they could meet for lunch. She'd sent a picture of herself at her last dress fitting—it had become a game almost, seeing what sort of text garnered a response from her mother. If the serious question about how to know when to trust someone with her heart got no response, maybe a pair of cute shoes would. Alex had begun to share her life with her mother whether Vivien wanted her to or not.

So far, Vivien had told her to have fun at the wedding and make sure she slept with a hot groomsman. Considering Ethan's groomsmen were his married brothers, Alex was so not going there. Maybe the key to having a relationship with her mother was not giving or expecting too much. If Alex was trying to connect, and all Vivien was going to give back was to encourage her to have a one-night stand, perhaps Alex could acknowledge that it was Vivien who had the problem, and not Alex.

Her Gran had told Alex to not take her mother too seriously for years, but Alex had always hoped a real mother resided in Vivien somewhere. But Vivien didn't even seem to care to know that Alex might be heartbroken, and maybe it was better that way. Alex had Juliet to talk to when she was ready, and maybe that was enough.

Alex sat up straight, keeping her attention on the road. Acknowledging that maybe she didn't need her mother freed a knot in her stomach, even as that unreachable spot beneath her ribs ached.

Chapter Twenty-Four

Rich's mother had a boyfriend. He was fine with it, really. She'd made no secret of dating while he'd been a teenager, and she'd had a couple long term relationships over the years. Rich had always been fine with it. Rich wanted his mother to be happy, but when he'd flown down to Savannah, he'd imagined it would be just the two of them. He had not expected to find Sawyer attached to his mother's hip or flirting with her in the morning over their coffee or slapping her ass as they washed dishes after dinner or holding her hand as they strode down the City Market.

He didn't blame them. It was all the things people who were in love did.

Really, Rich was happy for his mother. He could appreciate everything Sawyer brought to her life. She looked lighter and happier than he'd seen her in years. She even looked younger, which was probably a good thing, because the one thing Rich couldn't accept about Sawyer (other than the fact that he was a lawyer and Rich kept wanting to call him Sawyer the Lawyer to his face) was that Sawyer was thirty-nine.

Sonia was young for having two grown kids in their thirties, but she was still twenty years her partner's senior. Gina was thirty-six. His sister was only three years younger than the guy their mother was dating.

Rich knew he needed to get over it and not let his distaste for their age gap show, but sometimes it took him by surprise, and he'd caught his mother giving him the side-eye more than once. Sawyer, at least, was pretending not to notice, which Rich thought was the least he could do since Sawyer and his mom were at that stage of their relationship where they wanted to be together all the time.

Of the week Rich had planned to stay with his mother, he didn't get any time alone with her until Friday night, after he'd already been there four days. The wedding he hadn't been invited to would take place the next day. Whether Sonia had warned Sawyer that it might be a night she needed alone with her son, or if he did really have a standing poker game with his work colleagues, Rich didn't care to puzzle out. He was just grateful for the time.

Sonia spent the afternoon in the kitchen, creating Rich's favorite meal, homemade linguine with clams in a butter sauce, along with homemade bread and big green salad with slightly more olives and parmesan than romaine.

They opened the white wine that was meant for the pasta early and kept drinking while they picked at an antipasto platter. They spoke in Italian for the first time all week. They talked about their jobs, about Gina and the boys, about how his mother was bringing Sawyer the Lawyer to her mother's house for Christmas, and how she'd pay for Rich's ticket to Italy if he wanted.

Rich only said he didn't know what he wanted to do for Christmas.

"Well, the offer is still open, if you change your mind."

Before he could think better of it, he set his wineglass down on the distressed white kitchen table and said, "I might be going to France in the next few months instead."

Sonia cocked her head to one side. "*Francia*?" She drew out the two syllables of the word as if she'd never said them before.

Rich spun his glass through his fingers by the stem. "I've been looking for Dad. I think I've almost found him."

His mother's confusion melted into a frown. "There's nothing to be gained by looking for your father. He left us. He doesn't deserve your time or your energy. He doesn't deserve you."

Rich knew his mother meant well, that she was only trying to protect him, but he was grown now, and some things, he needed to learn for himself. "But I need to find out for myself whether I deserve him," Rich said.

His mother's frown deepened. "Is this about Juliet?" she asked. "Are you looking for something to replace her because she's getting married tomorrow?"

"No, Mom. This isn't about Juliet. I'm happy for her. I miss her, and I hope someday we can be friends, but that's it."

"Then I don't understand why you would be looking for your father."

He stared at his mother for a few silent, tense moments. She appeared truly distressed by the news, as if simply by looking for his father, Rich was bound to get hurt. Finally, drumming up his courage, he asked the question he wanted answered the most. "Do you think I'm like him? Do you think I'm destined to be restless and frightened and do what he did to us once I have a family?"

He watched as understanding bloomed in his mother's eyes, cascading down as she straightened her spine and set her shoulders back.

"You want to start a family?"

"I've been courting someone for the last few weeks." Rich grimaced into his wine glass. "It hasn't been going well."

A timer dinged, and his mother rose from the table. "Keep talking. Just because I'm finishing up dinner, doesn't mean I'm not listening."

By the time he'd caught his mom up on his history with Alex, they were almost finished eating dinner.

"How much of this story did you already know?" he asked when his mother nibbled on the end of her slice of sourdough.

"All of the early bits," she said, "Or at least the highlights your sister gave me—"

"Gossip," Rich said, but a smile curled his lips. Sonia met him with an answering grin.

"But nothing that had been going on this year."

"What should I do?"

Sonia picked up Rich's phone from where he'd left it on the table and held it out to him. Then she said, "I think you need to call Juliet."

• • • •

ALEX HAD FOLLOWED JULIET back to her suite after the rehearsal dinner. They were tipsy–well, Alex was tipsy. Juliet was only pretending to be tipsy after an evening of "vodka sodas with lime" something Juliet *never* drank. Alex had sneaked a sip when Juliet had run to the restroom and confirmed her suspicion that there was no vodka in that soda. Even so, as they burst through Juliet's door and collapsed onto her bed, Juliet was just as giggly as Alex who had gone way over her one to two ounces of tequila, and then thrown a couple glasses of champagne in there for good measure.

Juliet rolled onto her side, her hands covering her middle and blew out a deep breath. "Oh my God, I feel like I'm gonna puke."

"Getting cold feet?" Alex asked and Juliet scowled and sat up.

"Yoga will help. I've got an extra mat if you want to join?"

"I'll hurt myself if I try to do drunk yoga, but I will change into yoga pants." Alex peeled herself off the bed and swayed a moment before catching her footing. Juliet was already pulling a change of clothes out of the dresser as Alex tottered down the hall to her own room.

She took a few minutes to wipe the makeup from her face and munch on a piece of jerky, part of a pack Dale had given her to avoid roadside junk food. She felt almost halfway sober when she meandered back toward Juliet's room, but stopped outside the propped open door as the familiar, ethereal music Juliet did yoga to switched to a generic ringer.

"Hello?" Juliet asked, and Alex could just make her out, tapping her phone from downward facing dog. Alex smiled. It was good to see some things never changed.

"Hey, Jules," a deep, familiar voice came over the line and Alex felt all the blood run from her head and pool around her feet. Some things really did never change.

"Rich!" Juliet sounded excited but didn't miss a beat in her routine and she switched from downward dog to three-legged dog, raising her right foot into the air. "What's up?"

"I thought I'd call to say congratulations, since I can't be there in person. I'm happy for you." There was a pause, and then he said. "I hope Ethan realizes what a beautiful woman you are."

Juliet giggled a little as she shifted her right leg forward into a lunge, then straightened into a high lunge, then warrior two. "He's well aware but thank you."

"What about you?" He asked. "How are you feeling?"

Juliet leaned backward into peaceful warrior. "I'm all right. A little nauseous, but otherwise I'm happy as a clam."

"Getting cold feet?"

Juliet laughed and cartwheeled over into standing right angle pose. "That's what Alex said, but no. Probably just ate too much."

Alex had to stop her own snort. Juliet had barely eaten anything, moving her food around on her plate with her fork more than anything.

Rich went quiet, staying that way as Juliet worked through a vinyasa as if he were watching her move as well, and only began talking again once Juliet was back in downward dog.

"How is Alex? Is she doing okay?" He didn't ask like an acquaintance asking after someone they hadn't seen in a while. He asked with an intensity in his voice that made it clear he knew of a reason or two to be concerned.

Juliet took notice, pausing with her left foot in the air, her head cocking to the side as she glanced to her phone screen. "You know Alex, she puts up a brave front."

Alex shifted from one foot to the other, ducking out of sight as Juliet once again lifted into warrior two, this time facing the door.

"So, she's not okay," Rich said, his words weighed down by a sigh.

"She's mostly been her usual mouthy self," Juliet said. "But when she doesn't think anyone's looking, she stares off into space looking completely devastated. Do you know why that is?"

Rich sighed into the phone again, and Alex imagined him ruffling a hand through his wavy hair. "Has she told you anything about us?" he asked.

Alex could hear Juliet's knowing smile, when she said, "What do you mean by '*us?*'"

"We've been seeing each other—well, really more me spending most of my time convincing her to give me the time of day, and her giving in occasionally. But those times have been so good, Jules. Amazing. Phenomenal. Like, I want to do this the rest of my life phenomenal—" Juliet interrupted him with a squeal.

"Do you know how long I've been waiting for the two of you to figure this out? I was five minutes away from Parent Trapping the two of your together."

Rich let out a soft laugh, and Alex's stomach clenched. Juliet wanted them to be together?

"That's funny, considering you're our biggest problem."

Alex chanced a peek through the crack in the door and Juliet was working through another vinyasa as she said, "How's that?"

"For one, I think Alex is terrified of a repeat of what went down last time, and for another, she thinks you're so amazing that she could never live up to the standard you set and that a part of me will always be replacing you with her."

Juliet collapsed out of her pose, settling with her legs crossed. "Are you kidding? That's ridiculous."

"It's what we fought about last weekend. Basically broke us up, but I don't want to be done, Jules." The ache, the pain in Rich's voice had tears pinging in Alex's eyes. She could almost hear the mirroring tears gathering in Rich's eyes as he said, "I really, really need not to be done."

"Oh wow," Juliet said, picking up the phone and switching off the speaker. "I had no idea you guys were so serious. Gina said something about you two, and I hoped, maybe someday. Oh wow." Juliet took a deep breath and sat up straight. "Okay. Tell me exactly what happened. Let me see if I can help."

Alex stood in the hall, hearing Juliet's voice every few minutes, but not really listening to what she said as Alex tried to wrap her mind around the idea that Rich was calling Juliet on the night before her wedding, not to convince her one last time to run away with him, but for advice about how to fix things with Alex.

Alex's mind wandered back to when Ethan had done the same thing for Juliet, calling Alex every time he made a misstep—and there had been many in the beginning. Was that what Rich was doing? Fumbling to make things perfect because he was so in love that he was clueless? Rich had never struck Alex as clueless, but this was a unique situation they were in. Maybe he was as unsure about how to proceed as she was. A little flame of hope bloomed from that dark ache in her chest.

Maybe this thing with Rich wasn't completely ridiculous?

Alex became aware of quiet from beyond the door, then a slight rustling. When she peeked through the crack, Juliet was rolling up her yoga mat.

"You can come in now," Juliet said. And as Alex pushed through the door, she asked. "How much of that did you hear?"

"Everything until you turned off the speaker."

Juliet shook her head, then took Alex by the hands and pulled her to sit across from her on the big bed. "Why didn't you tell me?"

"Because the whole thing has been such a disaster. And it was a disaster the last time too."

"And you thought I'd be mad."

"Yeah."

Juliet pegged her with a wide eyed, sarcastic expression that said *are you kidding me*?

Alex felt herself blush and lifted her shoulders to her ears. "The last thing I want to do is mess things up between us again. You're the last real family I have, and Rich has been such touchy territory for years."

Juliet squeezed Alex's hands. "I just want you to be happy," she said. "And, yes, I have a history with Rich. A big, long complicated one, and while he'll always have a special place in my heart, that's all it is, Alex. An acknowledgement that we had something once upon a time. Don't let that stop you. If Rich is who you want, see him, sleep with him, marry him, have his babies. Please."

With tears welling in her eyes, Alex said, "It doesn't make me a hypocrite for telling you to stay away from him all those years?"

"Back then, you were right. But listening to him just now, I think you should go for it."

"What did he tell you?"

"Did he really let you put makeup on him, and then go out in public without looking at himself in the mirror?"

"He did."

"The Rich I knew was far too vain and far too masculine to go along with a scheme like that."

"You don't think he would have done that for you?"

"Never in a million years."

Alex's heart stopped, and she placed a mental bookmark on this moment to examine again when she was alone. Perhaps the makeup stunt had meant even more to Rich than it had to Alex. If he'd done it just for her. Maybe all his actions this past summer, the flowers, the gifts, maybe they weren't just the things Rich did to get a woman's attention. Maybe they were things he'd done specifically for her. And maybe she'd been doing him a disservice in not giving him more credit for his actions.

To Juliet, Alex said, "He hated every minute of it."

"And when he realized you'd only put a little bit of concealer on him?"

Alex felt her blush deepen. "I think he nearly proposed, but that's just because he was relieved I hadn't put him in blue eye liner."

"It was because he realized he could trust you in any circumstance," Juliet said. "But you don't trust him yet."

"Do you blame me?" Alex asked, but maybe, after hearing the longing in Rich's voice when she spoke of her, maybe she could start.

Juliet's miniscule shake of the head was all Alex needed. "But I think you should give him a chance, without factoring me into the equation. After tomorrow, I'll have everything I'm ever going to need."

"You mean Ethan," Alex said.

"And my job," Juliet amended.

Alex's eyes zeroed in on Juliet's abdomen. "And whatever bun it is you have baking in your oven."

One of Juliet's hands closed over her stomach, and a slow smile spread over her lips.

"How did you know?"

Alex scoffed. "Please, lady. I spent six years greeting pregnant women five days a week. I might not have made it through nursing school, but I can recognize the signs a mile away."

"Do you think anyone else has noticed?"

"I don't think anyone is paying quite as close attention to you as I do—except maybe Ethan, and I'm assuming he knows already."

Juliet's grin lit up. "I could barely keep him out of the bathroom long enough to pee on the stick the day after my period was late."

"You two are so domestic it makes me sick, "Alex said, but her grin almost neared Juliet's in radiance. "So, when are you due? How do you feel?"

Juliet's smile faltered a little, and Alex knew she was thinking of her losses, but Alex wouldn't expect her to lose this one too and wouldn't let Juliet think that way either. Not if she could help it, even if meant texting her pregnancy memes every day for the next several months. "I'm only eight weeks along," she said. "And I am miserable."

"That's a good thing."

Juliet pursed her lips. "And assuming this one sticks, we'll have an April baby."

Alex patted Juliet's knee. "No ifs, babe. You're gonna have an April baby."

Juliet rubbed a circle over her abdomen. "I really hope you're right."

"Of course I am." She pulled her friend into a hug. "I was right about Ethan, wasn't I?"

"Every time," Juliet said, then after a few minutes of silence. "I really hope this one's a girl."

"Me too," Alex said. "I've always wanted a niece."

Juliet squeezed Alex's hand. "Me too. You should probably get on that. Probably with Rich. Soon."

Alex groaned and covered her face with her hands. "Can I just put it on the record that you encouraging me to get it on with your ex is super creepy."

Juliet only shrugged. "I'm just saying, I am no longer a valid excuse for you to avoid him."

"Heard," Alex said. "Please let's never go there again."

"I make no promises," Juliet said, then broke off mid giggle for a mad dash to the bathroom.

• • • •

THE CEREMONY HAD BEEN beautiful. Watching Juliet surrounded by ferns and palm fronds as she and Ethan were married beneath the summer sun was a memory Alex was thankful to have. It had been a long time since Alex had cried from happiness, but when Ethan's brothers whooped like they were at ball game as the preacher pronounced them man and wife, Alex couldn't help the tears that sprang to her eyes. Ethan had joined them in the whooping and lifted Juliet off her feet, then swept her in a circle that had Juliet screeching in delight. The entire crowd cheered as Ethan lowered her back to her feet and kissed her without waiting for the preacher's permission.

Laughing, the preacher had said, "Ladies and Gentlemen, I present to you Ethan and Juliet Harvey."

Ethan and Juliet had stood facing the crowd, grinning at one another, hands clasped between them.

Alex hadn't even tried to hide her tears as she linked arms with Henry and followed them back down the aisle.

As Alex watched Ethan and Juliet dance together while the reception wound to a close, Alex again dabbed at her eyes with a cocktail napkin. It had been one of those weddings where tears had flowed freely down smiling faces. Alex was so distracted, watching Juliet bury her nose against her husband's shoulder that she didn't see Gina's approach, or Colleen close on her heels.

Colleen set a fresh tequila and soda down in front of Alex, then plopped into the chair next to her. "Gina and I are having a disagreement, and we need you to settle something for us."

Alex looked from left to right, at the two women flanking her, a little confused. Alex had been avoiding Gina as much as she could. Not only was the woman kind of intimidating, she was also the only person aside from Juliet who knew about Alex and Rich, and Alex did not want to discuss it. As for Colleen, Alex didn't really know her. They'd communicated about the wedding over the last couple of months, but Juliet's sister could be . . . surly, and Alex felt like any interactions with her were a potential land mine.

"What's that?" Alex asked as she reached for the drink, and looked to Gina, but she only curled her lips in a knowing grin as Colleen said, "Gina has been trying to tell me that you and her brother have been getting it on all summer, but I've been trying to tell her that you can't possibly be that stupid. Not after what went down a few years ago."

Alex pulled her powder blue skirt further down her thighs. Juliet had chosen tea length dresses for her afternoon wedding, but Alex felt like the satin dress was little more than a slip the way the slinky cut clung to her. Colleen, with her lush curves and wavy blonde hair looked like a pinup model, and while Alex had always been a tad jealous of women with big boobs, she wondered if Colleen felt even more naked than Alex did right now.

Alex took a sip of her new drink and said, "Twice isn't exactly all summer."

But Colleen propped her elbows on the table, seemingly oblivious to how it put her cleavage on display and said to Gina. "No offense, but your brother is kind of an asshole." Gina raised her eyebrows as Colleen turned her attention to Alex. "Which makes me wonder what the fuck you've been thinking. I mean, the guy better have a magic dick or something, because there is absolutely no reason to put up with someone treating you like shit all the time."

Gina choked on her wine, but Alex offered Colleen a half smile. "I appreciate your concern, but Rich—" tears pooled in the back of Alex's eyes again as her voice caught in her throat. The hope that had swelled after hearing Rich's voice last night had subsided as the day had worn on. He'd said he needed them not to be over, and even without Juliet in the mix, Alex wasn't sure they were salvageable. She swallowed, not wanting to shed another tear for herself, not when she still had so much to think about, and tried again, "Rich and I aren't together anymore, so there's nothing for you to worry about."

Gina's slender hand closed over Alex's shoulder.

"Oh my God, you're kidding me," Colleen said, and knocked backed the rest of her drink—what looked to be straight whiskey. "Are you telling me you actually like the guy?"

Alex swiped at her eyes with her wrist, no longer caring if she smudged her eye makeup, and sniffed the rest of the tears back. "Rich has changed—or, he's at least, he's left the cheating behind him."

Gina's reassuring hand slipped away with a quick pat in solidarity and Alex turned to her. "Has he told you about the private investigator he hired to find your dad?"

The color drained out of Gina's face, and her glass of wine hit the table with a dull thunk. "He said he was looking for him, but—"

"He's been looking for him for years, and I'm so proud of him for sticking with the search, even though I know it hurts him to know that Marius probably doesn't want to be found."

Gina shook her head. "He's just setting himself up for more heartbreak."

Alex nodded. "I think so to, but I think he needs to see for himself that he's more than his father—that he's not doomed to hurt everyone he loves."

Gina's face crumpled, and her fingers circled her temples. "I told him just a few days ago that he was a lot like dad, and it—he was upset."

Alex nodded. "That's especially cutting, coming from you, I think."

Gina pushed back her chair. "I have to go."

"What was that about?" Colleen asked, as Gina rushed from the empty barn turned reception hall.

Alex spun her glass, having lost all appetite for her drink. "My guess is she's calling her brother."

"Okay, but why?"

"Because she realized how badly something she said might have hurt him."

Colleen's brows furrowed as she gazed after the sliding wooden door Gina had disappeared through. "But why does he need a private investigator to find his dad?"

Alex felt like Colleen should probably know why, but she didn't ask why Juliet hadn't confided in her. The sisters hadn't exactly been close back when Rich and Juliet had been together. So, Alex told her the story of how Rich's dad had left, and Rich's years-long quest for answers.

"What a fucking coward," Colleen said when Alex finished her story, but there was a reluctant tenderness in her eyes that said she didn't want to feel sorry for Rich. "You don't just abandon your kids. Ever."

Alex nodded. "Rich isn't all bad, you see."

Colleen made a clucking noise in the back of her throat. "No guy is all bad. But his history doesn't do him any favors, you have to admit."

"No," Alex said. "It really doesn't."

"And I have a pretty low tolerance for douchebags and cheaters."

A laugh escaped from Alex. "Are these mutually exclusive categories?"

"Nah," Colleen pushed her curtain of blonde hair over her shoulder. "Usually they're one and the same, but not always. The douchebags are easier to dismiss. The cheaters—they're the ones that cut you deep, you know?"

"Yeah," Alex said, but then realized that maybe Colleen had her own heartbreak that she was referring to. "And you know from experience?"

Colleen shrugged, "I think everyone's got a little experience with betrayal."

Cryptic, but fine. Alex wasn't going to push the subject. And it seemed that Colleen was done with it as well. "Anyway, as fun as this little *tete a tete* has been, I spy a single, very attractive young doctor friend of Ethan's that looks like he might need some company." Colleen waggled her eyebrows at Alex before sauntering across the room to a group of men whom Ethan had invited.

That had been Alex once, brazen and unapologetic when it came to men. But now, if she couldn't have Rich, she wasn't sure what she wanted anyone.

Chapter Twenty-Five

Two weeks after Juliet's wedding, Alex still hadn't seen Rich. Though the texting had started the day after she'd returned from the wedding. When she'd finished at the gym, she had message from Rich that said, *I hope you enjoyed your weekend. My mother has a thrity-nine-year-old boyfriend called Sawyer who's a lawyer. I'd suspect of him of using my mother for her money, but his family is old money loaded, so that can't be it.*

Alex, who had spent the whole drive back to Kansas City stuck in her own head, had let out a snort of a laugh, and fired back, *Maybe he's just using her for her body.*

She could feel Rich's cringe when he texted back, *Funny.* Then, a few minutes later. *I've missed you.*

That had Alex's stomach clenching. She saw what he was doing. It was his usual routine for reeling in women: say something funny, then charm their pants off with a hint of vulnerability. She recognized it, while she realized this wasn't Rich trying to play games with her. He was trying to make amends, provide them with some neutral ground to start over.

Alex let his text sit for an hour as she worked. The studio was still quiet. Avery wasn't due to show until noon, and it was just Alex and Alastor listening to Perfume Genius on repeat as she attached fastenings to crystals. Alex had missed Rich, at first with the despairing ache of thinking she'd never see him again. Then, after eavesdropping on Juliet's phone call, she had dipped back and forth between burgeoning hope and bleak despondency. Somewhere between the Colorado border and Hays, Alex had decided she wanted to make this work. Hell, she wanted to show up at his door and lock herself in his apartment until they emerged with an armistice, signed and notarized and sealed with few orgasms apiece, but she couldn't. As much as Alex appreciated Rich's strategy, they'd said too many things the last time they'd been together to just pick up and try again.

Finally, when she'd strung all the pendants on their chains and hung them on the bar over Avery's worktable, she returned to her phone and texted him back, *I've missed you too.*

Her heart hammered in her chest for a full minute until she switched her phone off and shoved it under the cushion on Avery's chair, and cranked up the music. As easy as it would be to call Rich and moon over his sweet words, Alex was still sorting out how she wanted to proceed.

When Alex turned her phone on later that evening when she'd shut the studio door for the day, he'd sent her three more texts. He's asked how the wedding had gone, if she was busy this week, and finally, as if he had been working up to the last one, if she would be available for dinner soon. A thrill ran through her when she read the words. He wanted to have dinner, which meant he wanted to see her.

How about coffee? Tomorrow afternoon? Alex offered instead, then set up the time and place. He didn't object, though Alex knew if the situation were reversed, she'd be disappointed. Dinner was more intimate, and could easily stretch into more, whereas coffee at three-thirty in the afternoon implied a brief encounter, an hour at most in a public spot before going their separate ways.

Alex needed that cup of coffee by the time she arrived at the coffee shop the next day. She'd tossed and turned all night, thinking up different scenarios for how this would go in her head until she'd finally drifted off only a couple of hours before she was due at the gym. The day had been a haze of nerves of bleary-eyed sleepiness. Even though Alex had taken the time to make her hair all pretty and wavy, and to get dressed in her black ankle-length suit pants with a ruffly black silk blouse, she felt like she'd spent the day being flogged. Her sore arms from Dale putting her through the ringer this morning didn't help.

Alex forgot all of that when she stepped into the coffee shop to find Rich already there. He sat at a table near the back, but visible from the door. He too had dressed up for the occasion, wearing a navy shirt and gray pants. There was even a sport coat draped over the back of his chair, and Alex hoped he'd actually had an important meeting that day, because it was way too hot for long sleeves and a jacket.

He stood as she approached the table and leaned in to place a kiss on both her cheeks. That was how Alex could tell he was nervous. He was reverting to the European habits he'd learned as a child, not the more American detachment he'd perfected as an adult. "I ordered you an Americano," he said, and pulled her chair out for her.

"Oh," Alex looked at the table for the first time to see that there were indeed two steaming mugs of coffee there, and he'd even remembered what she drank. "Thank you," she said as she took her seat.

Rich joined her and smiled, even as he spun his mug on his saucer. "You look great."

Alex allowed herself a smile as she raised the coffee to her lips. The smell was familiar and comforting even as her heart was pounding so hard Rich could probably see it through her shirt. "You do too." She took a sip of the coffee, then squared her shoulders and met Rich's hesitant gaze. "Now let's talk about the abortion."

• • • •

RICH WAS GLAD HE HADN'T been sipping his coffee just then, because it probably would have come out of his nose. Of all the reasons he'd dreamed up about why Alex would want to meet for coffee, her letting him down easy once and for had won out most often. Not once had he imagined her opening their conversation with *that* topic.

"I'm sorry," he said.

"The last time we spoke, it sounded like you were harboring some resentment about me terminating that pregnancy, and I don't think that's a healthy way to build a relationship. I want to put everything out there. Figure out all the bad stuff and see if we can build a relationship from the rubble."

"You want to build a relationship? With me?"

Alex's smile turned shy. "I would like to try." She placed her phone on the table and unlocked it. "I made a list of all of our major issues that I feel we need to discuss first. And last time we were together the pregnancy and subsequent termination seemed like a big hurdle for you, so I'd thought we'd start there."

Rich couldn't help the twist of his lips. She was approaching this like it they were discussing business. While Rich found Alex and her attempts at compartmentalizing adorable, he also fundamentally disagreed with her methodology.

He pulled her phone across the table toward him and read her list.

None of the items surprised him. Juliet's name was second after abortion, then came kids, living situation, finances.

"You've thought a lot about this," he said as he handed her phone back to her.

"Haven't you?"

Rich nodded, taking her hand as she set her phone aside. He'd been doing real estate searches and contemplating the merits of sending her more gifts. He'd even looked up Airbnb's in Chicago, thinking it might make for a nice weekend getaway.

"Of course, I have."

"Then why do you look so amused?"

"Do you really think we'll be able to tick issues off a list and call them settled over one cup of coffee?"

Alex tried to pull her hand free, but Rich clenched his fingers down around her. "I suppose you think it's stupid to try."

He shook his head, holding her gaze. "It's not stupid. But it's only just a start, Alex."

She didn't say anything. Something like fear edged into her eyes, and Rich wanted to tell her not to be afraid, even though his heart pounded so hard he could barely hear his own thoughts. He gripped Alex's hand like it was a lifeline, and fought through the fear that she was going to leave and never speak to him again.

"To answer your question, yes, I was upset that you didn't tell me at the time. Yes, I would have tried to convince you to have the baby, and yes, I understand now why that wasn't an option for you, but mostly I've been angry at myself for the reasons why things wouldn't have worked out between us back then."

"Are you still angry with me?" she asked, the vulnerability in her voice not a characteristic Rich associated with Alex.

"No."

"Are you still angry with yourself?"

"Daily, but it's something I'm working on." She nodded, and Rich took the opportunity to turn the tables on her. "Do you blame me for having to go through that experience?"

She shook her head and screwed her eyes shut.

"Do you blame yourself?"

Alex nodded and swiped the lone tear she hadn't been successful at suppressing down her cheek. "I think. I mean, Dale keeps saying he think I should talk to a therapist. Not just about this. Or us. But about my mom. Gran. Everything."

Rich ran circles around her palm with his thumb, attempting to comfort her without being too overwhelming. "I've been thinking the same thing for myself actually. I am thinking about calling off the search for my dad."

"Why?"

Rich shrugged. "He doesn't want to be found," he said, even though it was more than that. A new fear had struck him, that his dad would have a family, and that he would deny Rich the chance to know them. The thought sent a shot of ice through his heart. That would be worse than not knowing.

"Perhaps you should talk to your new therapist about it?"

"It's not a bad idea."

Alex rotated her mug with her non-dominant hand so she could take a sip without slipping her hand from beneath his. Then she sighed into her mug the same way she did in the morning, like coffee was the magic ingredient missing from her life, and without it, she wasn't completely Alex.

"If the past isn't a problem between us and we're addressing our individual issues in therapy, what was next on the list?" Rich asked.

"Juliet."

"What about her?"

"I overheard the first half of your conversation the other night."

Rich cocked his head to the side. He couldn't help it. He'd known he'd been on speaker phone for a few minutes, he just hadn't realized Alex had been there. "You heard her say she wants us to be together, then?"

Alex blushed.

Blushed.

"Yes."

"Is that still a problem for you?"

Alex's blush deepened. "Aside from being a little surreal? No. We talked about it. And I realized she's been nudging me toward this for a while now."

Rich's grin stretched wide, and he brought her fingers to his lips for a kiss. "Then I think we have a good starting place. We can figure the rest out later."

With a squeeze, he dropped Alex's hand, took a long sip of his coffee, then stood.

"Where are you going?" she asked, whirling in her chair as he crossed toward the door.

Rich walked backward so he could face her, grinning even though he walked away from her. "I have a meeting at work," It was true, though the meeting wasn't for another hour. "Find your therapist and call me when you're ready."

Then he left the coffee shop. It was a gamble, leaving her there, but one he was betting his whole life would pay off.

Chapter Twenty-Six

A week later, Alex hadn't done anything but work. She channeled her energy into her business, just like she'd always done. First there had been all the orders to catch up on from her week off. Then she'd called Avery and Janet in to let them know they'd be scaling up operations over the next few months. Alex had known she'd need to do it eventually, and she was terrified of spending the extra money on renting a studio space and hiring *another* full-time employee, but the week away had given her perspective. How she'd been working just wasn't sustainable. She needed to be able to take a break, and while Alex hadn't been worried while she'd been away, the never-ending tasks that had awaited her upon her return had forced Alex to face some hard truths. She had more work coming in than she and her staff would be able to keep up with long term.

Janet was on the job of finding them a studio space while Alex trained Avery to make some of the simpler pieces, which Alex had been reluctant to do, even though Avery was more than capable. Alex was so used to doing the brunt of the jewelry making herself–afraid it would compromise her integrity not to make each piece herself–that the relief and freedom she found at being able to concentrate solely on the complicated pieces surprised and delighted her. She hadn't realized exactly how much she'd dreaded making the same necklaces over and over again, day after day.

She'd never been more fulfilled in her 'work as she was the day she allowed Avery to fill orders on her own. On the other hand, more free time only gave Alex more time to think about how she hadn't heard from Rich at all. She'd been so sure he was going to call her, despite his parting words, that she was getting annoyed at him for making her call him. They both had plenty of shit to work out on their own. Why was the ball in her court?

"I mean, if it was important enough for him to call Juliet on the night before her wedding for advice, shouldn't it be important enough to freaking call me already?" Alex asked in between punches.

Dale gave a quick shake of his head. "If you have enough breath left to keep complaining about this douche, I'm not working you hard enough. Double time it, lady."

Alex squared her feet and raised her fists. "He's not a douche, he's the goddamn love of my life—apparently."

"But you haven't spoken to him for a week."

"Minor inconvenience."

Dale tapped the bag. "Have I ever told you that you need a therapist?"

Alex only smiled, she hadn't found one yet. She'd been meaning to ask Chris for a recommendation, but hadn't seen him, and didn't want to put that burden on Dale. "How about I agree to come to sparring on Saturday instead?"

Dale grunted in approval as she put more force into her punches. "It's a step in the right direction anyway."

Alex had officially come to sparring for the first time the weekend before, and she had had her ass thoroughly handed to her by Evelyn in the ring. But afterwards they had gone out to coffee together and run into Avery at the coffee shop.

It had been one of the best days she'd had since her grandmother died. Alex had felt at home for the first time since she'd slept with Rich the first time—since she had pushed Juliet away all those years ago. Sitting in that coffee shop, arms heavy and abs aching, surrounded by laughing friends and receiving texted photos of Juliet and Ethan's mountain hiking honeymoon, Alex finally felt as though she had a family.

Maybe it didn't matter that she had an imperfect relationship with her mother, or that her grandmother's house had finally sold, and Alex really had no physical home to go back to. She could create her own family.

As she dabbed her face dry with her towel after her workout, Dale surprised her with an arm around her shoulders.

"Now, I wouldn't do this for just anybody," he said, squeezing her into his side. "But since you're so pathetic and everything, I thought I'd give you a hand."

He passed her an envelope and released her.

"What's this?"

"Tickets to a charity event. Invite your boyfriend and stop bothering me with your drama."

"What kind of charity?" Alex asked. She wanted to peek inside, but the envelope was sealed.

Dale rubbed the back of his neck. "Chris and I are part of a group that works with LGBTQ youth in the city. It's part gym, part community therapy, part safe space."

"You and Chris are doing this?" Alex asked. "Why didn't you ever say anything?"

Dale shrugged, his cheeks turning pink. "It's a pet project. And you've had a busy summer."

"How much are the tickets?" she asked, reaching for her purse, even though she knew it was in her locker. "You have to let me pay for them."

Dale waved her off. "It's a cash bar." When Alex opened her mouth to protest again, he said, "Throw in one of those fancy necklaces you make for the silent auction, and we'll call it even."

"I can do that," Alex smiled. "Thanks."

She settled into her car a few minutes later and opened the envelope. The event was a week from Friday. That should work. Now all she would have to do was dredge up the guts to call Rich.

· · · ·

RICH HAD TOLD HIMSELF that if Alex didn't call him within three days, he would call her in case she'd gotten the mistaken impression that him leaving the coffee shop the way he had had been him walking away. Waiting those first three days for her had been torture, but then, when it was his turn, Rich couldn't bring himself to pick up his phone and call her. He wanted to. He longed to see her. His body ached to touch her, taste her, slide inside her and tell her he was never letting go.

But every day he found another excuse to put it off. Every single reason he gave himself was bullshit. Preparing for the semester was old hat by now. He would be busier once school started, even though he was back in his office every day. He would just get his thoughts organized on the paper he was supposed to be writing or the article he was supposed to be reviewing, and then he'd get distracted looking at real estate listings for houses in Midtown and Westport.

He didn't have plans to move anytime soon. He'd been in the same apartment since he was an undergrad, and he was happy with it, but some part of him knew he couldn't ask Alex to live there with him, not after he'd lived there with Juliet.

Rich wanted to go to Alex with a plan, a file organized and neat like he would put together if he were going to a bank with a business proposal. He wanted to list out for her all the ways he would make sure she was happy, give her options for where they would live. He wanted to detail how they would afford it, show her which schools were the best, which neighborhoods had the easiest commute for them both.

Rich knew Alex would kick him out for trying to plan their life without her, but he also knew he couldn't go to her empty-handed. Rich didn't know what else to do, he supposed he understood her approach to their coffee date better.

What he hadn't expected was for Alex to call him before he could make up his mind. A week after their coffee date, he'd been headed out of a department meeting when he flipped on his phone to find a missed call and a voicemail from her.

He listened to her message on his way back to his office, his heart pounding so loud he could barely hear Alex's voice.

So, I'm donating some jewelry to this charity gala thing to help raise money for LGBTQ kids who need a safe place to hang out, and they gave me two tickets to the event, and I was wondering if maybe you'd like to be my plus one. It doesn't have to mean anything if you don't want it to. We can just go as friends.

Then she rattled off the date and location, finishing with an awkward, *Let me know. Kay. Thanks. Bye.*

Rich closed his office door behind himself, and leaned back into it, unable to pull the smile from his face as he clicked on the icon to return Alex's call.

· · · ·

ALEX WAS WITH SIMONE at her shop on the plaza, discussing another line of rings when "I Want Your Sex" by George Michael began to play in her hand. A photo of a sleeping, scruffy, and snuggly post-coital Rich popped up on her screen.

"I should take this," Alex said, snatching the phone out of sight and hiding the photo against her chest.

"I'll say you should," Simone said with a wink, while Alex turned her back and tried not to blush. She'd only set that ringtone because Rich never called. He always texted. The photo, she wouldn't apologize for though. Rich was hot—she just didn't want anyone else to see him like that.

"You know you're interrupting a very important business meeting, right?" Alex answered the phone, not bothering with a "Hello." She'd been planning what she would say to him when he called her back all morning—how she would be playful, familiar, but not affectionate, just in case he'd changed his mind.

"What if I want to go to this thing with you as more than your friend?" Rich asked.

She appreciated the straightforwardness of his question, the lack of hesitancy in his tone. "That's fine too."

"What if I'm late?"

"Why would you be late?"

"Because I'm part of a committee planning a modern languages conference, and we have a meeting that night that probably won't be over until seven, and I really can't show up to it in a tux when I'm already the youngest, most attractive person on the committee. It'll be like rubbing their faces in it."

Alex wanted to laugh, but that could be construed as flirting, since that's exactly what Rich was doing. She bit her lip to contain her smile, and asked, "Who plans a meeting for seven o'clock on a Friday night?"

"Busy professors trying to fit one more commitment in before the semester starts."

"You guys aren't busy," she said. "You're just lame."

"I can be there by eight-thirty," he said. "And I definitely want to come, if you'll still have me now that you know how lame I am."

Yes. Rich was definitely flirting. "Late is fine. Dale can keep me company until you get there."

A low growling noise come from Rich before he said, "Your trainer's going to be there?"

She giggled. Just because she wasn't flirting didn't mean she couldn't tease him a little. "It's his thing. He's one of the organizers, so yeah, he'll be there all night."

"Great," Rich said.

"He's married," Alex reminded him.

"When has that ever stopped anyone?" Alex didn't miss the misery in his voice as he spoke.

"For most people, wedding vows actually mean something."

Rich sighed. "You're right. I'm sorry. I've been thinking about my dad lately."

"Any news on that front?"

"Nothing new. Waiting for my guy to send me his latest installment of dead ends."

"But it's still a thing? You didn't call it off."

"Not yet."

"Good," Alex said, and glanced over her shoulder. "I should get back to work."

"Where are you?" He asked. "Maybe I can meet you for dinner."

"I'm at Simone's shop on the plaza. I'm designing a line of engagement rings for her for the holidays."

"Perfect," Rich said. "I can be there in an hour."

"No," she said. "Not this time. If we're going to do this, I want to take it slow. I'll see you at the gala."

There was silence for a beat then Rich said. "Alright, but I'm texting you later, *Piccolina*."

"That's fine. No dick pics though. That's not moving slow."

Rich chuckled low and seductive, as if he wasn't making any promises and hung up the phone.

Simone was still rearranging her ring display when Alex returned. "Please tell me that was the man I met at your party, and that you took that picture the morning after."

Alex shrugged and mimed zipping her lips and throwing away the key, before saying, "Show me what you've been working on lately." But inside, Alex was congratulating herself on remaining in control of that conversation and not allowing her libido to overtake her brain. Perhaps she was capable of having an adult relationship after all.

Chapter Twenty-Seven

Over the past week, Rich had learned that he didn't know how to go slow with Alex. He'd had to stop himself ten times a day from sending her teasingly lascivious texts. It's what they'd always done, and while he couldn't deny how fun it was to excite her, he also didn't want to push her too hard too quickly.

Instead he kept in touch, asking questions about her day, sharing small frustrations or triumphs in his own day. He screenshotted all the stupid texts he received about the conference he was planning and sent them to her. Questions like *Can the Spanish teachers have their own lounge since there are so many of them?* And six different people wanting to know how if they could book enough hotel rooms so no one needed to have any roommates, which was a question Rich didn't even want to touch, so he directed them to the committee in charge of rooming and refreshments.

Alex complained back about a custom order she was working with, a woman who claimed to have a nickel allergy and tried to tell Alex there was nickel in sterling silver, despite Alex telling her that there was nickel in *some* sterling silver, but not in Alex's sterling. The woman wanted Alex to use twenty-four karat gold, but at sterling silver prices, and Alex was about ready to give her deposit back just so she didn't have to deal with her anymore.

Texting with her was entertaining, but it wasn't the same as being in the same room as her, taking in her smile, smelling her sweet tropical scent, burying his nose in her hair, pressing his lips to hers. Rich missed her so much he wouldn't even mind it if she punched him in the chest again.

Funnily enough, that was exactly how he felt when he laid eyes on her at the gala. She stood between two men, laughing. The shorter, broader man was laughing too, and the taller, more handsome one only wore a sly grin. Jealousy tugged at Rich's stomach as he watched them. He figured the broader one with the sandy hair was her trainer. He didn't think the taller one, who matched Rich in leanness as well as skin and hair color, was a boxer. But then again, he wouldn't have pegged Alex for a boxer either.

Rich took the time to get a drink from the bar, cringing as they handed him his manhattan in a martini glass. He should have asked for a rocks glass.

As he approached Alex and her friends, they were laughing again, though Rich was too far away to hear what was so funny. He examined her companions again. The taller one was handsomer up close, his jaw squarer than Rich's, skin and hair a shade lighter, and his nose was maddeningly straight. Rich hadn't liked Alex's teasing about her trainer, even if he knew it was only teasing. That didn't explain why Rich had fought jealousy while waiting on his drink, unable to keep his eyes off the taller man, as if Rich might have been replaced by a doppelganger while he'd been giving Alex space.

Rich had wondered often if he had any half-brothers wandering around, more since he'd heard from his P.I. earlier today that he'd found something and was overnighting him the documents. But close up, it was easier to tell this man was not Algerian, and definitely not related to Rich.

Even better, when Alex's eyes noticed his approach, they brightened, and her smile softened, causing the other two men to turn their attention to him.

"You made it," she said, crossing to his side and looping and arm around his waist. She wore the same black dress she'd worn to her party, but with some of the funkier, chunkier jewelry from her collection.

He looped an arm around her shoulders and placed a quick kiss to her forehead. "Of course I did."

Alex winked at him before taking one careful step away from his side, motioning toward the broader one. "Rich, this is Dale Callaghan, my trainer, and this is his husband, Chris Demir."

Rich stopped himself from doing a double take at the word husband, and shook first Dale's hand, then Chris's as Alex said, "Guys, this is Rich Durand. The man currently trying to get in my pants."

"It's a little more noble than that," Rich said, even as everyone sniggered.

"You're the one who sent the teddy bear," Dale said.

Rich looked at Alex in confusion. He had sent a teddy bear, but how did her trainer know that?

"I tried to give him the bear because of the boxing gloves. He was too macho to take it, but he did have the very good idea of pretending the punching bag was your face."

"Do you find that a helpful training strategy?" Rich asked Alex, but it was Chris who answered.

"It's not the healthiest solution, but it helps to release frustration in the moment."

Alex rolled her eyes. "Chris is a therapist, and he wants to be my therapist for whatever reason."

"Sweetheart, you're a doll, but you're also a nut."

"And I'm secure in my nuttiness, thank you very much." A secret smile passed between the two of them, and Rich wondered if maybe he really was her therapist. Before he could ask, she held out her hand to Rich. "I'm going to take this guy around to bid on the silent auction items and make sure he pays his way."

Chris looked him up and down as Rich took Alex's hand and turned away, and said, "I bet we can help lighten those pockets."

Rich ignored him. He was used to people assuming he had money, like his name was a description of his bank account. He almost said something about how he was wearing a rented tux but decided to ignore the other man.

"You look amazing," he said, turning his attention back to Alex.

She looked him up and down, far more critically than Chris had. "I liked the blue suit better. You look like you should be playing cards against James Bond in the French Riviera with that martini glass in your hand."

"Why can't I just be James Bond?" he asked, more than aware that the villains were usually the ones who were vaguely ethnic, and never the title character, but Alex only said, "James Bond doesn't drink whiskey."

Rich's laugh surprised him, and he squeezed her hand as they approached the auction tables. He bid on a set of boxing lessons from Alex's gym, a handwoven shawl he could see his mother appreciating, a bottle or two of wine, but when he came across Alex's jewelry, he had to stop and admire the pieces.

"Are these one of a kind?" he asked, motioning to the necklace, earrings, and ring that all already had high bids on them.

Alex shrugged, and said, "I didn't want to give them something people could just buy online, you know?" like it was no big deal.

He pulled her into an embrace right there in front of the auction table. "You are immensely talented."

Alex eyed her display. "It's nothing."

He tilted her chin back so she was staring up into his eyes. "It's not nothing, Alex. Your work is amazing. You are amazing."

Alex's eyes shimmered for a second, before a whispered, "Thank you," slipped from her lips. She motioned toward the table with her handbag as she pulled from Rich's arms. "And my necklace has more bids than anything else, so I guess I'm winning."

Rich let her wander down the line of tables as he bid on the earrings, a pair of cascading crystal stars Gina would like. Then, when Alex had excused herself to the restroom a while later, he went back and bid on the ring, because he'd never seen anything like it. It was a waving cluster of raw diamonds in various sizes set in rose gold with two rough-cut golden-brown stones he thought might be topaz nestled into both crests of the wave. He wasn't sure how valuable the topaz was, but it was the same exact color as Alex's eyes. Rich couldn't bear to see her give it away.

Rich found excuses to sneak back over and up his bid Another person was warring with him for the ring, but just before the bidding ended, Rich wrote down a price that on par with the rings he'd gone down to the plaza to see. Simone had recognized him, tried to sell him one of Alex's own rings to propose to her with, but he'd said he wouldn't have her make her own engagement ring. Now that he'd seen this ring, Rich had changed his mind. He would never find a better ring than this one.

Rich couldn't keep a smile off his face as the bidding ended with his number the highest on the page, and he had to keep Alex out on the dance floor and moving to hide his triumph. She didn't seem to object, standing close, laughing. Since this was a gala and not Tokyo Nights, they played a song or two slow enough for Alex to nestle her nose into Rich's shoulder as they danced. She inhaled, then let out a relaxed sounding sigh.

He understood and ran his hand down the length of her spine, pressing his palm against the small of her back to hold her closer. Rich lowered his lips to whisper in her ear, "I've missed you, *Piccolina*."

She stretched her neck back just far enough to meet his eyes. "I don't like being apart," she said.

"Then let's endeavor not to be apart very often."

"Starting now?"

Rich nodded, then brushed his nose against hers. "Starting now."

Alex giggled, then pressed up on her toes so she could whisper in his ear, "That means you're taking me home with you tonight, yes?"

"Whatever you want, *Picollina.*"

"I want you to take me home now."

Rich didn't need her to say it twice. He pulled her off the dance floor and toward the door. They stopped to say their goodbyes to Dale and Chris, then they were gone. It wasn't until they were in the quiet darkness of his bedroom that he kissed her and said, *"Sei tutto ciò che voglio. Ti voglio sempre avere al mio fianco. Con te voglio invecchiare. Te amo,"* against her lips.

Alex giggled, and tangled her hands in his hair. "You've already got the girl in your bedroom. No need to pull out the Italian to impress her now."

"But it sounds so much better in Italian."

"Except I have no clue what you're saying."

Rich kissed along her jawbone and slipped her glasses off her face and onto the nightstand. "I'll tell you in the morning."

"Not fair," Alex said, but then his lips were on hers again, and neither of them spoke for the rest of the night.

• • • •

ALEX REALIZED SHE WAS in an unfamiliar bed as soon as she stretched, and her fingers hit wall instead of her wooden headboard. This bed was softer than hers, the sheets better quality, the pillows down instead of microfiber. A quick glance to her left showed that she was alone in Rich's bed.

The sun was up, and she thought she could make out the scent of coffee wafting up the stairs from his kitchen. Alex snagged a blue button-up from his closet and made her way down the stairs from the loft into the shabby main level of his apartment. The building Rich lived in was old, older than even the one Alex lived in, and it looked it. The exposed brick walls everywhere made it cool even on the warmest of days. The finish on the hardwood was worn off, and even the rugs Rich had spread over the living room floor, and under the dining room table were worn thin.

The stairwell let out at the juncture between the kitchen and living room, but the only thing that separated the two rooms was a large square island with a cooktop on one side and two stools on the other.

Rich stood behind the cooktop, laying bacon into a frying pan. He wore a Jesuit University t-shirt and athletic shorts and smiled at Alex as she seated herself on one of the stools with a yawn.

"You're up early," she said.

"It's almost ten." Rich rounded the island and handed her a cup of coffee, and kissed her forehead as he said, "Good morning."

Alex plucked at his t-shirt. "You're all sweaty."

"I just got back from a run."

"Overachiever."

Rich only kissed her forehead again and asked, "How do you want your eggs?"

"Over easy."

She watched him work as he hummed along to the Les Baxter he'd switched on. Alex grinned into her mug. He looked happy. Content. Confident.

Alex flushed as he realized she felt the same way. That was new, and possibly an afterglow from their lovemaking the night before. And that's what it had been—not the messy, passionate coming together they'd shared earlier in the summer, but a reverent sort of gentleness had tinged every move they'd made together. Alex thought maybe it was too early to decide, but she had the feeling this morning that this things between them just might work.

When Rich sat down next to Alex at the island, she leaned into him and ran her fingers through his still damp hair. Then she kissed him just for the joy of kissing him.

"You're perfect," she said, when he pulled back to look into her eyes. There was a minute shake of his head, and he opened his mouth to say something, but Alex pressed her index finger to his lips. "To me, you're perfect."

He swallowed, and his eyes turned serious, and a little glassy, and all of Alex's nerve endings sparked to life, as if a cloud of static electricity were surrounding her. Something big was happening.

Before they could do anything or say anything, someone pounded on the front door. Rich grazed his knuckles over her cheek before he stood. "I almost forgot," he said as he stood.

"What is it?" Alex asked.

But Rich was already answering the door. He signed for something and returned to the table carrying a thick packet that bore the marks of international post.

"This is everything the P.I. was able to find on my dad," he said.

"Oh my God. Open it!"

Rich took a deep breath and ripped the packet open, settling the contents between them on the island so they could read as they ate. Rich set the main report aside to rifle through the document copies included, as if afraid to read it all at once, or saving the surprise of where his father was now for last.

There was a copy of a birth certificate, a few news articles Alex couldn't read because they were in French, but Rich said they were unflattering write ups of protests his father had been involved in. They'd been nonviolent protests about rights for North African refugees, but he'd been quoted in them.

"Your dad was North African?" Alex tried to remember if Rich or Juliet had ever said anything about his father outside the obvious, but she couldn't recall anything.

"My grandparents were Algerian. I never knew them, but there was plenty of intermixing with the Algerian and Pieds Noirs—French settlers in Algeria—before my grandparents came along, because they've been Durands for generations, but both my grandparents emigrated with their families to Paris after World War II."

"How do you know all that?"

Rich shrugged and shoveled a bite of cold eggs into his mouth. "My dad used to tell us about what it was like to live in France after the Algerian War. How he was the first person in his family to go to University. He would talk about how most of his family converted to Christianity out of fear rather than true devotion. How jobs were hard for his parents to find, and even sometimes he'd show up for an interview and be turned away, even for teaching positions. It was easier for him to get teaching jobs in Italy and the US, because they wanted a native French speaker."

Alex was going to have to sort through all this information later. There were more layers to this man than she expected, but she felt on some level that she should have known. She wanted to know everything. "Why do you think he went back?" Alex asked.

"If we don't find the answer in here," he tapped the pile of paper, "That'll be the first thing I ask him."

They sifted through some more documents, university certificates, the Italian marriage license from when Rich's parents were married, some Italian newspaper articles announcing Sonia's marriage, then birth announcements for both him and Gina. A copy of the divorce decree. Then employment information from a small private school in Paris dated from 1999, and Rich sat straighter beside Alex.

There was an attached photo ID, and Rich his fingers over the face. "That's exactly how I remember him."

He looked remarkably like his son. They had the same eyes and nose, but Rich's jawline was softer, more rounded, his black hair wavier.

Next there was another marriage certificate from 2001. Marius Durand to Genevieve Meursault. She was younger than he, only twenty-nine when they married, making her thirteen years younger than her husband.

As if he was thinking the same thing, Rich said, "She's closer in age to me than she is to him."

Alex didn't say anything to that, besides, "Let's see if they're still married."

Rich flipped to the next page. The birth of a son, Alexandre, in October of 2004. Rich stared at it for a few minutes, before saying, "I have a brother."

Alex rubbed his arm. "And look, we have the same name."

"He's fourteen," Rich said. "A fourteen-year-old brother I've never met, who probably doesn't know about me either."

"Do you want to know him?" Alex asked. "I bet if we keep looking, we'll find their address, maybe a phone number at the end of all this."

Rich nodded and flipped the page. Alex wasn't entirely certain he hadn't gone into shock.

The next page was another birth certificate. A daughter this time. Manon, born in December 2006. Rich covered his mouth as if holding in a sob, and that's when Alex noticed that tears had sprung to his eyes.

"I've never known what it was like to have a brother, but I've always known what a gift it was to have a sister." He traced the name on the paper, first and last, Manon Durand, again and again. "I'm missing so much of her life."

Alex stood then, the same height standing as he was sitting on the stool and held him for a few minutes as he battled through the emotions she could only guess at. Anger at his father for leaving and keeping this new family from him. Grief at all the missed years. Relief at finally having some answers. Joy at finding new siblings.

The next piece of paper was a short article from the newspaper which Rich translated for Alex. The headline read "Teacher Collapses During Lecture." The article detailed how Marius Durand, 57 collapsed during class and could not be roused on the scene. He was transported to a local hospital for treatment. Rich flipped immediately to the next page which was a memo from the school Rich's father taught at, saying that he had been diagnosed with lung cancer and would be taking a leave of absence as he pursued treatment.

They were down to the last page in the file, and Alex held her breath as Rich flipped to it. She didn't need him to translate the words for her. She could tell immediately that it was an obituary lying on top of a death certificate. The photograph was more recent than the one on the ID, but Marius still looked young and healthy, though with distinguished silver streaks running through his hair.

Alex searched for the date as Rich sat in silence. The obituary had run in April. They were four months too late.

The arms Rich still had wrapped around her drew her in closer, and he wept.

Chapter Twenty-Eight

Outside of work commitments, Alex hadn't left Rich's side in the last week, and he was grateful. She'd held his hand as he'd called his mother and told her what he'd learned. She'd gone with him to Gina's for dinner on Wednesday night and sat beside him when he'd told Gina about Alexandre and Manon. Alex had retreated to the kitchen with Colin so Rich could have a moment alone with his sister.

It had been one of the most difficult weeks of Rich's life. Of all the scenarios he'd pictured of finding his father, that Marius would no longer be living had never been one of them. The sorrow and regret about not finding him sooner—at least soon enough to say goodbye—had kept him awake long after Alex had dozed off beside him. What if he'd hired an investigator a year ago instead of waiting? What if he'd started searching for him sooner? What if he had put more effort into it? What if he'd pressed his mother for information? If he'd been honest about how important talking to his father just one more time had been to him, maybe Gina and his mother would have understood. Maybe they even would have helped.

Regret drove him from his bed. They'd been spending most of their nights at Alex's because of the cat, but Rich had had some work he needed to finish, so Alex had packed a tackle box full of jewelry supplies and loaded Rich down with a litter box and cat food, and they'd all spent a cozy evening in his living room as Rich tried to figure out how to fit both the cat and his laptop on his lap.

Rich kissed Alex on the forehead before pulling on a pair of shorts and a sweatshirt. The nights were already growing chilly, and it was only the beginning of September. The cat chirped as he headed for the stairs and rose from his perch on the ledge overlooking the kitchen and followed Rich down the stairs.

Alastor wove between his feet as he drank a glass of water. He'd left his laptop on the breakfast bar, and his mind drifted to the folder that still lay atop his desk upstairs. Included with the report had been his step-mother's phone number and email address. The clock on the stove read two-sixteen, which meant it was just past eight in Paris. Not technically too early to call, but he'd wake Alex. And Rich wasn't sure if he was ready to talk to the woman. There were too many unanswered questions. If she hadn't known about him before the investigator had contacted her, she was likely adjusting to her new reality too, on top of dealing with the recent loss of her husband.

An email would be better. A softer approach that she could answer at her leisure—or ignore, he supposed. As Rich snuck up the stairs and grabbed the folder. He hoped she didn't ignore his email.

He sat at the breakfast bar with the cat in his lap and typed a short, quick email in French to a woman he had never met.

Genevieve,

You don't know me, but your late husband, Marius was my father. I've been looking for him for years and have been heartbroken to find him too late. I am sorry for your loss. I know this must be a difficult time for you and your family. I'm sure a learning of a long-lost American son has also been a surprise for you, but in lieu of reconnecting with my father, I would like to get to know the people who were important to him. It is my hope that you would like to know me too.

Regards,

Riccardo Durand

He'd included his phone number, but he did not expect a return phone call. He didn't even expect a return email, but as Rich slipped beneath the covers and pulled Alex into his arms, he felt a little of the burning grief settle into something more manageable.

"You're so cold," Alex said as she pulled the covers in tighter around herself at the same time she burrowed further into Rich's side. Indeed, her skin almost felt like fire against his chilled limbs.

"It's good you're here to warm me up then, *Piccolina*."

"Smooth talker," Alex murmured before sleep washed over her again. "You're lucky to have me."

"Yes, I am." Rich held her as sleep slowly claimed him too.

• • • •

ALEX WAS ALONE IN HER apartment for the first time in a week. Since she and Rich had set aside everything that was keeping them apart, she hadn't had a moment alone. If she wasn't with Rich, she'd been working with Avery and Janet. Trying to keep up with workflow during their expansion meant that one or both of them were hovering at the edge of Alex's work bench with questions or suggestions, or just to talk about all the amazing things Sparkle & Shine could become with the Alex & Co line taking off and more space and more hands. The excitement had been palpable but balancing that with Rich's grief had been exhausting.

Two weeks ago, Alex would have despaired of another night alone in her studio, but she was thankful for Rich's meeting. She needed the quiet.

So much had changed in such a short amount of time. She'd felt as though she'd spent this whole last week keeping up. Rich had vacillated between an insatiable hunger for her and a withdrawn despondency that meant he was thinking about his dad. He'd told her over breakfast that he'd emailed his father's widow in the night, and he'd seemed lighter when he'd left for work that morning. Alex hoped it would last. She didn't begrudge him time to mourn his father. What worried her was the mental beating he'd been giving himself for being too late. She hoped emailing his step-mother meant he was moving past that now.

She had loved this past week. Had loved going to bed with Rich every night and waking up with him every morning. She'd loved the energy of moving on to new things, she'd even enjoyed her evening at Gina's, despite her nerves. But what Alex needed now was quiet.

She hadn't even turned on the studio's stereo when she sat down. She just plopped onto her chair and pulled out one of the many tiny drawers on the cubbies that lined her work table. They were the kind of thing meant for nails and screws in wood shops, but Alex used them to store beads and stones and fittings. The drawer she pulled out this evening was full of little bits of raw rose quartz. She'd designed a necklace almost four years ago now that featured a single piece of lightly polished rose quartz dangling from a long chain. The pieces that were shaped like the usual obelisk style crystals always sold the best, because th cards she'd displayed them on read that rose quartz was the stone that represented love, and every relationship was as unique as every hand-polished stone, they'd always been her bestseller.

Alex wasn't going to lie and say that hand-polishing the stones hadn't become tedious sometimes over the years, but the piece had been her signature design for so long now, Alex didn't dare get rid of it. And yes, washing the little pink stones in vinegar and sanding them would be one of the tasks she'd pass along to whoever she ended up hiring, but she wanted to do them herself this one last time.

She'd originally started polishing the stones herself because buying them raw was so much cheaper than buying them cut and polished, and then she'd made it work for her with the marketing. But Alex had also always loved watching the stone transform from dusty and dull to something that sparkled.

Her Gran had always called her a rough-cut stone. She had told Alex she was too sharp around the edges, that with a little polish she'd settle down nicely. But Alex thought her Gran was wrong about that. Alex had exactly the edges she needed. She'd been afraid of sanding off the wrong corner and becoming her mother, but what Alex had realized over the last few months was that she was multi-facetted, cut just right to give off maximum sparkle, and that she should be proud of who she'd become.

Alex was so transfixed by the transformation of one stone that barely needed any sanding to come to a perfectly imperfect shine that she didn't hear Rich come in until he said from behind her, "I thought you were going to take the night off?"

Alex switched off her tiny sanding tool and smiled up at Rich before realizing he couldn't see it through her mask. She pulled it down and stood. "That was purely recreational stone polishing."

He placed a quick kiss on her lips and tapped her safety goggles. "You should wear these more often. I like the double glasses look."

Alex snorted and pushed the goggles over her glasses to rest on the top of her head. "I'll be sure to put them on the model the next time we have a photo shoot."

Rich's grin was like coming home as he pulled her against his chest. He pulled the goggles off and buried his nose in her hair. They stood like that for a few minutes, just enjoying the feel of each other. Their relationship was brand new, but it also felt years in the making, and Alex didn't need any more convincing. He had flaws, sure, but so did she. The imperfections only made him more beautiful.

"How's the conference coming along?" she asked.

Rich groaned. "I'll be happy when it's over."

"Only six more months of planning." Alex patted his back and made to step out of his embrace, but he held her close. "What's up?"

"She emailed me back."

Alex didn't need to ask who he meant.

"What did she say?"

"Remember how you told me I should take someone with me if I went to visit my dad?"

"Yeah?"

"How do you feel about going to Paris?"

Chapter Twenty-Nine

Rich had only been to Paris three times before; each time had been on short trips while he'd been visiting Italy. Once when he was a kid with his family, a second time in college before Juliet had moved in with him, and the last, a quick visit during his last school trip to see if he could locate his father in the city. All previous trips had been during the summer. On this fourth visit, so close to Christmas, he found he liked Paris more in the winter. It was cold and overcast, but that hadn't stopped he and Alex from strolling the Champs Elysee, ice skating at the Eiffel tower, and having long, leisurely dinners at sidewalk cafes with heaters warming the small patios.

They'd been here four days already, and Alex was having a hard time adjusting to the time change. She'd been tired since they'd arrived, and she'd been alternating between an upset stomach and a ravenous one. All hallmarks of someone who didn't travel often. Alex hadn't been feeling well the night before, and after a quick trip to the pharmacy, they'd gone to bed early. She'd slept like the dead and woken an hour after he had.

They were staying in a small apartment overlooking the Seine with a kitchen just big enough to make coffee to go with the croissants from the patisserie on the corner. He'd already had most of one pot and read a local newspaper while he waited for Alex to wake. When she did, she headed straight for the bathroom, and the sounds of retching reached his ears.

That was new.

He crossed the small kitchen to the hallway and rapped on the door. "Are you alright? Can I get you anything?"

"Do we still have any of that fancy fizzy lemon water?"

It had been Alex's preferred drink since they'd arrived. "I'll get you a glass. Are you going back to bed?"

"No, I'll be out in a minute."

Rich retreated to the kitchen, poured a glass of the sparkling water and waited. When Alex emerged from the hallway, she looked a little pale, but otherwise alright. She wore the shirt he'd worn yesterday with a pair of heavy wool socks. Her hair was pulled up in a ponytail, but since she'd slept on it, it was coming out of the elastic and falling on her face and over her shoulder. Her glasses were a little crooked on her nose, and she straightened them as she took the stool beside him.

"Did dinner not agree with you?" he asked after she took a tentative sip of her water.

"Dinner was delicious," she spied a box on the counter. "Did you get *pain au chocolat* today?"

Rich felt his eyebrows draw together into a frown. "You want to eat?"

Alex took another sip of her water, then another. "I'm going to puke again if I don't, I think."

Rich couldn't help his chuckle as he stood. "You have the strangest reaction to traveling I've ever seen." He grabbed the box off the counter by the sink, and held it open for Alex. Inside were two *pain au chocolat* and two croissants. Alex grabbed one of the chocolate pastries, and groaned as she bit into it.

"I'm going to get so fat," she said with a full mouth.

"Just think about how much Dale is going to scold you when you get home and tell him you ate croissants for breakfast every day."

Alex chewed, pursing her lips to the side while Rich poured himself another cup of coffee, then grabbed the butter and one of the croissants, leaving the second *pain au chocolat* for Alex, should she want it.

"I'm not sure how much I'm going to be seeing Dale for a while. I'll have to call Juliet this afternoon and ask her."

Rich blinked. He loved her, but she wasn't making any sense. "Why wouldn't you see Dale? He's your favorite person."

"You're right. We'll have to invite him and Chris over for dinner more often."

They'd been living in Alex's apartment for the last two months. She'd moved her business into a studio space in the West Bottoms, not far from her apartment, and Rich had moved in with her while they looked for a place they could buy, loft, condo, or house, they hadn't decided yet.

"Sure. But why wouldn't you see him at the gym?"

Alex took a big bite of her pastry, followed by a gulp of water that was so big it looked painful when she swallowed. "You know how I lost my IUD a few weeks ago?"

Of course he did. They'd been using condoms since she'd noticed it was gone. Apparently, it was a thing that they could just fall out. How it could fall out and Alex never notice Rich wasn't sure, but her doctor had said she'd most likely flushed it down the toilet. She was supposed to get her implant after the new year.

"Yes," Rich said cautiously.

"Turns out we didn't catch it soon enough."

"What?" His coffee mug plunked onto the counter, slopping hot coffee over his fingers as his stomach landed on the floor near his toes.

"How do you feel about being a daddy?" she asked, her grin wide and teasing.

"Are you serious?"

Alex narrowed her eyes as if to scold him for doubting her, but she'd done that in jest before too. "What did you think I bought at the pharmacy last night?"

"The French equivalent of TUMS."

Alex shook her head, barely keeping her amusement at his shock under wraps. She had to be messing with him. "The test is on the bathroom counter if you want to see it, but remember, I peed on it. And I might not have read the instructions perfectly, but I'm pretty sure it's positive."

"You're not joking."

"Not even a little bit."

Rich dropped onto the stool again. "You're pregnant."

"Pretty darn sure."

His brain immediately went to the last time. How he hadn't known. How keeping the pregnancy had been so little of an option for her she hadn't even told him. "And are you—do you want to—are you going to keep it?"

Shock registered on Alex's face this time. "Is there a reason why I shouldn't?"

Rich felt his brain firing and tripping over itself just as much as he tripped over his. "Last time, I thought, maybe, I mean—"

"We're light years away from where we were the last time this happened."

She was right. They were. And they'd both put in a lot of work to get there.

He met her eyes again, allowing himself to hope when she grinned and pushed her glasses up her nose. "You want to have this baby?" he asked.

Alex leaned into him, and he wrapped an around her shoulder. "I want to have *your* baby," she said.

He kissed the top of her head. "That's—this is amazing."

"Merry Christmas," she said.

He chuckled. Christmas wasn't for a few more days, and they would be back in the States by then. Rich had his own Christmas surprise planned for her. The night before they left, he'd planned a romantic dinner from a restaurant with a view of the lit Eiffel Tower, and over champagne, he was going to get the ring he'd won at the silent auction out and ask her to marry him. Though he guessed the champagne was out now.

"It's the best gift I've ever received," he said, kissing her forehead again.

"Does my Christmas gift have anything to do with that little black box in your shaving kit?"

Rich sat up straight. "You've been snooping?" Had she seen the ring. Why hadn't she said anything?

Alex only snuggled into him farther, nudging his arm more closely around her shoulders, encouraging him to relax.

"I was looking for TUMS," she said. "But you should probably answer my question."

Rich had to think back a moment to remember what the question was. "Yes, that's part of your Christmas present."

"You're not gonna hold out on me now, are you?"

Rich checked his watch. "We're going to be late if we don't get going now."

Alex grabbed his wrist and checked his watch for herself. "We have plenty of time."

They were meeting his step-mother and his brother and sister for lunch. Though they'd been emailing for months, this was the first time they were all going to meet in person. Rich was full of anxious, nervous energy, and the coffee wasn't helping. He wanted to be out and moving around. Not putting his entire life on the line.

Then again, he doubted there was much question of her saying no. They were going to buy a house together. They were, lord above, they were having a baby together. Why should he wait?

With a pat on her hip, he disengaged himself from her hold and retrieved the ring from where he'd been hiding it, apparently unsuccessfully in his shaving kit.

Despite his pep talk, Rich's heart pounded as he made the short walk back into the main living area. Alex, still disheveled from bed, but her color already returning, grinned at him from the stool.

"I'm curious to see what kind of jewelry you bought for someone who designs it for a living."

Rich ignored her, and with the ring box tucked in one hand, he cupped her cheek with the other. "You are everything I've ever wanted. The only person I want to grow old with. The person I want to share my life with."

Alex's mischievous grin faded, and tears filled her eyes as her jaw dropped open. Rich tilted her chin up, closing her lips so he could place a quick, firm kiss to her mouth.

"I love you, Alex. Will you marry me?"

He stood back a step so he could open the box and show her the ring. Alex let out a sound that was half sob, half laugh as one hand covered her mouth and the other reached for the ring.

"I can't believe you bought this," she said, pulling the ring from the box.

"The second I saw it, I knew it had to be yours," he said. "And I knew I had to be the one to give it to you."

"I almost kept it for myself," she said, sliding the ring onto her finger to admire it. "I was thinking of you when I made it."

"As long as you're not mad you made your own engagement ring," he said, entwining his fingers with hers.

"Not gonna lie, I probably would have altered anything else," she said, resting her head on his chest and sighed. "I love you."

Alex's *I love yous* were rare and it was only now that they'd been together for months that they weren't sounding tentative and cautious. Rich knew she hadn't had much to love in her life, or many people giving her love back, but Rich was going to change that.

"I love you, Alex. I love your mouth, your sass, your confidence. I want to spend my life being good enough for you."

Tears were dropping from her lashes, and Rich flicked them away.

"You're perfect," she said. "But we have to get married soon, because otherwise I'll hear my grandmother telling me I'm a bad example for this kid for the rest of my life, okay?"

Rich pressed a soft kiss to her lips. "Whatever you want, *Picollina.*"

Alex bounced on her toes in the damp grass. It had rained that morning, and she'd been anxious all day, even after the cloud cover had cleared at noon. The sun had warmed the air into the low seventies, but the grass under the rose-covered arbor still soaked her toes. Janet, the genius, had stuck some sort of disc support on the end of Alex's heels so she didn't sink into the wet earth, but her open white sandals didn't do much to keep her feet dry.

White sandals.

White.

Alex still couldn't believe she'd let Juliet and Avery talk her into wearing white. She smoothed a hand over her new baby bump. At five months along, she'd only just started to show, and couldn't get enough of how the slinky silk fabric draped over her belly. Her baby. The baby she and Rich had made together. And today.

Today they were finally getting married. It had taken about four months longer than she wanted to get here. She'd wanted to elope the moment they'd returned from Paris, but Rich had convinced her to wait, to plan something special, even if it was just a small ceremony.

And she'd gone small. They'd only invited their closest friends and family, not including the photographer. Neither of them had much family, but Gina and her family were there. Rich's mother and her boyfriend stood next to them. Two of Rich's colleagues loitered near the back with Roland Calgary. Simone was there. Janet and Avery were filming the vows so they could send them to Rich's family in Paris later. Chris chatted with Ethan, who held baby Viola. That was the real reason they'd waited so long to have the wedding. Because Alex couldn't get married without Juliet there, and neither Ethan nor Juliet had wanted to travel with their precious daughter before she was a month old.

Baby Viola had turned four weeks old on Thursday, and she was most precious pink yeller Alex had ever met. It had been worth waiting the extra months to have her wedding, not only to have Juliet present, but to meet the newest member of her family.

Waiting for the baby had made planning the wedding difficult, but Alex had found a way around that.

She'd gone guerilla.

The stupid garden wanted two months notice and six hundred dollars for two hours for a corner of the garden that they wouldn't even let Alex cordon off, because quote – *it was a public park and they couldn't keep the public away* – unquote. Well screw that, if they couldn't control the public, they couldn't control Alex having a twenty-minute ceremony under one of the arbors with fifteen of her closest friends.

Dale checked his watch and nudged Alex's side. "If your groom doesn't hurry up, somebody is going to catch on."

Alex shook her head and scanned the lanes that wound through and around the rose garden, searching for Rich. He was five minutes late.

"He'll be here," Juliet, who stood to her left, said.

Alex knew she was right. They'd had dinner with Dale and Chris and Ethan and Juliet last night and signed all the documents. They were technically married as soon as Dale signed and submitted the paperwork, but Rich was late, and Rich was never late. He always showed up precisely on time, and Dale was annoyed.

"If I get arrested for violating permit law, you're paying all my legal fees."

Alex rolled her eyes. "Fine."

"It's just a thousand dollar fine," Juliet said. "They only arrest you if you don't pay that."

Alex socked Dale in the shoulder. "See, just a grand, buddy. I'm good for it."

Dale grimaced. He hadn't liked the guerilla wedding idea from the start. He was a tried and true rule follower, and being the officiant, he'd been convinced he would be the one to get in trouble, despite Alex's insistence that no one would even notice.

"Any word?" Alex asked Juliet.

Alex had stowed her phone and wallet in Viola's diaper bag and had given Juliet strict instructions not to let her touch her phone. True to form, Alex hadn't heard from her mother about the wedding outside of her initial *Congratulations!* text. Alex had told her precisely when and where the event would take place, but Vivien had never responded. She hadn't even told her mother she was pregnant yet. She could only handle so much disappointment at once. First she'd get through the wedding, then she'd work on her feelings about how her child wouldn't have the kind of grandmother Alex had had in Gran—not from Vivien at least. Sonia was going to spoil her grandchild rotten. She'd come with a whole suitcase full of girl's clothes, blankets, and bedding. Alex had spent more time than she should have over the last two days folding and refolding the tiny clothes, imagining her daughter in them. She was only halfway through her pregnancy, but already Alex was anxious to cradle her baby in her arms the way Ethan held a sleeping Viola. She wondered if he even realized he was swaying and bouncing as he spoke with Chris.

Ethan and Juliet and Viola had stayed wit,h Alex last night, while Rich had stayed at Gina's. The baby had cried half the night, and Alex didn't know how Ethan and Juliet were awake and alert. Alex had gotten up and made them all breakfast, then taken a two-hour nap before Juliet had woken her to get ready for the wedding.

"Nothing," Juliet said, as she tucked Alex's phone back into her bag. "He's probably just looking for a parking space."

Alex nodded. Parking did suck in this neighborhood.

"Ten minutes late now," Dale muttered, and Alex's stomach turned with worry. What if something had happened to him?

Dinner had been awkward last night. It was bound to be, having Ethan and Rich in the same room and interacting for the first time perhaps ever. Ethan had been surly and on edge, because it was the first time they'd left Viola with someone, and Rich had been both withdrawn and so touchy-feely with Alex that she'd wanted to smack his hands away. He was nervous, and he was trying, Alex knew, but Chris and Dale had kept the conversation flowing until the two old rivals had warmed up to the situation. The night hadn't ended badly though. Ethan and Rich had even shaken hands before then end. Though admittedly Ethan had looked like he was going to punch Rich in the face when he leaned in and placed twin kisses on Juliet's cheeks. He'd backed off when Juliet had placed her hands on Rich's shoulders and said, "Be good to her," and Rich had answered with, "For the rest of my life."

That had made Alex go all gooey on the inside. She felt a distinct loss as she kissed Rich goodnight and watched him get in his car and drive away. It was only a few blocks to his sister's house. The house they'd purchased in March was in the same neighborhood, so their kids could grow up together.

Alex recalled the conversation she'd had with Juliet when she'd stayed with them before their wedding: Juliet's hand resting on her abdomen as she'd said, "This place. This job. This man." That was exactly how Alex had been feeling for months. She'd infused all those feelings into the ring that waiting in Dale's pocket.

She'd crafted Rich's wedding band out of gold, with veins of rose gold twining across the surface in a way that mirrored the waving motion of her own ring. It was masculine, but still held some of her usual boho flair, and the only piece of men's jewelry Alex had ever made. She'd imagined how right it would feel to slide it onto his finger today, and now she was worried she'd kissed him goodbye for the last time last night.

She clutched Juliet's arm. "What if he was in an accident?"

Juliet looked over Alex's head, and she could tell she and Dale were rolling their eyes at each other over her. "He's fine. He'll be here."

"But Rich is never late," Alex said, standing on her toes again. It didn't make her any taller than she already was in her four-inch heels, but it felt like she was doing something more than standing around waiting for her fiancé to show up to their wedding. She tried to peer over the heads of the other people in the park, looking for Rich's wavy black hair, but he was nowhere to be seen. Except—was that Edgar?

A tall silver-haired man in a gray suit stalked down one of the paths and Alex thought she caught a flash of her mom's wild steel gray hair. She bobbed to her right to get a better look, and her modified stiletto came down on one of Dale's loafers.

Dale cursed and picked Alex up beneath her arms and moved her a foot away from himself, but she only hopped back up on her toes. "That's definitely Edgar." And then a family moved over on the path, and there was Vivien, her loose hair long and blowing in the wind along with the panels on her long blue tunic. She smiled and waved at Alex. That's when Alex saw him, hurrying her mother along like the mother hen he was at heart. Rich met her eyes with a wide smile, and the tension in her shoulders eased. He was here, and he'd somehow corralled her mother here too.

He met her halfway to the arbor where everyone was waiting and pulled her into his arms. He smelled like her mother's cigarettes, but also like Rich, the sandalwood and soap smell that somehow permeated all his belongings. "I'm sorry I'm late," he said in her ear, then placed short, desperate kisses along her jaw until he reached her mouth. Alex curled into him then, almost purring at the heat and pressure of his embrace.

"I thought something had happened to you," she said. As she pulled back to take him in. But he was whole. He was dressed in his navy suit, and he'd styled his hair, but left the stubble he'd worn the night before, and there were dark rings under his eyes.

"I've been to Chicago and back since I saw you last," he said.

Alex reared back, looking between him and her mother. "What? How?"

Vivien wrapped an arm around Rich's waist, and one arm around Alex's shoulders, pulling them in for a triangle hug. "Rich rescued me, darling. I missed my flight and couldn't get a car to drive. We didn't think Edgar would get here in time, so Rich drove out to pick me up. He and Edgar got there at the same time, so we all drove back together." Vivien was beaming, but Alex looked between them, trying to overcome her confusion.

"But why didn't anyone tell me?"

"I wanted it to be a surprise!" Vivien said, like this was funny. "I'll bet you thought I wasn't coming."

"Well, no, I didn't. I'm glad you're here but," she turned to Rich and Vivien stepped back, still grinning in triumph. "Did you drive all night?"

He shrugged it off, "Edgar drove so I could doze in the car on the way back."

"Are you okay?"

Rich's lips parted in a slow smile. "I made it back to you, so yes." He ducked his head, touching his forehead to hers. "You are beautiful."

"I missed you."

"How's our girl?" he asked, flattening his palm over her belly.

"I felt another kick this afternoon, I think."

Rich flexed his long fingers, and Alex knew he was hoping to feel something, but Alex was barely registering them yet. It would be a few weeks before he he'd be able to detect anything.

"All right. Come on, you two," Dale clapped the same way he did during training. "Canoodle after your married. I don't feel like going to jail today."

Alex shot him a glare. "Nobody is going to arrest you."

He only motioned for them from his place beneath the rose arbor. Rich offered Alex his arm, and the two of them walked down the aisle created by their little crowd parting to make way.

Alex barely registered anything after Dale's joke about not being qualified to marry anyone, but how logistics had never stopped Alex in anything before. She was too busy registering the feel of Rich's hands in hers as she smiled up at him. Minutes later, Dale had pronounced them husband and wife and was shooing them out of the rose garden and toward the parking lot. "Let's get this reception underway, I need a drink."

They had booked a private room in a locally owned steakhouse for their reception. It had been the simplest option on short notice. On the drive there, Vivien and Edgar sat in the back of Rich's jeep, which now also smelled of her mother's cigarettes.

Once she was buckled in, Alex rotated around to see her mother. "Thank you for coming, Mama," she said. "It really means a lot."

"Of course, darling. I wouldn't miss your wedding," Vivien said as if she were offended now that Alex would even consider it. "But why haven't either of you mentioned my grandbaby?"

Alex met Rich's eyes before he put the car in gear, and the both looked toward the sky. It was going to be a long night.

But really, it wasn't. Edgar chided Vivien and asked when the baby was due.

And when they arrived at the restaurant, the evening passed in a flurry of toasts and laughter and sparkling white grape juice. Alex snuggled with Viola and joined Juliet in teasing Ethan. She held Rich's hand and kissed him every time her mother, who'd had too much to drink, tinged her fork against her glass.

They only left the restaurant after Edgar had nodded off in the corner of a booth and Rich couldn't stop yawning.

After dropping her mother and Edgar off at their hotel, Alex sat Rich down on their bed and first undressed herself, then him. Alex's couldn't look away from the delighted contentment in his eyes as she pushed him flat on his back and lowered herself down on top of him in a long, slow slide that set the pace for their lovemaking.

Afterward, as they lay tangled together on the bed, Rich twined his left hand with hers so their new rings clinked together in the dark room.

"I can't believe you drove to Chicago to rescue my mom," Alex said.

"Well, she called Juliet, and Juliet called me."

Alex rolled her head on Rich's shoulder. "I do not understand her at all. Why keep it a surprise?"

Rich kissed her finger, just over where her new wedding band rested. "I have no idea, but you wanted her there, and if pulling an all-nighter made it happen, I was happy to do it, *Picollina.*"

"I'm glad she was there."

"Good."

"But I'm even more glad you didn't die in a car crash or change your mind at the last minute."

Rich hiked up on his elbow so he could meet her eyes in the dark. "I knew I wanted to marry you the second I saw you standing on the hill by yourself in your cap and gown."

Alex laughed. "It took me a bit longer."

"When?"

"When you came out of the bathroom laughing at Novel. I was terrified."

"I remember."

Alex smoothed a hand over her bare baby bump. "I don't think I stopped being afraid until I found that ring box in Paris. I knew I wanted to be with you, and I suspected that I was pregnant, but I was afraid I wouldn't be enough for you until I opened that box and saw that you'd bought one of my rings."

Rich kissed her forehead and collapsed back onto the pillows. "I knew you peeked."

"Of course I did. It was a fucking ring box."

Rich stretched out with a loud yawn, and Alex knew she should let him go to sleep. "But you pretended you didn't."

"Hey, you're mostly perfect, but your ego still needed to surprise me with the ring, so I let you have it."

"How charitable of you."

Alex snuggled into his side again. "I do what I can."

Rich didn't respond, his breathing had evened out, and her husband had fallen asleep.

Keep reading for a preview from book three in the Try Again Series,

Read & Wright.

Here's your chance to find out what's got Colleen all twisted up.

Read & Wright is available now![1]

THANK YOU FOR READING!

I hope you enjoyed *Sparkle & Shine*. I always meant to write Alex and Colleen's stories, but when I told my husband my plans were to get Alex and Rich together in book two, he told me it couldn't be done. He thought Rich was too much of a villain. And I said, "Hold my coffee. I got this."

So yes, I set out to humanize Rich, and I hope you were able to forgive him for his sins and maybe fall in love with him just a little bit too. And does anybody else want to join Alex's gym? I'm on the lookout for a real-life Dale. If I find one, I'll let you know. In the meantime, give yourself credit for all that you do. We all have different struggles, but we all work hard in this life, and you friend, are rocking it. *fistbump*

• • • •

The third and final book in the Try Again Series, Colleen's story, is coming your way in 2019. Sign up for my newsletter[2] to get sneak peeks and extras!

• • • •

Want to Connect with Me?

---

2. http://BookHip.com/QFDZZK

I am @marlaholtauthor[3] on Instagram. I'd love to see your bookstagram posts or just chat about the book. I can't wait to meet you!

FINALLY, LEAVING REVIEWS is one of the best ways you can support the Indie Authors you love. I'd be forever in your debt.

As Alex would say, get it, badass.

---

3. http://instagram.com/marlaholtauthor

Chapter One

Colleen parked in the farthest space from the entrance out of habit. That she needed to walk the extra steps into the grocery store was one of the many habits her mother had expected of her since childhood. Sherry Hawthorne reminded her daughter of the rest through helpful text messages like an unwanted fitness app. *Park as far back as you can. Always take the stairs. Take walks on your lunch break. Always leave food on your plate. Drink more water. Eat more vegetables than anything else. Save sugar for special occasions.*

Her mother lived by those rules. Colleen did not. That Colleen neither kept a journal where she tracked her food intake, nor cared if her calories burned measured more than her calories consumed, had always a point of contention between her and her mother. She'd always told Colleen that it was a woman's job to be conscious of her figure. A woman's appearance affected her place in the world. And since Colleen had lived up to her mother's ideal, her mother had always been quick to pick at Colleen's eating habits, especially in public. She would criticize the food on Colleen's plate no matter who was listening while Juliet, Colleen's naturally thin older sister, was allowed to eat as many pieces of pie as she liked.

Colleen had always been on the round side of thin growing up and had only recently crossed over into being plus-sized. A person could only juggle so much and when she felt like her entire life had been falling apart, a few pounds had seemed the least of her worries.

Now that she was back in Goodland though? It had been the only thing her mother had talked about. In truth, the first few days it had almost been a relief. She could compare step counts and food journals with her mother instead of discussing exactly *why* her youngest daughter had given up her apartment in Denver and was living in the studio above the garage.

It was only a stalling tactic. Colleen knew that. Because even if being thin was one of her mother's measuring sticks, it wasn't one of Colleen's.

No, what made Colleen feel like as failure as she tripped out of her boat of an old Buick and into the blustery Walmart parking lot was that she'd been asked to resign from her underwhelming day job and just flat out fired from her "just for fun but I really need the extra money ha ha," barista gig. Which was bullshit. She had not been rude to that guy. She'd called him out on staring at her boobs, which she considered harassment. But when had anybody ever taken the woman's side in a harassment case? Easier just to fire her and not deal with it.

Luckily, the people at Holy Grounds, the coffee shop where Colleen worked now, thought Colleen moving back home to Kansas from Denver showed good sense. Which was good, because without the tips she'd made this last week, she wouldn't be able to afford this trip to the grocery store.

Just like she hadn't been able to afford much of anything since Derek had moved out last year. No. She wasn't going there.

Colleen shoved any thoughts of her ex out of her mind. She didn't have the energy to waste on him right now.

So, here Colleen was, at twenty-seven, kind of, almost, not really living with her parents and working as a barista—again. She'd left her umbrella in a half-unpacked box by the door, so she was also getting slowly soaked by the cold, misty October rain. Colleen pulled her denim jacket tighter around her waist and jogged as fast as her heeled booties would let her run.

The lights were too bright, like noon in July compared to the dank bluish gray cold outside. Colleen had to blink as she spun in a circle, gathering her bearings in the massive store. She hadn't been in a Walmart since she'd come home last Christmas.

Colleen had expected to be stopped by every person she met and interrogated about how her life was and what she was up to and how magical Juliet's wedding had been, and how were the bride and groom? Any babies on the horizon? How perfect was it that their little hometown midwife had found a baby doctor of her own? They were going to be so happy, and when was Colleen going to settle down?

She'd been through the same conversations six times a day at the coffee shop since she'd been back, but Walmart was different. It was big, sterile, anonymous. She could have been at any Walmart anywhere in the world. She didn't even recognize the elderly greeter by the door who pointed her in the direction of the shopping cart bay.

As much as Colleen was appalled by the idea of Walmart being the only real grocery store in town anymore, she was thankful to be someplace where she could be alone. She didn't want anyone to remind her about her perfect sister and her sister's perfect husband and her sister's perfect house in the mountains and the baby Juliet was going to have in the spring. Colleen didn't want to be reminded that no matter what Juliet did, she succeeded and no matter what Colleen did, she failed.

She picked out some new kitchen towels and roamed the aisles for the ground turkey. She paused in front of the vanilla Oreos, her hand almost grasping the yellow package before her mother's voice rang in her head, citing again how much weight Colleen had put on recently. She forced her back straight and her chin up. She didn't need her mother's voice, and she didn't need the damn cookies either. She might be home with her tail between her legs, but she had a plan damnit, and that started by not spending money on extras.

Saying no felt good. And hey, Katy Perry was playing on the store radio. Colleen bopped along to Katy's encouragement to be a firework as she turned into the spice aisle. She had brought all the kitchen essentials with her from Denver when she'd moved but had tossed most of her spices. She hadn't cooked often even though she'd had a gorgeous kitchen with a stainless-steel range and long, granite countertops. She hadn't had time. She'd spent all her time at work to be able to afford the gorgeous kitchen that she didn't have time to cook in. Takeout had been so good and so varied in Denver, it hadn't really mattered.

But in Goodland? The choices were pizza, fried chicken, fast food burgers or the all you can eat buffet. There was the one Chinese place, but Colleen hadn't eaten there since the summer after her senior year, and she still couldn't think about that night without her stomach rolling, so cooking it was.

At ten o'clock on a Tuesday morning, Colleen was the only person in the aisle. She was debating whether she should buy the Walmart brand curry spice blend or the name brand kind when she caught a movement out of the corner of her eye. Colleen glanced over her shoulder to see a man and his young son. But then she did a double take.

A man bun? She hadn't seen a man bun yet. It was so common in Denver, she never would have noticed, but in this sleepy Kansas hamlet, this Norse god had her full attention. He was tall with strawberry blonde hair pulled back in an artfully messy bun. He'd complemented that with a sculpted beard just a touch redder than his hair. Broad shoulders and a muscled torso pulled his black t-shirt tight across his chest. The predictable logo printed over his impressive pecs read *Wright's Gym*. Of course he wore a gym logo. Nobody got a body like that without considerable time lifting ridiculously heavy things.

Yup, it was like someone had walked into her mind and pulled out all her favorite attributes and molded them into one gorgeous package. Colleen checked that she wasn't drooling and tried to turn her attention back to her spice purchases. She'd go for the expensive curry blend. If she was going to eat butternut squash, she was at least going to do her best to pretend that it was takeout from her favorite curry shop back home.

The Norse god and his heir stopped in front of the powdered sugar. According to her eavesdropping, they were making a cake for Grandma, which made Colleen's ovaries jingle to life. She felt herself edging closer despite her resolve to stay away from anything that gave her mother more cause to complain. Father and son were going to make the frosting from scratch and were debating whether they needed one bag of sugar or two. Colleen wanted to swoop in and give them the best cake baking advice they'd ever heard and then be invited over to help them bake said cake and . . . possibly other things once the kid was in bed, but alas, Colleen had never baked a cake. She wished she had, because this man obviously hadn't touched sugar in years, and he was likely more clueless about baking than she was. She at least could make cookies.

She dumped the rest of the spices she needed into her cart, then made her way down the aisle. She paused just on the god's left to grab a bottle of the vanilla stevia that had to be beyond reproach. And would you look at that? No wedding ring. She offered the man a small, sweet, but apologetic smile for invading his space. He nodded at her, then stopped, cocked his head to the side as something like recognition lit in his eyes. He finished his nod and turned back to his son as Colleen navigated her cart away.

"Let's get two bags just in case," he said, and Colleen booked it into the next aisle. That little kernel of recognition had shaken her, and her heart pounded in her chest. Colleen would have remembered if she'd encountered that level of physical perfection before, wouldn't she? There was really only one person she could think of. One voice with that particular timbre, one man of that extreme height with hair that color. With a child that age. But she wouldn't let herself believe it.

Colleen leaned against a support pole in the coffee aisle, fanning herself as she tried to convince herself who he wasn't. The most damning evidence was his shirt, because he almost had to be one of the Wrights by stature alone. Colton and Court had gone to school with Colleen and Juliet, and they had both been as tall and as thin as telephone poles back then. The Colton Colleen remembered had been boring and obsessed with Juliet. She had always found Courtney more interesting, cute even—before he'd turned out to be a total bastard. But both brothers had moved away for college and never come back, and Wright's Gym was one of those big franchises wasn't it?

No, it couldn't be *that* Wright.

Maybe he'd thought she was someone else. She was fifty pounds heavier than she'd been high school and had way better fashion sense now.

Colleen looked down at her skinny jeans and brown suede booties. She'd paired them with a sage green tunic that matched her eyes. Because of the rain, she'd worn her denim jacket with the gray triangular scarf Juliet had given her for Christmas last year. She looked fucking amazing—if she didn't think too hard about those fifty extra pounds. Colleen knew she'd thought about them a lot less before she'd moved home, and her mother hadn't stopped reminding her about them on a thrice daily basis.

It was part of the reason that she was here grocery shopping instead of at home putting the finishing touches on her freelance website. Because if Colleen had to share one more meal with her mother as she made passive aggressive comments about the amount and type of food she ate, Colleen might commit matricide. And she liked her mother—sort of. She didn't really want to kill her, but one more comment about butter or white potatoes, Colleen was likely to lob her butter knife right into her mother's forehead. She was pretty sure she'd be found not guilty by reason of grave provocation, but still, Colleen didn't want to be sad unemployed chick who'd killed her mother. Nobody would ever hire her to be their social media manager.

Colleen needed work that wasn't coffee shop work. Colleen refused to be the aging barista who still lived with her parents. That wasn't an option. Even the apartment over the carriage house was a temporary arrangement. Colleen had given herself six months to get her freelance business off the ground and then she was hoofing it back to Denver just in time for the snow to melt and enjoy the sunshine through her balcony window.

Colleen grabbed a box of organic green tea and smiled as she pictured herself tapping away at her laptop, sipping the tea and looking out the window to see Pikes Peak in the distance, and then writing the best fucking sentence of her life. Of course, in the fantasy Colleen was writing fiction and not web copy, but she couldn't be too picky about that. No one was going to pay her to write the romance novels she only touched in the dead of night. Everyone needed a social media manager these days.

Ooo. That was a good niche market to target though. Romance authors would probably rather spend more time writing and less time marketing, she could think of two different promotional packages she could offer off the top of her head, and a good brainstorming session could churn out something for everyone at any price point.

Colleen dug out her phone and started tapping out notes before she forgot. See, she was fantastic at this marketing and promotions shit. She just needed to work for cool people who liked the word, "Fuck." Turned out History Colorado, where she'd tried to be conservative and educational for three years hadn't been much of a fan of the hip, edgy perspective that had got her hired in the first place.

Whatever. She was gonna rock as an indie.

Colleen had just dropped her phone back in her purse when the Norse god and his dark-haired son passed her aisle. The little boy, who had to be seven or eight, pointed down the aisle. "Didn't Gramma say we were out of coffee?"

One huge, rugged hand steered the boy toward the next aisle over. "Not that crap. I'll stop by Holy Grounds on the way home from work tonight and grab some of the good stuff."

Colleen's heart almost stopped. She didn't hear whether the kid also had an opinion on coffee. She was too busy thinking about how she worked tonight, and how she would be able to convince Thor to meet her in the supply closet for some moka java and a quick grope.

Unless he was who she thought he was, in which case the only option was a swift kick in the shins, and by shins, she meant balls.

And if it wasn't him, he probably wasn't interested in her anyway. She looked down at herself again, noticing the tummy pooch and wide hips. Not for the first time, jealousy over her sister's naturally lithe, lean yoga instructor's build swept over her. The Norse god probably only went for women like Juliet. Thin. Beautiful. Perfect.

Whatever. Colleen didn't need him. Didn't want him. What did she need a god for? She didn't. Especially not one with a kid. She was so not mother material. That was one thing Colleen would cede to her sister. Juliet could have all the babies. Colleen's one run in with pregnancy had been more than enough for her. No thank you. Never again.

• • • •

SEXY MAN BUN—WHO DEFINITELY wasn't Courtney Wright, aka the man who'd broken her heart at eighteen—hadn't come into Holy Grounds that evening. Not that she had been looking for him or anything. Because she totally hadn't been. Colleen had been too busy being interrogated by Ms. Wrathbone, the elderly woman who had been her Sunday School teacher and who was so desperately curious to know about Colleen's life in Denver that she stood right beside the register while she stirred extra cocoa into her hot chocolate and smacked her scone.

"Big city wasn't all it was cracked up to be then, huh?" had been her opening line.

Colleen had shrugged and attempted the same vague answer she'd given to most people who'd asked her about why she was back so far: "Denver was fun, but it was time for a change." Most Goodland natives had taken that to mean that it was time for her to come home to where she belonged, but Ms. Wrathbone just kept on spitting scone and yammering while Colleen counted out her change.

"Big cities aren't for soft girls. You have to be sharp to make it out there."

Colleen did her best to ignore the insult, not sure if she'd just been called fat, or stupid, or both. The old Colleen would have said something smart and cutting, but today, Colleen didn't have the energy.

Vi, the only other coworker she had that wasn't eighteen, plunked a latte on the counter next to Colleen. "And what do you know about big cities Ms. W. You're still living in the house you were born in."

"My Hal was from the city."

Colleen frowned, and she felt a little bit of her old self perk up as she remembered that Ms. Wrathbone's long dead husband had gone to school with her grandfather. Her parents were from a town in west central Kansas that seemed big compared to Goodland, but still only had a population of around 20,000. "Well, I understand Hays was rough back in your day, what with all the gunslingers and the cattle rustlers and the brothels, but there's plenty of space for savvy curvy girls to make their way outside prostitution these days."

Ms. Wrathbone's jaw gaped for a moment, showing the attractive sight of her partially chewed blueberry scone. "Well, I never," she said, as Vi edged Colleen off the register with a bump of her hip.

Colleen took up her position at the espresso machine, thankful for the save, though Ms. Wrathbone remained undeterred. She stood by the register, talking over the line of customers looking for an afternoon pick-me-up talking about the last girl she knew who came home from the big city. She'd been pregnant and penniless because she'd been living as a kept woman and her sugar daddy had left her for somebody else. She'd actually said, "Sugar daddy."

"You can't trust men from the big city. They're vain and fickle as a feather," Colleen heard her say over the grinder. She shared an eyeroll with Vi, but her heart panged in her chest. Colleen hadn't been a kept woman. She'd worked hard to pay her half of the apartment she'd shared with Derek. But he had been fickle, and her being destitute and depressed had been a direct result of him moving out to date a younger, thinner blonde than Colleen. He hadn't gotten her pregnant though, so at least Colleen had that point in her favor.

She was still working on forgiving herself for trusting him, and it was made even harder by the fact that he'd somehow gotten wind of her moving. He'd been texting her three times a day for the last week.

Eighty percent of Colleen knew that he was only reaching out because Younger and Blonder had dumped him, but the other twenty percent still stupidly missed him and the fun they'd had together. That had been their pattern for years. How many times had Colleen let him back into her bed? She'd called it a convenient arrangement with her best friend because it made her sound less pathetic, but really it had been Colleen taking whatever scraps of affection Derek spared her. Now she knew better.

"I suppose you know that from experience?" Colleen said, just loudly enough for Ms. Wrathbone to hear over the phlegmy sound of steaming milk. Colleen actually hadn't known anything about Ms. Wrathbone's personal life, but the way the woman stuck her nose in the air and turned on her heel, suggested that Colleen had struck a little too close to home.

When the cranky woman had disappeared out the front door, Vi high-fived Colleen. "Score one for us, City Girl."

Colleen liked Vi a lot, even though she hadn't expected to make any friends in town. All her high school friends had either moved away or were busy being married and pregnant with their second or third kid. And really, Colleen had been kind of a loaner in high school. She'd worked with her dad, did her best to fit in at youth group, but spent most of her time hiding behind books so nobody noticed how much she didn't fit in at all.

It hadn't been until that summer after her senior year that Colleen had really felt seen by anyone. When it had been Courtney Wright who had seen her.

"The girls and I are heading out to Taylor's tonight around ten. You should join."

Taylor's was a country music club in Colby where everyone went line dancing. It had been the place to sneak into in high school, since it was eighteen and over. Colleen had only been once, and it had been awkward and lonely. She'd grown up listening to country music, since that's what her parents listened to, but she'd been more into Pulp and The Killers. Anything intense and glittery.

And besides, Taylor's had been a fifteen-dollar cover when she was sixteen. It only had to have gone up since then. If she couldn't afford a three-dollar package of vanilla Oreos, she definitely couldn't afford a night out with drinks.

"Maybe in a few weeks," Colleen said.

Vi gave her a sympathetic look, but only said, "I'll hold you to that."

Vi was only a year younger than Colleen but working her way through school part-time. She still hung out with the newly-of-age drinkers. Colleen could drink. She was able to knock back whiskey with the best of them. When she was in a mood, she ordered top shelf bourbon neat and drank the man who had put her in that mood—usually Derek—right under the table.

Just another reason Derek had never been good for her.

"I know you will." And really, Colleen wouldn't mind going out, even if it was country music. She preferred writing until the dead of night then collapsing into bed with her head so full of her characters that she dreamed of them, but she wasn't beyond needing a girl's night every now and then.

She'd been working so much her last few months in Denver that she hadn't hung out with any of her friends. And that was the kicker about break ups, all the friends ended up choosing sides, and all hers had chosen Derek.

Since heroes in romance novels were always better than men in real life, Colleen asked. "Did you read that book yet?"

"Holy shit," Vi said, and Colleen's face broke out into a devious smile. She loved this part of getting friends hooked on romances. She'd loaned Vi one of her favorite slow burns a couple of days ago.

"You finished it didn't you?"

"I stayed up until midnight reading, before I got to my psych homework. The textbook wasn't nearly as exciting."

"I have the next book, if you're interested."

"No. Yes. Well. I need to study for my test on Friday. But after that?"

"Absolutely." Colleen and Vi high fived. The satisfaction of getting someone hooked on reading carried her through the rest of her shift.

She was mopping the floor after close when a jolt of satisfaction stopped her mid-wring. If she went with her idea of promoting indie romance novels, she'd be doing one of her favorite things: introducing readers to books they loved.

Colleen smiled to herself. She'd finally found her niche.

<u>Buy Here</u>[1]

---

1. https://books2read.com/u/mYKZgY

About the Author

Marla Holt grew up wishing the heroines in the fairy tales she loved had more to choose from than marrying the prince or utter devastation, so now she writes modern day fairy tales with a feminist flare. She's living her own dream come true, writing and knitting in Topeka, Kansas with her husband and three boys.

Read more at tinydinostudios.com.

www.ingramcontent.com/pod-product-compliance
Lightning Source LLC
Chambersburg PA
CBHW051609100726
47898CB00001B/290